The Grace NOTE

Jaqi Anderson

WESTBOW
PRESS®
A DIVISION OF THOMAS NELSON
& ZONDERVAN

WestBow Press books may be ordered through booksellers or by contacting:

WestBow Press
A Division of Thomas Nelson & Zondervan
1663 Liberty Drive
Bloomington, IN 47403
www.westbowpress.com
1 (866) 928-1240

Because of the dynamic nature of the Internet, any web addresses or
links contained in this book may have changed since publication and
may no longer be valid. The views expressed in this work are solely those
of the author and do not necessarily reflect the views of the publisher,
and the publisher hereby disclaims any responsibility for them.

This is a work of fiction. All of the characters, names, incidents,
organizations, and dialogue in this novel are either the products
of the author's imagination or are used fictitiously.

Any people depicted in stock imagery provided by Getty Images are
models, and such images are being used for illustrative purposes only.
Certain stock imagery © Getty Images.

ISBN: 978-1-9736-3055-5 (sc)
ISBN: 978-1-9736-3054-8 (hc)
ISBN: 978-1-9736-3056-2 (e)

Library of Congress Control Number: 2018906880

Print information available on the last page.

WestBow Press rev. date: 12/26/2018

Grace note

(n.) ornament used to decorate or embellish a melody

"Earth's crammed with heaven,
And every common bush afire with God,
But only he who sees takes off his shoes;
The rest sit round and pluck blackberries."

—Elizabeth Barrett Browning

'Exquisite. An absolute gem!'
Julia Immonem, author of *Row for Freedom*, **and founder of Sport for Freedom**

'This unforgettable book really got under my skin. I just didn't want it to end, and felt full of grief when it did'.
S.Jackson

'What's in a note?! Often something powerful and profound. This book is both. You're in for a treat! I was hooked from the first paragraph – characters so full of life, in a story that twists and turns, taking you on a journey full of serendipity and delight. A truly "graceful" debut from an exciting new author..who effortlessly reveals the profound, amidst the everyday. An exciting read from start to finish.'
A.Kennedy, Actress and Theatre Director

'Sometimes there is an unspoken chasm between the seen and the unseen. Jaqi explores this theme with touching honesty, and tender clarity. A satisfying quest'.
The Right Reverend Richard Jackson, Bishop of Lewes, UK

'There is a depth to this beautifully composed story which filled an ache in my soul. Charming, compelling and an absolute page turner. Find your quiet place to curl up with this book – you will not be disappointed'.
F.Cox

'This book has a powerful melody which will not leave you untouched. A wonderful book.'
H.Khoo

'The best book I have read in years – I became attached to all the characters. They were so real and beautifully described. I could not put it down as I wanted to know what became of them all. This is a book with both heart and impetus…a rare find.

S.Emsley

'The Grace Note's intricate interweaving of everyday lives through believable characters is masterfully handled by Jaqi in her debut novel. With a warm tone and fascinating narrative, the story takes you on a journey as lives intertwine through those serendipitous moments we can all identify with – leaving the reader wanting more!'

J.Brice

'What a feast! At last – a novel which masterfully connects the musical with the divine. I cannot recommend this book highly enough'.

A. Buckland, Opera singer and Director of Opera Brava UK

Acknowledgments

Firstly I would like to thank the wonderful WestBow team for all their wonderful assistance in turning a dream into reality. No words of thanks enough for your wisdom, patience and support shown towards this relic writer!

Emma, your help with the cover design has been magnificent. I am so indebted to you.

To all those faithful friends who have listened without yawning, kept me laughing, and cheered from the sidelines – an awesome team effort! You each know who you are, and I am *utterly* grateful to you. Without you all goading me on, I would have surely given up long ago. Truly, iron sharpens iron.

With hindsight, I would like to thank the Guildhall School of Music and Drama for inadvertently giving me a springboard to write this story. What a wonderful silver lining.

For all my music teachers and pupils: remember, education can go sideways. Bravo to all of you!

Nazike, my Albanian friend and advisor. You have truly given this novel credibility, and I thank you.

For all those valued individuals who generously offered crucial advice and help in Tirana, and beyond. I hope this book does justice to what you have been through, though I suspect it doesn't even scratch the surface.

Sophie, for rescuing my dangerous French. Tu es magnifique!

Oana, Ceausescu child, incredible survivor, and treasured

friend. Your authentic story has empowered me never to forget. I owe you a huge debt.

Deborah, if prayer is the rudder that moves the ship, then your prayers and countless others have made this book possible. An eternity of thanks to you for accompanying me on this journey.

Sharon, for your exceptional kindness in letting me stay at the breath-taking Carn Eve in Cornwall, to complete the manuscript. You simply provided the boot camp I needed. Nothing like a cliff on Land's End with hurricane winds to inspire creativity. Awesome! Your constant generosity and support stand completely apart.

To my awesome and experienced 'proofers'. Your encouragement has been immense and humbling to say the least, and your insight invaluable. Thank you for all your patient reading and advice!

The Warnham Court Women. I can't leave you out. Your wild enthusiasm is infectious, and your love is insane. Literally.

To my dear friend 'Pastor' David Grice. David, I have no words of thanks enough for your persistent, dogged and exceptional encouragement over many years. You deserve the credit for so much, so here it is.

Kirsten, incredible adventures can start over a drink. Here is one of them!

To my parents and brother. This journey has been utterly enriched by your incessant loving and concrete belief in me. You also gave me the puzzle box in which I found The Grace Note jigsaw pieces. Chance?

GGG, (my precious late grandmother), who assured me when I was only seven that I would one day be a writer. How did you know? I'm sorry it's taken me so long.

To my dear godchildren and precious nieces. You are each jewels, every one of you!

To my children (children?): My diamond, song, rock, anchor, smile – and angel. In that order. You have provided inspiration enough for a lifetime of writing, and without you I would be utterly incomplete. Parents do strange things sometimes don't they? I can't wait to see what you all decide to do in mid-life. Never say never. Mama loves you!

Not forgetting my little Surprise, and all that follow her. Grandmas also do strange things don't they? Bibi's prayers surround you always, so that you too can chase your destiny. And catch it!

Finally to the one person who has literally placed this book into your hand, and made it all possible. My rib and heartbeat, closest friend, truest critic and biggest fan – my husband Ian. My life coach. You're the absolute best thing a girl could wish for. (Even when she's a Granny).

And finally.. finally. I need to thank Babi above all. You really set me up for this didn't you?! You truly are the Lord of the Dance. Do I detect a roar of laughter?

Chapter 1

Kitty stirred. The warm, comforting womb of her bed was still and secure. She savored the softness of the duvet around her body and nestled further within, cocooned in her private space. Her mind slowly began to filter out sleep, her body resisting. Somewhere downstairs, a phone was ringing, jarring and insistent. *Bordering on rude*, she thought. An invasion of silence, unwanted and unasked for. Like an irritating insect buzzing around a room, it should be swatted and removed, especially during school holidays. Yes, most definitely during school holidays.

Slowly, she swung over and sat up. Her middle-aged body wasn't so lithe these days. Muscles ached after a night's prolonged inaction, and she was aware of a morning stiffness that was becoming annoyingly familiar.

She padded through the bedroom and descended downstairs. Ribbons of light streamed in through the front door's patterned glass, attempting to pry her eyelids open. All her life, waking up had been a struggle. She slept so deeply that it felt like a tortuous assault, this transfer from her world of dreams. It had to be done slowly; that was the only way. Her husband teased her every morning, but it was no good. She simply couldn't catapult from one world to the other in nanoseconds. That was just barbaric. Once when she was a student, she had slept through a bomb scare; the entire building was evacuated, doors hounded, and sleepy inhabitants evicted. But she never heard a thing. How they had laughed at her. Drugged on sleep, that's what she was. A sweet morphine of wonder, that's what the nocturnal elixir yielded in wondrous regularity. And she was grateful.

But there would be no jibing this morning. Nick, her husband was at work, and the house was deliciously silent. The kids wouldn't surface for hours. Not even they could rib her Medusa hair, wild and torn into frizzy disarray by copious pillows. She had sat up slowly when she first awoke, confronted by her reflection from the dressing table mirror. What a sight. The mirror was never kind first thing in the morning, so she avoided it as a rule of highest principle, certainly for at least an hour.

The dogs were comatose and upside down in their basket. At least they, too, understood. Roger's short legs were stuck vertically upright and resembled an upturned coffee table, comically rigid. Basil was twisted into a ball of soft fluff and had cleverly hidden his eyes and tail so that it was impossible to decipher front end from rear. There they were, oblivious to the outside world. *Just how it should be*, she thought. *Disturb the sacredness of slumber at your peril.*

She reluctantly picked up the inconsiderate phone, clearing her throat quickly to sound awake.

"Hello?" she said stiffly.

It was Helen, her mother-in-law. Inside, she knew what was coming, and she slipped into a familiar rhythm of listening and nodding, tutting and murmuring, which was always the pattern of these calls. There was absolutely no need whatsoever for her to speak, which was usually a mercy. Yet she knew instinctively there would be no coffee for at least half an hour, by which time her stomach would be in knots.

She had often wondered if this absence of telephone etiquette should have been addressed earlier in their marriage. Twenty-one years later, she hadn't remotely conquered it, and now it was like a buried splinter, a dull annoyance that she had learned to live with. Yet she also knew, with a growing sense of sadness, that these phone calls had a finite life. For Helen was fighting a losing battle against an incurable and pernicious illness, and now it would be Kitty who was rude not to stop the world, however inconvenient, and listen. Truth was, she would miss the silence most of all. She chuckled to herself at the irony.

Forty minutes later, she replaced the phone receiver and looked longingly over at the kettle. Her body was now craving its assistance. Basil had opened one eye and shifted his warm body, half-burying the other dog, who had evaded suffocation and hadn't appeared to notice. That was the thing about dogs. She envied their simple satisfactions, their visible appreciation of comfort and warmth. It was there to be celebrated, and their basket was a picture of contentment. She loved the sheer simplicity of it all, their lack of anxiety and poochy incoherence of oppressive deadlines. She had learned much from them during this routine morning observation. No words to get in the way. Just sleep—pure and undisturbed. Her eyelids clicked an imaginary photograph.

She flicked the kettle switch and grabbed the steel coffee pot. She had her caffeine fix down to a fine art, a selective choice of South American coffee and milk heated in a warmer that she had probably wasted money on, although she could never get quite the same froth from the microwave. Next, she attended to her porridge. This was a relatively recent habit, acquired in no small part by the advice of her gym-obsessed son, and hailed as a gold-star cereal that would add at least another five years to her life if she started eating it *now*. Change habits slowly, she had warned herself. Trouble was, she had to admit she was really quite enjoying it. Especially with some muscovado, there was no escaping the fact that porridge staved off hunger pangs till nearly midday. Breathing in, she willed her disobedient tummy to stop spilling over her trousers and sighed. She must remember to ring her friend Jen about that new Pilates class next week.

Carving a space on the breakfast island, she tried to ignore the detritus of last night's mess and wished, for about the millionth

3

time, that she wasn't surrounded by the hideous clutter and accessories that accompany a houseful of adolescents. No amount of bleating or nagging had made the slightest difference; the boys seemed incapable of noticing their trail of destruction. Her older daughter's contribution was different, possibly worse: Lucy left neat and beautifully ordered piles of rubbish. Hair bands and grips graced every worktop, and her mobile phone, which never stayed in the same place twice, was therefore always and infuriatingly lost. An assortment of handbags added to the confusion. "Tidy mind, untidy workspace" she'd heard once. Well, it was all tosh. She practically had to enter Sam's bedroom every six months with a gas mask and rubber gloves and a peg on her nose. The poor defenseless hoover had the worst job, though, and she simply tried to shut her eyes and finish the wretched job as quickly as possible.

Such were the joys of sons. She loved them to her very core, but why she had ever thought that by the age of eighteen, they would be clean, independent, and sensible adults was completely beyond her. *They ought to warn you about this in antenatal classes*, she thought. It was all a test of psychological stamina. *One day, I'll have no one to tidy up after,* she realised mournfully. *It'll probably kill me.*

Her thoughts were interrupted by a sudden bark. The postman had the ability to rouse the dogs quicker than anyone, and they tore to the front door with predictable excitement, crashing over a pair of trainers and a basketball that had been left dangerously for the next victim to trip over. The rustle of letters gave her an expected sense of anticipation, although she had no reason to suspect that today would be any different from any other day. A concoction of typed letters and flyers, invoices, and business letters addressed to her husband, with dull address stamps and no incentive to open.

Why is it no one bothers to write handwritten letters anymore? she mused. *Worse still, why don't I write to anyone anymore?*

It was a question that disturbed her, a twenty-first-century cultural shift, no doubt, but she truly doubted whether the joy of receiving an interesting and personal letter had been lost in the mists of time, never to be recaptured.

As she suspected, the familiar shape of white envelopes and a charity magazine looked up at her from the doormat. Oh, and a postcard for Lucy from her friend on holiday in Magaluf. She wearily picked up the pile and made her way back to the kitchen, fingering her way through the envelopes and wondering whether the laundry pile was the next job to attend to, when she stopped. An unfamiliar handwritten letter had neatly been sliced between two bank statements. It was addressed to her.

The rarity of this event necessitated a return to the forgotten coffee mug on the kitchen table. She seated herself slowly into a chair, feeling a welcome rush of what could only be described as hopeful curiosity. Letters usually fell into three categories that she knew: the good, the bad, and the boring. Best not get too excited, she warned herself. Probably a bland and reasonable letter, devoid of any drama. However, there was something about the script that frankly just puzzled her. It wasn't the slanted, loopy handwriting of one of her transatlantic friends; neither did any family or friends' insignias immediately lay claim to the envelope's invisible contents. It was mysterious and inviting all at once. The stamp had a picture of two boomerangs on it, twisted together, making a sort of cross. She picked up a knife sitting next to her porridge bowl and slowly slit the envelope open. Inside she pulled out a page of neatly folded file paper, covered in black ink, and already she could see a neat small hand had been responsible. Still no clues, no cognitive nudge. She tugged at the letter, pulled it out, and began to read:

Jaqi Anderson

Dear Katherine,

I know this will be unexpected and almost certainly a shock, for which I sincerely apologise, but I was wondering if you would kindly agree to meet me?

I know we have never met, but I have only recently discovered that I am, in fact, your brother.

Yours sincerely,
David Simpson

Chapter 2

Somewhere, halfway over Paris, David awoke. There was a spot of bumpy turbulence, and the seatbelt lights interrupted a fitful dose. His legs ached abominably, and he needed a pee. The sight of the toilet queue up the aisle ahead of him made him sigh, and he realised he would have to wait. Plus the lady on the aisle seat who had been overflowing into his seat all night would require awkward navigation to hurdle over, and he simply didn't have the energy.

He consoled himself with the thought of an espresso in the airport terminal. He glanced across his sleepy teenage neighbour to the left and looked out of the window. A pale slate sky made his heart sink. How like England, he thought. Those iron skies which wrapped around you like a blanket and took you down to a place of sullen heaviness, the familiarity of which reminded him of why he had left there in the first place. He had simply been unable to face another long, dark winter in England, where the autumn days seemed shorter every year of his life, this belief settling in layers and gradually moulding into concrete certainty that he was chained like a prisoner to this place. Working as a busy medic had offered little respite. His window of opportunity had come in the form of a chance conversation at work during a monotonous lunch hour in the hospital canteen. That had in itself reassured him that exit strategies can leap out at you at the most unexpected moment.

'My daughter's emigrating,' one of the theatre nurses, called Terry, had announced triumphantly, on a day when horizontal sleet slashed across the dirty expanse of window that separated the hospital from the bleakness of the car park, where even now, figures with inverted umbrellas and wet hair were scurrying through the rain to their cars.

'Really?'

David hadn't even looked up from his sandwich. He was finding it increasingly harder to engage with colleagues outside of theatre, and Terry was no exception. He just wanted to switch off.

'Yeah, they got a visa no problem. Crying out for health workers in Oz. You should think about it, David. It's gonna kill the wife losing the grandkids, but I talked her round. Only one life, eh?'

Only one life. The phrase struck him forcibly, like an idea of seismic proportions; it had been a seminal moment.

Putting his lukewarm polyestered tea slowly down on the ugly plastic table, he smiled bleakly at Terry, mumbled something about needing to get back for the afternoon list, and made his exit as politely as he could. Was this a sign?

Only last night, he had stayed up too late, watching a gripping documentary about a garage worker who had heard about street kids in Lima, sold his house and car, and moved straight out there to start a new life, fuelled by the boredom he was leaving behind. Frankly, he admired his guts. It all sounded so plausible when neatly wrapped up on a TV screen. So do-able, yet so wildly impossible. Just the thought of explaining it to Dad was enough to terrify him. Mum would understand, but she was gone, prematurely snatched by a savage cancer three years earlier. He missed her more than he dared admit. Grief is a strange thing, he thought during most of his waking hours. Always there, following him like a dark shadow, blocking out the sunlight he desperately sought. Maybe that's why he felt restless and confined. He was longing to escape this jail of sadness, but try as he might, he simply couldn't.

Maybe a change is just what I need, he thought. But if only he had the courage. His divorce, the year after his mother's death, had been no easier to bear. A short-lived marriage that had started on the wrong foot, and for all the wrong reasons, and never picked up. He simply had nothing left to give in the aftermath of bereavement, and she hadn't put up a fight to keep him. It was entirely mutual, amicable, and horribly wrong, but that's all there was to it. He conflated his grief in one fell swoop and dived into work like there was no tomorrow. This kept him sane and functioning, but only just. Inside, lonely empty nights in his unwelcoming and unadorned apartment threatened to derail him every time he stepped through the door.

But he had done it. By some extraordinary mustering of an unknown reserve, he had knocked on a few doors, and they had swung open easily. Far too easily, he often thought since, though his regret for not having acted earlier seemed rather brief. Once he stepped foot in the land Down Under, filled with sunshine and promise, his clinging mood had dried up as quickly as wet paint on a hot day. Not that he was able to forget his losses, but they just didn't chain him anymore. Even his dad had shown a rare streak of encouragement, holidays for him no doubt, and he had jumped on it as a final confirmation. His confidence had returned like an empty glass being refilled, and within a few short weeks, he had sold up his flat and the few possessions Laura hadn't wanted, taken years' worth of old winter coats and clothes to the charity shop, and bought a one-way ticket to Melbourne.

That was eighteen months ago. He now had a new and interesting girlfriend, worked a job which didn't curb him unduly, and spent every weekend on the beach or at the golf club. The transformation had been startling, he had to admit. And yet, three weeks ago, all that had been shattered by an email he had picked up from his dad, late one night, when his head was fuzzy from

9

beer and his neck was scorched and humming from an evening stroll on the beach with Evie. He had only glanced at his screen on his way to a bed that was drawing him like a magnet.

'*Dear David*,' he read:

I want to show you a letter from your mother, which I should have sent you a long time ago. Somehow I can't bring myself to send it, but maybe you could find it in yourself to come and receive it in person. Please don't be angry at me. I have kept this secret for far too long anyway. Grief has paralysed me and I ask for your forgiveness. Know that this changes nothing between us, and I remain ever, and always affectionately, your Dad.'

Chapter 3

Kitty sat motionless at the kitchen table, adhered by some invisible force to the words in front of her. It was completely surreal. She stared ahead of her for a very long time, distilling the moment, drip by drip, into her consciousness. Her coffee cooled without notice. She was only aware of being transported from her domestic world to somewhere far away, somewhere that felt huge and ominous, unknown and uncharted. Her present world was spinning around, and she was being lifted out of it effortlessly, her disconnected thoughts darting like flickers of sunlight on water. Nothing threaded together, and she felt at sea, tossed around by nauseating waves which pounded against her on all sides.

Upstairs, she heard a toilet flush and then a slow and heavy thunder of footsteps down the stairs. Momentarily, she jolted back into the present. One of the boys was awake, but she desperately needed space to process this bombshell. She stuffed the letter back in its envelope and hid it on top of the dog cage, wedging it under a small sack. On the back door of the kitchen hung her waterproof jacket. She was still in her pyjamas, worn and barely decent—but there was no time to change. She flung on her jacket, which almost covered them, and grabbed her purple wellies. She glanced at the dog leads hanging on a peg, debating whether to risk taking them, but the footsteps were drawing closer.

No, she thought, *I must escape without them.*

Without looking back at the dogs' reaction to the rustle of her jacket, she slipped noiselessly out of the door.

Outside, a soft drizzle touched her cheeks. She pulled her hood up, grateful for an extra excuse to mask her frenetic hair. She knew she must get into the woods as soon as she could, to avoid passers-by. It frankly wasn't cool to be walking round the village in your pyjamas, but if she made a dash for the woods, she could hide. Quickening her step, she cut across a small cul-de-sac and snaked round the back of a cluster of new houses. On top of each other, they looked like Monopoly pieces in uniform rows. Same doors, same windows, and same postage stamp-sized gardens—only space for a clothes dryer, a couple of chairs, and a patch of grass no bigger than two bed sheets. That's why she loved the countryside so much, an ocean of freedom in comparison, a delicious expanse where both her legs and thoughts found fluidity and space. Whole fields, abandoned now by cattle or sheep, were edged by ubiquitous bramble hedgerows, brown and darkened now their berries had fallen. She crossed a road, pushed open a stiff gate, and followed a short narrow path which tunnelled down to another gate, which had a flimsy sign attached to it saying 'Keep dogs on leads.' She lifted the latch. Before her lay a large, empty field … and freedom.

Only now did she try to assemble any of her shooting thoughts. There was an email address he had given, so that was how she would reply. In truth, that was the only way she could reply. He'd left no other address or phone number. She shuddered at the thought of phoning him. Perhaps that's why he hadn't left a number; he didn't want contact that way, either.

She thought of her parents, now both dead. *Were they watching this?* she wondered. What on earth would they make of this? What should *she* make of this? She just couldn't grasp it. There were too many missing pieces.

She began mulling over her life. *I suppose it never* was *conventional*, she thought honestly. Her adoption at two weeks old to older parents had been a resounding success; she knew that much. Surely, no child had been more loved. Growing up in the perfect childhood soil of unconditional acceptance, with wonder lavished upon her from her earliest memories, had indeed been fun. *I was the answer to their disappointment,* she thought truthfully: she fully understood that. *I wanted to make them happy. And I did.*

She hadn't suffered with the usual agonies of an adoptee, at least not till she became a mother herself, as she had been too settled, too secure to want to rock a boat from which she never wanted to fall out of. Her blunt logic had simply been: if they didn't want me then, why would I want them now? Childish instinct, maybe, but it had protected her very well for umpteen years.

She had reached the end of the field and came upon an antechamber to the woods ahead. Here she would find privacy and quiet, and she hoped she wouldn't bump into another walker. She pushed aside a nagging feeling of guilt that she hadn't taken the dogs. By now they would be darting ahead of her, sniffing wildly in the undergrowth, chasing each other in secret detective work that she could never be part of. Especially with this rain, which had turned into a steady, if not unpleasant smattering. It always seemed to ignite their senses, offering smells more satisfying, more alive and alert. She felt their enjoyment of this place as much as her own. Still. At least Sam would be with them now, onto his fourth bowl of cereal and a second cup of tea.

I wonder if he will remember to feed them, she thought. Almost certainly not. They will be scrabbling under his feet, chewing his socks, and he will miss the cues entirely. He will simply be getting irritated by their attention.

She set off on a familiar route which would lead her back full circle to the field she had started from. A short but satisfying thinking time, she decided. Twenty minutes to begin absorbing the enormity of this news and start to formulate a plan, yet not long enough for the kids to notice she'd gone. She wasn't ready to share this with them yet; it would have to wait. Life was too full of their precarious hormones for them to be able to support her wobbling emotions today.

Thinking back, she tried to separate out the facts like separate jigsaw pieces. She knew little about her adoptive circumstances, other than that her young parents had been unable to support her, but the facts were meagre and thin. Her adoptive parents had always seemed guarded on this subject, so as a child, she never had the courage to ask the big questions. The passing years only increased this inner longing for information, but each time she had mustered the courage to start an exploration, she had fallen pregnant again and became utterly lost in the aftermath of the new arrival. A pathetic excuse which she had chided herself for, but somehow, ten years and more babies than she could have imagined had happened. A decade of total and unceasing activity, where basic survival was the order of each and every day. Feeding and burping, washing and exercising, sleeping and safety. Mountains of smelly nappies, and then the endless entertainment. Counting the sleeping heads in their beds each night, and realising with a deep gratitude that they were all still alive by some miraculous means, which she couldn't totally take the credit for. Never had she been more convinced of guardian angels than when she had her babies. You would have to have more than eyes in the back of your head to keep constant watch over five small children. You needed to be a Dalek.

So it had just happened. Nothing more than that. No premeditated decision, no ulterior revenge, no convoluted psychological reason, just simply that life had got in the way, so that by the age of forty-five, she was still no nearer to solving the riddle that was her origin. It was not that she didn't think about it, or them, from time to time. Truthfully, she felt sorrier for them than for herself. Give up a baby? She'd rather have an arm chopped off. It was as inconceivable that she could have handed over one of her peachy babies as it was that the moon might turn green.

Even so, questions kept knocking on the door of her mind. How had he got her address? Who had told him where she was, and why now, of all times, was he trying to find her? Was he a stepbrother? She assumed so, but there was simply no knowing. She considered that he might even be a fake, some hideous psychopath hunting her down. Her imagination had always had a bit of an inclination to go off-piste, and she had no reason to doubt his authenticity, but still. The letter had been very brief, no real explanation. In a bizarre way, it seemed like the strangest practical joke; certainly not the sort of letter you would expect every day.

'*I am your brother,*' he had simply said.

But she already had a brother, and a very good one too. Max may not be her own flesh and blood, but she never thought of him as if he weren't. They had shared a childhood and their parents, and had come to a deep understanding of each other that only siblings have. Theirs was a relationship forged through childhood squabbles, fights, and the monotony of everyday existence, life lived in parallel for long years on end. Partners through the daily tedium of school, they had even shared many friends, being only eighteen months apart. No. She was quite sure she didn't really want another brother, and yet she couldn't ignore the implications if the reality was true.

The path twisted through a deeper valley of brambles and cleared into a wider path, the tall trees above shielding her impressively from the rain. Here the leafy canopy of green created a waterproof tunnel, and she let her hood slip down. No one could see her here. She suddenly was poised on a particular shelf in time, which felt good. After all the years of waiting, this was the right moment. This had all happened for a reason, she felt sure; maybe a higher hand orchestrating events, even? Her belief in God was as unshakeable as a rock. She only had to look at the detail in a flower or gaze at the fingers of a newborn baby to believe. She knew she was lucky in that respect. There were a multitude of things which didn't make sense, but raw faith was not one of them. Her life was still a mess of tangles and knots, but deep down, she trusted that it would all work out somehow. The opposite of that belief was frankly too depressing to contemplate.

So I will meet him, she concluded, with resolution gaining momentum in every step. *It will be an adventure, and it will be my secret. I will write back to him today, and who knows? I may just discover I even like him.*

The field was soaking up heavier rain by the time she got there, so she raised her hood again and quickened her pace. She would get home, attack the laundry and chores with renewed vigour, and pray for a window of opportunity in the afternoon to hide away from the children and compose her email. Suddenly, all sorts of ideas flooded her about how to disperse the children with maximum speed and minimum effort. The cinema. This would be the perfect day for a film. She would drive them all there and arrange a rendezvous afterwards. Who knows? She might even treat them to a pizza.

She practically raced up the road to the house in her enthusiasm, unlatching the garden gate and bounding up to the back door, letting herself in. The rain was now falling heavily. She burst into the empty kitchen before stopping abruptly in her tracks.

Basil was lying on the floor, wagging his tail furiously, surrounded by a mound of paper pieces. The letter had been torn to shreds.

Chapter 4

The airport terminal seemed busier than ever. *A world population exploding out of control*, David thought glumly, feeling chilly even before he started to sidle off the plane.

He queued an age for his suitcase, grateful as he looked at a burka-clad mother with four small children that he only had one bag to retrieve. He fished around in his rucksack for the thin blue sweater he had brought with him. Practically unused at home, he now realised that it would be woefully inadequate. He would just have to borrow one of his dad's, smiling at the incongruence. Clothes were just one of the many things that disconnected them, more than just a generational thing or fashion preference. In practically every respect, he thought ruefully, they were just so … different. He sighed as he realised that there would be no cheery welcome from him today as he rounded the corner to the arrivals lounge. Brian's arthritis was too troublesome now, and driving such a long way would be out of the question. David had called a fortnight ago, saying he was planning a visit to coincide with his father's birthday, but they both knew it was a smokescreen. He hadn't been back since the day he had set off on his big adventure and probably would have left it another year, but now there was this mystifying letter. An enormous elephant in the family room. He couldn't bring himself to talk about it on the phone or on Skype. It was too huge, too puzzling. A million questions had weaved their way through his mind since he had picked up that email. The answers to his questions could only be found face to face. He knew that intuitively.

He made his way through customs and out into the main terminal building. Outside, the sky was threatening, and he didn't relish the thought of having to delve into his suitcase to find another jacket. He made his way to the station terminal, queued for a ticket, and headed down to the platform, grabbing an espresso and noting its price with disdain. His train left in twenty minutes. He would head into London and catch the nearest available train to Sheffield, hopefully arriving in time for tea. He thought about this for a minute. In the old days, it would have been unthinkable for Mum not to be putting a meal on the table, bustling with the joy of seeing him again. She would be fixing his favourite dinner, fussing around for a fresh tablecloth to cover the worn dining room table, and invariably placing a little candle or flower at the centre of it all. Her special welcome. She could always do that, he remembered clearly. With her, he felt truly wanted, whilst his very presence always seemed to put a spring in her step. It pained him to think he had never really thanked her for the vast tranche of these little big things, and how many other things he had failed to appreciate, blindly taking her mother's love for granted until, after a few short weeks, time had run out, and she was rendered unconscious by the diamorphine pump. The hole in his heart was almost too big to bear.

And now, going back to the house where every single object had her memory attached to it was going to be an internal struggle which he would have to try and conceal. He loved his father deeply, but there was always some distance between them: part character, part upbringing, part habit. For Brian had never been a chummy type of dad. He was essentially deeply private. David learned to respect that, not tripping into no-zone areas without permission, tiptoeing around sensitive subjects as he had done ever since childhood. What he was afraid of, he wasn't quite sure; it was just an established boundary which, though invisible, always held him in check. Mum, of course, had been the opposite. Her warmth and emotional magnitude had been as wide as an ocean, her arms of embrace just as boundless. And no amount of wishing could bring her back. The best response he could think of was to mirror her memory, clothe himself with her legacy, incorporate the little habits and qualities which he had admired so much in her, and limp on, hoping that in some mysterious way, she would be noticing. Pleased with him, and perhaps relieved.

The train finally reached its destination, and David felt an old tug of pleasure at being home again. Not that he especially loved Sheffield; it was just the overwhelming familiarity of the place. Each building, road, and park had a memory attached, a ghost on every corner. But there was no one at the station he recognised, no one at all.

He had phoned from St. Pancras to say when he was arriving and was relieved to see the welcome sight of his father's car, waiting for him behind the taxi rank. He sped up to reach him, realising with some relief that he was actually glad to see his father again. He noticed how Brian heaved himself out of the car more cautiously than he remembered, placing both feet steadily on the pavement before rising to greet him. His hug was warm and wonderful. He looked older, David noticed. More stooped and less hair, but seeing him in the flesh again was just indisputably preferable to looking at his photo on the sideboard in Australia. Yes, it was good to be home.

His gaze was momentarily distracted by a flitting movement he noticed in the back of the car. He saw a coloured scarf float across the window. David frowned. So he had not come alone? He suddenly felt uneasy. There was no reason to bring anyone; his brother was miles away in London, and Brian hadn't mentioned bringing anyone. And if anything, it was a woman's face he saw smiling up at him. A round and pasty kind of face, totally unfamiliar. She was looking up at him in silent appraisal. Brian detected David's confusion.

'Oh, David,' he said. 'I'm sorry. I should have mentioned. I've bought a special friend I want you to meet.'

He coloured slightly, with a mischievous if slightly guilty smile on his face. Then he opened the back door of the car somewhat triumphantly, as if opening an oven door to reveal the Christmas turkey.

'Maureen, I'd like you to meet David. And David, I'd like you to meet Maureen, who is, well, Maureen. My new girlfriend.'

Chapter 5

David was completely taken aback. Nothing had prepared him for this. For the second time in only a few weeks, the ground beneath his feet was swaying precariously. *'Woah, steady on,'* he wanted to say. *Girlfriend*? On whose watch? He knew that this was an instinctive and immature response; Brian's decisions were not his to make, not even remotely. But he just wished he'd been consulted. It felt all wrong. It should be his mother hopping out of the car, enveloping him in one of her famous squidges, telling him how fine he looked, or how tired, or whatever. But here was this stranger, this very … unwanted stranger, being imposed on him without warning. And he was supposed to be what, delighted?

From a subconscious depth, his manners kicked in, a professional mask coming to the rescue.

'Oh, I'm sorry, yes, er—hello, Maureen. Pleased to meet you.'

"Like absolutely not," he really wanted to say. He offered out a hand, and she took it, smiling. She had a kind sort of face, not unpleasant really, and she seemed a fading version perhaps of what she might have been; it was hard to tell. She was bundled in a thick burgundy coat, with a twirly silk scarf round her neck, which always made David imagine women of a certain age who only wore scarves to hide their double chins. Only she didn't really have one of those; she was quite petite, really, and seemed small and fragile beside Brian's tall frame. He coughed.

'Maureen is my big new secret, David,' he started, but aware

21

this wasn't going to suffice, he added, 'I thought it would be nicer for you to meet her face to face, rather than imagine someone. I've been longing to tell you. His eyes were bright, and nervously hopeful.

Maureen was smiling at him appreciatively. Can't be easy for her, David had to admit. It wasn't easy for any of them, though, this awkwardness, this unexpected scenario, pregnant with the unknown. He smiled weakly back.

He had so hoped for a quiet evening with his dad, to unlock the contents of his mother's letter over a bottle of wine or some beers. Now there would be a barrier to this most intimate of conversations, which he felt so desperately needed to be had. Suddenly, he felt weary. The journey had been long and would be catching up with him soon. The thought of an evening of enforced and polite conversation was just too much to contemplate. He automatically put a hand on the car door.

'Let's hop in, shall we?' he said crisply. 'I must get home soon, Dad. I will probably be asleep before we get there.'

It was a warning to Brian and a personal code that no, this really was not okay. Shutters were going down fast. He knew he was being rude, but he had never been one to disguise his feelings cleverly. Another one of their contrasts, he thought. Brian was as hidden as a closed book, he had increasingly realised, and this unexpected relationship simply justified his belief. Holding the door open, Maureen bundled herself inside, whilst he hopped round to the front. Small comfort that they'd reserved his usual place beside his father's driver's seat, but it didn't offer much help in the face of his swirling emotions. After all, Maureen was still, inescapably, sitting in the back seat.

They drove home in awkward and stilted silence, with David lacking the energy or motivation to say much. Brian looked determinedly ahead of him as he drove, his brow furrowed, exhibiting an undisguised knot of anxiety. Soon, they turned up a final hill and into the road which he had known all his life, and ahead of them, the pale mustard-coloured terrace that had been his beloved launch pad into the world. So he was home again, but what home was it now? This question seared itself across his mind with an acute stab of pain.

What a difference a day makes, David thought, as his dad reversed into the drive, and the car came to a final halt.

Chapter 6

Tess checked her watch. Another forty minutes, and her shift would be over. She busied herself collecting charts together for handover and made a final check on her patients. All were happy and settled. Relief descended. The breakfast trolley had arrived, and the sleeping ward was waking to the sound of the cleaner's clatter and the trundle of the medicine trolley. A faint smell of bacon and antiseptic fused over the airless ward, in competition with the omnipresent waft from the sluice. She tried to disguise a yawn. Night duty had never been her thing. Her body was aching for a foam bath and bed. And even better, the four days off she had earned, after a gruelling few nights at work with a menopausal and less-than-enthusiastic colleague. It had felt like a single-handed run of shifts, and she simply needed to stop. Now.

On her way out of the hospital, she stopped at the kiosk to buy a paper and some milk, impulsively adding an almond croissant by way of reward. Fatigue and nausea were kicking in fast, but only a ten-minute bus ride, and she would be home. She ate the croissant hungrily on the bus, frustrated at her limp willpower and impatience. *This would taste so much better with tea*, she thought. She stared at the paper, unable to concentrate; after reading the same paragraph three times, she stuffed it back in her bag. She hoped there would be enough hot water for a bath, but on reflection was not sure she even had energy for that. Her legs were humming and screaming for relief, but she feared she may fall asleep if she surrendered to the caress of the bubbles. She put a key into the front door and practically fell inside.

The answer phone was flashing, and she wanted to ignore it. Against her better judgement, she pressed the button. A woman's voice with a French accent followed the beep.

'Hello Tess, this is Giselle returning your call. Please do call me to arrange a lesson when you get a moment. Thanks.' Beep.

She stumbled up the stairs, forgetting that she had even called her. Now was definitely not the time to be thinking about music lessons. She went into her bedroom, drew the curtains, and collapsed into bed. Within minutes, she was asleep, not even the sound of a vicious cat squall immediately below her window disturbing her.

Chapter 7

Kitty froze in disbelief. *No, no, NO!* she screamed to herself. This couldn't be for real. Basil looked as though he had tipped a paper shredder upside down, clearly ecstatic with his new game as he continued to rip the letter into yet more pieces. How had he managed it? But the stupidity of that question simply vanished as quickly as she asked it, knowing full well that she hadn't had time to think before she'd left. She had been in a panic to conceal the letter from Sam.

She rushed over and picked up a few of the chewed gummy remnants. But it was hopeless. They were beyond all rescue. She frantically tried to search for a piece with the address, but it was nowhere to be seen. At best, odd words could be identified, but nothing more. Her one and only ever link with her unknown past was now starting to digest in a dog's stomach. *Unbelievable.*

She slumped down on a kitchen chair. Sam's breakfast remains were littered on the table, with cereal crumbs and splashes of milk resembling giant and unwelcome blobs of glue, which had missed the bowl entirely when he poured. *What was it with his dexterity, or lack of it?* she wondered. The vital connection between dirty bowl and the dishwasher was just not a concept that she had succeeded in passing on to her eldest and most messy of sons. Still, she smiled to herself. At least he had put the milk back in the fridge. Hooray for small mercies.

She steered herself stoically towards the sink and began to run the hot water, squirting some cleaner into the bowl. Bizarrely and only in abstract odd moments, she knew she sometimes relished the satisfaction of clearing up after them all. That she had made her own rod was almost certain, but it still gave her the primal and maternal satisfaction of being needed. Being appreciated was another thing altogether. That was something she could only assume but never really gauge amidst the seasonal teenage grunts and glares. *Maybe they'll be grateful one day*, she sighed to herself, determined to swat the buzz of self-pity away like a mosquito. *Don't expect too much, Kit*, she scolded herself. *Just hold onto the small blessings. At least you don't have to spoon-feed him anymore.*

Quickly and mechanically, she cleared the decks. Deflation was settling in as quickly as a sudden coastal mist, and she needed to remove herself from Basil's presence before murderous thoughts overcame her. She wandered into the lounge. Ignoring the scene of disarray on the sofa, where more cushions were on the floor than on the couch, she looked over at her beloved piano, covered with piles of music in equal disorder. The piano subconsciously drew her, like a magnet, to sit down; she would always retreat here when perturbed. Only she knew, with profundity, its depth of companionship. The best friend you'll ever have, one of her teachers had once told her, and in some ways, it was true. As her fingers slid over the keys in search of consolation, she felt the familiarity of their response rise to meet her, and her spirits stirred. Remembering the sleeping household, she shut the doors and windows, playing very softly. Here, she was at rest in her quiet place, safe from critical ears who were now forbidden from having a nosy peep into her soul. Solace surfaced from somewhere deep within. There would be a way, she decided. Somehow, she would track him down.

Her thoughts spiralled upwards, twisting and concocting themselves into a prayer. *Please God, let him find me again. Please.*

With a tentative certainty, she started to play one of her favourite pieces, letting it touch her deepest core, and as the notes came alive under her fingertips, so did her hope.

Chapter 8

The meal over, David fumbled excuses to get to bed. Maureen had made a brave effort to welcome him and had even cooked a half-decent supper, but the strain amongst the three of them hung oppressively. He resented being forced to make polite conversation with his own father. It just seemed strange and plain odd to be sitting around the table, his father glowing in the presence of another woman, when pulsating through his entire being was the burning conundrum of his mother's letter. Did Maureen know more than he did? That thought just ignited an inner and tortured fury. He struggled not to glare at Brian over his glass.

Yawning, he pushed back his plate and reversed his chair with a squeak.

'I think I'd probably better hit the sack,' he said, smiling anaemically. 'Thanks, Maureen. That was a really good pasta. I hope you didn't go to too much trouble.'

He winced at his pretence. Even he could tell that the sauce was homemade, and the salad had been carefully pared and dressed. He felt a pang of guilt. Of course, his father was free to befriend any woman now; he just wished he'd been warned. Especially now, in the light of this mysterious letter. He ached to know what was in it. It was going to be impossible to discover anything more tonight, and he knew he should get some sleep before he disappointed Brian or himself any further.

'Night, Dad … Maureen.' He nodded to them both as he heaved himself out of his chair, avoiding his father's gaze.

He knew it would be hiding some pain, one that neither of them wanted or had asked for. He so wanted to share his father's newly found happiness, if that's what it was, but his heart was too raw and unprepared. He simply wasn't ready for Maureen, not yet.

He felt like a hypocrite. Evie had swept into his life wondrously, with as much force as surprise. She had set to work like a dogged and faithful cleaner, dusting out the cobwebs accumulated by grief and opening the windows such that the blast of fresh air took him by surprise and left him scratching his head. He sometimes wondered if he was more of a project than lover, her sanitary zeal determined to place him in a better position than when she found him. That he had welcomed the abrupt change she had brought wasn't in doubt. He was very fond of her; yes, he was indeed grateful. But as time went on, he detected a growing ripple of resentment within him which he couldn't always quell. He had no desire to be micromanaged, however worthy the intention. He wondered if he might just lose part of himself in time, and that with the years, he would become squeezed into a labelled container that bore his name. He would be placed in a box that suited her, an achievement from which she would derive deep satisfaction; whilst he would be left hollow, vacuumed dry, and utterly obsolete.

He made his way up to the half-landing and caught sight of his face in the long mirror that hung like a sentry on the faded wallpaper. The face that stared back at him confirmed the inevitable. His temples loomed naked and exposed, his forehead a stave of lines, and the white flecks in his sideburns and stubble all visible proof that the vibrancy of youth had indeed passed. Irretrievably. He knew he ought to be grateful to have a woman like Evie, who was prepared to invest in this middle-aged relic whose shelf life was stamped with undisguised clarity every time he caught his reflection. Yes, he knew what he ought to think, and yet. He sighed. Was this a sign of ageing, he wondered, just being prepared to settle for a score of six or maybe seven out of ten? Accepting someone who wasn't exactly what he had dreamt of, but which, when all was considered, proved agreeable and safe. It was that practical mediocrity which he had spurned in Brian during his youth. That orderly and risk-averse approach, not daring to dare, which had speared his dreams and aspirations with a silent deadliness. A subtle poison which had infiltrated his ambition, but now, as he reflected, was probably only symbolic of Brian's age that he found himself at now. Evie was the sensible option. He would let it be, for now.

His bedroom welcomed him like the long-lost traveller he was. He fell onto the bed, which had cradled too many weary nights to count, his sacred oasis and resting place. Dolefully, he undressed and pulled back the covers. Again, his thoughts turned towards his mother. Her presence was everywhere in this house; her fingers, which had lovingly folded his bedspread, were now stilled and absent; her fragrance still lingered in the furniture, pictures, and familiar objects which surrounded him now. He climbed under the worn but clean eiderdown and suddenly felt as if he were climbing into his child's body again. The hole she had left began to pull him down again, and he felt himself falling and falling, like Alice; his mind spiralled downwards, and his weightless body dropped until he fell yet further into a sad, lonely, and oblivious sleep.

Chapter 9

The next morning, he awoke to the muffled sound of the radio coming from the kitchen beneath him. He stirred slowly. The initial and pleasant ambience of being in his old room was quickly overtaken in his consciousness by the thud of the previous evening's events. He sat up heavily.

He could hear his father whistling downstairs, and part of him just wanted to rush down and join him. To enjoy the appreciation of his smiling face, and wishing so desperately that he could turn the clock back so that Mum could be here too, enjoying their morning coffee altogether. How she used to love his visits, he thought with a momentary pang. He would be treated like a royal guest in his own home, a world away from the obligations of childhood ritual and habit.

He paused as he remembered her cooing to make his favourite dishes, the house spic and sparkling, her love and care oozing extravagantly out of every action. His morning paper carefully laid out, and tidy geraniums paraded healthily outside the windowsill. Once, she had even hung a little bird box on the apple tree outside the kitchen window, chosen simply for the pleasure of those sitting at the table. Those little touches were actually the big things, he realised with alacrity. Details that had been lost on a boy were finally appreciated by the man. Her utter selflessness and pleasure in giving had exceeded all cost to herself, or so it had always seemed. He had never yet met anyone so innately sacrificial. Perhaps she had set a bar that was too high for him to duplicate in a wife, he thought sadly. Certainly, her memory had crystallised into virtual perfection. This was a trend which he knew accompanied bereavement, though try as he might, he could not really summon much negativity about her from his memory bank. This, too, was a welcome balm of grief, this focus on the positive. It gave him a legacy which he knew he must replicate, or her memory would be in vain.

He entered the kitchen and was surprised to see his father, standing alone at the sink, filling the kettle.

'Thought that might be you stirring,' he said, smiling at his son.

David smiled back.

Why he had thought Maureen would still be here, he wasn't sure. But before he could answer, Brian seemed to have read his thoughts.

'I'm so sorry I didn't tell you about Maureen,' he offered hesitantly, flicking on the kettle. 'I really should have told you before yesterday. I just couldn't bring myself to tell you on Skype. It was just too … big. I'm so sorry, son. I know your mum meant everything to you. Anyway, Maureen went home last night, so it's just the two of us now.'

He cut a solitary figure standing at the sink, his tall and regal frame bowed slightly with the years, his stature more frail and diminished now that his ninth decade had recently commenced.

David smiled again, appreciatively.

'I'm sorry too, Dad. Guess it was all just a bit of a shock. Shock and jet lag, you know. You'll have to fill me in. Clearly, I can't keep you safely out of my sight!'

He walked over and switched the radio off, as if to end the overture of an epic performance about to begin. Brian grinned.

'Yes, well, these things sometimes creep up on you unaware, son. It's not like I was looking, you know.'

This admission comforted David a little, as he started to put bread in the toaster.

'Anyway, I know that's not why you've come, and I do need to show you this letter. I know that's what you want to ask me about. Thank you for coming, David. It does mean a lot.' He paused. 'And I'm grateful, I really am.'

Suddenly, David felt like a priest about to hear a penance. Brian looked weary and heavily weighed down by the secret he was about to shed. He pushed his glasses back onto the top of his head and rubbed his eyes, revealing the saggy skin which surrounded them. David, for his part, felt a twitch of nervousness. What else had this most private of men not told him? He cleared his throat.

'Dad, it's okay. I mean, I wanted to come and see you anyway, but I can't think what Mum could have wanted to hide from me.' The thought of such duplicity made him wince. 'I can't really imagine there's something I don't know about her, about you, about everything, I mean, we've never really hidden anything, have we, Dad?' He wished it weren't so blatantly untrue.

David looked questioningly across at Brian, who poured the hot coffee into two mugs and splashed in some milk.

'Come here, son,' he said, beckoning to David; he pulled a chair out from the kitchen table and retrieved an envelope from the mug shelf on the faded dresser. 'This letter will come as a surprise, I know, but I wanted to be here when you read it. I haven't told Richard yet, but I will shortly.'

This seemed highly unusual in itself. Richard was David's older brother, who had always basked in his seniority. His absence in this moment simply added to David's unease.

David slowly put out his hand and took the letter. With slightly trembling fingers, he blanched at the sight of his mother's handwriting. It was addressed to both his brother and himself. Slitting open the envelope with his unused toast knife, and clutching coffee mug in hand for necessary but insubstantial moral support, he began to read:

Dear David and Richard,

It is as hard for me to pick up the pen to write this letter, as it will be for you to read it. I only hope that in time you will come to understand and forgive me for concealing the truth. I never meant to hurt either of you, least of all now. I know I won't be here when you come to read this, and that thought makes me unbearably sad and concerned for your reaction, as I know I will be unable to comfort and explain further. Please ask Dad all the questions you need to ask. We agreed together to tell you this way, although we both know it falls far short of the ideal.

The truth is, you both have an older sister. This will come as an enormous shock, and how I wish it were not so and that events had not turned out this way.

Your father and I had a child five years before we married, whilst we were still young and incapable of supporting her. I know it must sound Dickensian now, but that is just how it was back then. Our parents both strongly disapproved, and we had no other option but to give her up for adoption. You must both know that I could never have considered any alternative, even if there had been a safe alternative back then. My heart was truly broken by having to give up our beautiful baby, and not a day has gone by when I don't think of her and wonder what became of her.

We have very few details of her whereabouts, as we were barred from any contact. You may well ask why I have left it this late to either tell you or try to find her. The thing is, I had decided the time had come to trace her, when I fell terminally ill. I knew that it wasn't fair to either of us to meet me in this state. I didn't know how long the process would take, or how long I would have left. So you see, our reunion never happened, and nothing has made me sadder than this. Please know that I will love you both from beyond my grave, and her too. I hope you will find it in your hearts to forgive us and try in some small way to understand.

Maybe there will be a chance that you someday find and meet her, which would be my dearest wish, but who can know? Families are meant to be together. I know that truth now, and I have certainly paid an agonising price to discover it.

With my deepest and most profound love for you both,

Your grieving, yet ever loving
Mum

Chapter 10

The phone was ringing insistently in the hall. Tess jerked awake quickly. Years of shift work around unsavoury hours had acutely sensitised her to the dictatorship of the alarm clock, and she woke a mild panic now, momentarily afraid she might be late for work. She relaxed quickly as consciousness returned. Her block of nights was done, thank goodness. The phone would just have to wait.

As was her habit after days of nights and nights of days, she had slept through the entire day and most of the night, but it was early now, early for a phone call. It couldn't be much past seven.

She turned over and wondered if she was tired enough to try and sleep a bit more. Hard to tell. The phone seemed to be stuck in volume as well as persistence. Knowing that if she made a dash for it, it would ring off just as her hand picked up the receiver, she determined to ride it out. Answer phones were a necessary evil, she reasoned. Any minute now, her voice would click in and halt the invasion. From where she lay in bed, her ears couldn't tag the caller, so she chose to ignore it.

Trying to keep her eyes closed, she already knew there was light in the room, sensing the morning warmth breaking through her cheap, thin, and unlined curtains. She surrendered. Gazing at the window, a soft smile spread across her face. She hadn't really seen sunlight for over a week. The thought of a hospital-free day and blank diary was completely luscious, the sunshine only further making it a perfect prospect. She sat up in childlike excitement, her active mind already formulating plans and ideas which began to cascade wildly and compete for first place.

First things first, she remonstrated with herself. Nothing was going to stop the luxury of an unhurried breakfast, and she fairly bounced downstairs in her tattered fleecy dressing gown, a cast-off from her sister but unrivalled in comfort, if not style. Her eye caught the flashing phone. She deliberated. Not wanting to be responsible for anything or anyone at that particular moment, her common sense urged her to keep moving into the kitchen. But an innate sense of duty made her pause and press the answer button.

'Hello Tess, this is Giselle here again. I called yesterday about meeting up for a lesson. If you are still interested, perhaps you could give me a call? I look forward to hearing from you.' Click.

Tess sighed. Was she really interested in pursuing this, she wondered, or was it just another of her stupid whims? She had caught sight of Giselle's advert in a local newspaper, an intriguing offer of 'cello lessons for beginners.' Beginner, she most absolutely was. She had never had the luxury of music lessons, not ever. Her parents had endured one long financial struggle after another for as long as she could remember, her father more out of work than in. Then he had left them all when she was barely ten and had started all over again with a young barmaid, which had broken her mother's heart and left psychological carnage for both Tess and her older sister, Lizzie. Men were at best to be treated warily, they had long concluded. Her mother had been forced to work two and a half jobs round the clock to keep them intact, although that barely. The thought of her mother, still alone and now working in her mid-sixties at a local care home, aroused huge protective sympathies in her. Not that she had much else to occupy her, Tess knew. Work was a blessing rather than a burden, but even Sylvia couldn't keep it going forever. Still. Whilst it was there, it was good. She recognised the drive and survival instinct she had inherited, fuelling her own determination to leave school and earn a qualification which would give her regular and safe employment.

She had chosen nursing over hairdressing because she had been offered accommodation with the former, and at eighteen, her desperation to leave home and have some independence had taken precedence. Sylvia had done the best she could raising them in the circumstances, but Tess needed to be free from her sad and languid bitterness, which she was never allowed to forget whilst they lived under the same roof. Lizzie had moved out of town at the earliest opportunity, leapfrogging over a succession of unsatisfactory relationships, and was now working tables on a cruise liner, which kept her abroad for months at a time. Tess wasn't really sure she wanted to contemplate Lizzie's lifestyle too much. From time to time she would conjecture, but the sisters weren't close, not in the sense that Lizzie would ever come to Tess for advice or remotely value her opinion.

Neither could she begin to pry into Lizzie's personal life, nor did she want to. Lizzie, headstrong and wilful, had carved her own trail, leaving Tess to field Sylvia, until the nursing opportunity provided a natural break in the cycle, affording Tess her escape. Guilt had kept her training at a hospital nearby, but it suited them both: the half-hour bus journey between her flat and the rundown suburb where Sylvia lived in her drab council house, with Buster: a vintage tom cat incapable of demise or destruction, and her daily pack of Marlboros. Sylvia's aunt, a relatively unknown and peculiar widowed pensioner (Tess could only recall a hazy memory of blue hydrangeas in her front garden), had died in Bexhill last year, two years after Sylvia's own mother. It was only when Sylvia had had the unfortunate task of clearing out her bungalow that she had stumbled across an old 'cello case in the spare room, with a tired-looking instrument inside. The valuation hadn't amounted to much, and Sylvia was less inclined to take it to auction, so she had offered it to Tess, who had reluctantly put it in her spare room with a mental note to self to dispose of it when she had time. She didn't really want to sell it, at least not yet. For a few months ago, something odd had happened.

She had been in a taxi from the station, when quite by chance, she had caught the sound of some classical music playing from the driver's radio. It had suddenly disabled her. Never before had she experienced anything quite like it. It was especially alarming because she never, *ever* listened to classical music: instead, she lived off the bop and froth from the local radio which formed a constant banal backdrop on the ward, and television talent shows, which exhibited adrenaline-jerked wannabes trying to sing songs that had almost certainly been sung better by the original artists. It had been a violin sort of sound but not quite, lower, perhaps a 'cello? Her inexperienced ears couldn't tell. The sad and haunting melody woven with the piano had immobilised her completely, eliciting an emotional response that she neither knew she had nor remotely understood. To her great embarrassment, juicy big tears had formed in her eyes. She had stared at right angles out of the window for fear of detection. What was it? What exactly had extracted such a deep and sudden guttural reaction, communicating in a language she had no words to describe?

She had been torn between wanting to exit the taxi as quickly as possible to conceal her damp face and hoping the music would never stop. It was the most beautiful sound she had ever heard. She was paralysed by the sheer emotional force of it and the visceral response it demanded of her. She felt powerless in its wake.

As she scurried into work, she suddenly remembered the dusty hard 'cello case sitting in her little box room. Now instantly, the image of that object had taken on a new and profound meaning. She determined then and there that she would find someone to teach her how to play it. A crazy, ludicrous, and wild idea, but there it was. That is exactly what the music had done to her. An intoxicating madness, but a most sweet and enticing insanity, all at once. So when she stumbled across Giselle's advert, it had seemed by divine predestination that the 'cello had found her, rather than the other way round.

So it was, before she had time to think otherwise, that she had left a message on Giselle's mobile number, remonstrating with herself that she could always say she'd changed her mind if her courage decided to desert her at the eleventh hour.

Now she was faced with a choice and two voicemails which she couldn't very well ignore. Her sense of obligation exasperated her at times like this. Most of her friends wouldn't bother to pursue something they weren't sure about. This was way out of her comfort zone. She wasn't at all sure what she thought a 'cello teacher would look like or *be* like, for that matter, or what they might even have in common. Most worryingly, she doubted she any latent talent for music at all. No one had ever spotted her at school, but then there had never really been any chance for that. Her only recollections of class music had been of Miss Jeffries attempting unsuccessful crowd control, hopelessly trying to prevent the boys from vandalising the keyboards and playing light-swords with the drumsticks. Her friend Alice had had piano lessons, but she had been so teased and bullied with her plastic round glasses and horsey teeth that she had swiftly found more congenial security at the local grammar school. Tess had missed her. Her dedicated commitment to piano lessons had intrigued her, an unknown world that she was both jealous of and unsure about. Giselle certainly sounded foreign, but her voice was gentle and beguiling, soft and unthreatening. Her accent was suspiciously French, yet it was soothing. Nothing to be afraid of, she consoled herself. And yet. The risk of appearing a complete and unqualified moron now loomed very large.

She went into her shoebox-sized kitchen and filled up the kettle. Outside, she was pleased to see that the road was pleasantly quiet, the sky blue and cloudless, even if autumn was in full swing with fiery colour and exclamation. The perfect day for not being indoors, she said to herself. Sylvia would be working today, so she had no compulsion to visit, and she wanted to indulge in a spot of retail therapy at the new shopping mall. It was also, she couldn't deny, the perfect day to have a 'cello lesson.

She drank her tea slowly. What could possibly go wrong? Fortitude rose as her breakfast settled inside. It would be something to tell the girls at work, she chuckled.

'You did *what*?' she could hear them jibe. Yeah. It would be worth the response. She paused.

C'mon, Tess, she told herself. *You can do this. What's to lose?*

She went into the hall and picked up the phone.

'Giselle? It's Tess Gibson here. Sorry not to get back to you, but I've been working.' Pause. 'Yes, er, yes. I am around this afternoon. Three o'clock? Yes, that's fine. Sure. I can find you, don't worry. Okay. See you then.'

She replaced the handset and, slowly and deliberately, went upstairs to shower and dust down the hard bottle-green 'cello case which now, she felt sure, stared back at her impressively.

Chapter 11

The next week, Kitty had thrown herself back into the usual cacophony of her busy, chaotic life. Her level of despair had been tempered somewhat by the sheer joy of knowing about David's existence, and she had buried all thoughts about the practicalities of finding him by imagining him in her mind: his looks, his character, and a thousand loose ends which only he could untangle. Her prayer had been sincere and real. She didn't now doubt that she would somehow make contact with a brother who only a week ago she didn't know existed.

She had even tiptoed into an old village church a week ago, silently and quietly kneeling down in the vestry on an unforgiving cassock, making an appointment with the only One who could possibly help her now. The cool quiet air inside the darkened church had soothed her spirit, as she observed the carefully arranged flowers and watched the sun making a kaleidoscope of colours through the stained glass window, shafting pretty darts of light into a pool in front of the altar. The patterns were alive as they moved, kindling into flame her own small flicker of faith. She had dropped a coin into the box and lit a small candle, which she placed in the sandbox. For David, she offered. And peace had come, descending on her soul with wordless comfort and invisible assurance. '*All will be well*,' St Julian seemed to be whispering. Kitty felt it to be true.

She had recently started volunteering at a day centre in

village, realising with both joy and despair the resonance she had with people nearly twice her age, which she viewed as a useful dress rehearsal for her own senility she felt sure was advancing prematurely. But despite that, she was really loving it. There was rarely a day she didn't saunter home with a grin on her face and a story to tell. Kitty was a natural comedienne who could craft a joke out of most situations, much to the delight of Nick. To be fair, he was drowning in overwork and a business that regularly kept him awake at night, but this was not a fact he often shared with Kitty. He needed her verve and sunny disposition more than she realised, and she, unaware of this fact, often viewed his seeming disinterest with disdain.

It wasn't that she didn't love him deeply. He was the rock of her life, even if at times she wore him like a familiar and well-worn cardigan rather than a smart suit. They had married young after university, but despite that, the exacting years of parental survival had forged a deep companionship that was the curiosity of their friends, who often viewed their survival with incredulity in the light of their multiple offspring. For Kitty, Nick's calm stability was a prize beyond price. She had told him, of course, about David's letter, and predictably, he had reassured her that David would try to contact her again (even though secretly he believed it was unlikely). Despite all appearances to the contrary, he was still her biggest fan. The growing insecurities of her adoption had made him extra protective towards her. He did not want to see her hurt, and especially not now. He could see how much this letter had meant to her, and if Kitty had felt violent towards Basil, then he found himself feeling so too, only possibly more so.

During one of those surreal exchanges with a hearty nonagenarian at the lunch club, Kitty's attention was drawn to a concert that was coming to town in a fortnight. The said gentleman, a delightful if slightly confused retired colonel, had been telling the interested but totally deaf ladies on his table about an Albanian pianist who was coming to play at the Town Hall very soon. He of course was lamenting the fact that he wouldn't be able to go himself, now that his driving license had been annulled, but he wondered if they would like to go. The obvious fact of their auditory and mobility limitations had completely escaped his notice.

Kitty listened in sympathy. *It must be hard to have one's social life so curtailed*, she thought sadly. The concert was on a Saturday, and she had strictly insisted she didn't work weekends. Taxi duty always seemed to rule then instead.

She found herself initially drawn into the conversation as an interpreter, but seeing the delight of everyone round the table, she had, to her own astonishment, offered to drive anyone who would like to go. This so often happened with Kitty. Words would tumble out unfiltered before her brain could follow, and it had landed her in untold trouble on too many occasions. But there it was. The offer was now on the table, and there was no going back. She knew it would require some major domestic juggling to pull it off, hoping earnestly that Nick wouldn't be playing golf that morning, or she would be stuffed. She rather relished the thought of a concert, forgetting how many years it had been since she last went to one. Plus it would be so good to give some pleasure to these dear old folk she was becoming rather attached to.

'Whad'ya think, Nick?' she had asked him cautiously, late one night in bed as he was reading the paper.

'Huh?'

'The *con*cert. Do you think I can do it?'

Nick reluctantly tore himself away from the headlines.

'Concert?'

'*Nick*! The one I've told you about like every day for the last week?'

'Oh … yup. Sure.' He smiled across at her, pretending to understand. He vaguely recalled the idea.

'Well?'

'Go for it, Kit. I've got you covered.' He blinked slowly, willing himself to remember.

'Thanks, my man,' she said, pecking a kiss on his shoulder and slipping gratefully under the covers.

The day of the concert dawned chilly but bright, the sun's appearance balancing the nip in the air and illuminating autumn's display of ruby extravagance. She had collected their addresses and had planned a circular route to collect them. First she would drop the two children off at the swimming club; she had begged Jenny, her best friend, to retrieve them. She couldn't put into words the depth of her friendship with Jen. She was a true soulmate, the sister she had so longed for but never actually had. They had met at primary school and were still inseparable. School to university, then weddings and births: they had all been shared and dissected, lived and borne. At times over a pint or two, their husbands had admitted exasperated frustration at their closeness, but both had to concede their wives would be incalculably poorer without each other. Neither could they deny the massive benefits to them both of having an extra parent on hand when need demanded. Such as now. With Jenny around, Nick was free to escape to the golf course, and by a stroke of good fortune, the other three kids had been sleeping over at friends on Friday night, so all he had to do was honour the dogs with a quick walk, before heading off to the golf club to enjoy a few hours of coveted child-free sanity.

Kitty drove to the town hall and sat in the car park, deliberating. The various assortment of walking sticks, yet only two hands to support all five of them into the building, got the better of her. Mrs Gunthorpe had talked incessantly for the entire journey, and Kitty made a mental note to remind her about the importance of keeping quiet during the performance. The colonel was also in high spirits, giving Mrs Penn a word-by-word account of a concert he had been to in Gibraltar during the war, when Myra Hess had been playing and they had had to listen in virtual darkness because of the enemy blackout. Kitty turned the car round and headed for the front entrance of the town hall, which she parked in front of. She hopped out swiftly to explain to the attendant, who right now was frowning at her from the doorway.

Finally, after a Promethean effort—and a lengthy toilet stop (during which Kitty vowed to herself that she would never wear a corset)—she had them all sitting near the front, with herself stoutly seated at the end of the row. She had separated the colonel and Mrs Gunthorpe by putting Miss Trimble between them, whose total deafness would hopefully ensure they looked straight ahead rather than left or right at each other. Mrs Penn, once sat down, had closed her eyes and was nodding off peacefully before the concert had even begun. Mrs Watson, sitting next to her, was quietly and serenely looking at her programme with an ornate, bone-handled magnifying glass. Kitty shot a glance over her shoulder at the programme. Two Bach preludes and a fugue, then some Mendelssohn and Bartok in the first half, followed by a Rachmaninov 'dessert' after the interval. *Heaven*, she thought dreamily.

Kitty had long harboured hopes that she would one day pick up where she left off with the piano, before a career in journalism and five successive children had eclipsed that plan. She had grown up with an old walnut-cased upright piano, on top of which her mother had squeezed every conceivable photo frame, such that if she ever played too loudly, at least one of them would topple off. She had learnt from a sweet old lady called Miss Larkham, who used to pop round after school on Tuesdays with a large jar of smarties for every scale she could play correctly and a toffee if she played her pieces without a mistake. Kitty wasn't sure how many calories she must have absorbed over the years, but the results had been worth it. By eighteen, she was playing proficiently enough to accompany friends or play for the annual carol soirées which her mother insisted on hosting, before university had come and swept her away with errant distraction. But like a bird always coming home to roost, she would eagerly savour the holidays. Digging out her old favourite music from inside the ancient piano stool embroidered with yellow roses, she would mobilise her fingers again, much to her parents' adoration. Yes, the piano had always been her friend. And now, she had the next hour to enjoy the charms of a professional. It would be worth it. She breathed a deep sigh of relief.

A ripple of applause started to sweep through the audience. From the left of the stage, Kitty could see the soloist come onto the platform. He made a short journey to the front of the piano and, with bowed head and swishing raven hair, saluted the crowd with a curt nod and half-smile, and then he turned decisively to the piano and sat down.

Yani Belushi, Kitty noticed from the programme. A total stranger. She assessed him with respectful scrutiny, a novice to an expert.

The maestro stands from his seat and puts out a hand to steady him on the corner of the piano. He is trembling, his hair wet, and his back a rivulet of sweat cascading down his back under his jacket. He is utterly spent. The final force of Sergei's passion has demanded more from him than he is able to give. For he can only play that piece with her there with him. She is alive in every bar; in every phrase and line, he traces her grace and poise in the exquisite beauty which the notes afford him, her image in his mind unleashing the full depth of his heart. For this is the only place he can feel her now, in his fingers. She is lost to him in every other way. The music has prized open a wound, again. He nods and takes his bows. Then, turning, he leaves the stage abruptly, swiftly gathers his music and coat from the small backstage room, and before further ado, for he is incapable of speech now, slips out through a side fire door, and out into the street.

Chapter 12

David had written his letter. With Brian's help and after three days of long walks on the moors surrounding the city to clear his head, he had framed what he wanted to say to this mystery sister. He had an overwhelming desire to see her, feeling sure that her very womanhood would somehow bring him closer to his mother—their mother, even. He just couldn't get his head around that thought. In his mind, he imagined a younger version of Mum, someone who she was reincarnated in, someone who he would automatically love. It was hard to conceive of having an older sister. He tried to imagine how that would have played out. Maybe they wouldn't have got on, after all. Maybe she would have been overbearingly bossy, or nerdy, or just plain irritating. Maybe none of those things; or maybe all of them.

And so he posted his letter. Brian had done his research well, and it hadn't actually been that hard to track her down. He had wanted David to send his letter first, planning that as events unfolded, his own letter would flow on afterwards, but David suspected this was all a smokescreen. He knew only too well that his father was on a precipitous emotional journey; he sensed that this was too immense and raw for him. For Brian was indeed struggling without success to deal with the enormity of tracing a daughter he had abandoned. The guilt which had seeped into his entire life ever since now threatened to overwhelm him. It was better and easier for David to go first. So it was that David had discovered that she was living in Kent, many miles away, and that she had a different surname, which made him suppose she was married. That led him to think about children. Which led him to think about nieces and nephews he knew nothing about, his own childlessness having only recently registered to him as being a state he might wish to alter.

He had phoned Evie to fill her in with the dramatic turn of events, supposing she would be transfixed, but to his surprise and ill-concealed disappointment, she simply listened and then moved on hurriedly to tell him about her work and possible promotion, and how it had been since he left. Her job consumed her with the same urgent desire for improvement that she applied to him. He felt abandoned. This was too big to him for it not to be important to her also. It was all he could do not to yell at her on the phone, but knowing this would cause more problems than it would solve, he bit his lip and was glad she couldn't see his face.

He paused before the postbox, keenly aware of the dynamite hidden between the white sealed envelope he held in his hands. He placed the letter on the lip of the box, held it for a few seconds, and felt his heart lurch as his fingers released their grip, then heard it drop irretrievably and inescapably to the bottom.

Walking home, he detected both a lightness of spirit and a twinge of apprehension in equal measure. Now it was done. There was no going back, and he steeled himself with thoughts of the unknown future which now faced him. He kicked through the damp leaves, which were fast making a moist carpet on the pavement, and breathed deeply. The fine autumn day was invigorating him, and the moist air a welcome change from the sweaty Australian heat he had sought to escape to. He realised that he did in fact love the seasons here, after all. It was just the in-between bits he couldn't deal with, the smoky skies which offered nothing back except to compound a sense of melancholy.

But today, the sky was both fresh and hopeful, softly blue with a few latticed streams of barely visible cloud, making streaks across their wide canvas. He quickened his pace and thought of Brian, at home and waiting for him to return for lunch. He only had another week now before he would need to go home, and he had an overwhelming urge to spend more time with him, especially now that a dam seemed to have burst between them. His sister's existence had imperceptibly yet incredibly destroyed a barrier of silence that David had thought was irreversible. He noticed a new Deli across the road and impulsively crossed over and went inside. He chose an expensive piece of cheese and some fresh olives, keen to please Brian in any way he could and knowing it would. It was those little things again, he could almost hear his mother whispering in his ear. The little big things.

He turned round the final corner which led to his street. His house was still a few hundred yards down the road, but looking towards it, he stopped instantly. Unmistakably, outside where he knew his house was, an ambulance was parked. His heart lunged forward for the second time that morning, feeling that it had fallen down a mine shaft. He clutched his jacket pocket for his phone and then, cursing himself, remembered he'd left it behind. Quickly, he started to run.

Chapter 13

Tess paused outside the shiny black door of the terraced Victorian house, balancing the 'cello on the top step. It was heavy, and she was glad to put it down. It didn't feel much bigger than she was, and in truth, it wasn't. She cut a slight, trim figure standing there, her scarf wound twice round her neck in shades that magnified two big denim blue eyes. She had dug out an old winter coat that she thought looked vaguely smarter than her puffer jacket, and her augmented blonde hair, cut to a neat shoulder-length bob, swayed tidily in the wind. She had been in a quandary about shoes but had finally decided on ankle boots that gave her a bit of a height advantage over the cumbersome instrument. She took a deep breath. For all she knew, Giselle was probably peeking out the window right now; it never occurred to Tess to think that she might be as nervous as she was herself.

This was partially true, for Giselle had already caught sight of a small figure struggling up the hill, looking every bit like Pilgrim carrying his burden upon his back. Her heart sank a bit at having to resort to desperate measures. Not that teaching could entirely be classified as desperate, she corrected herself. It was just Giselle knew that in all honesty, she was not a natural teacher, quite apart from speaking English being an uphill struggle. It was merely something that moving here had necessitated. She had been in town for two months now, had signed up a short-term rent, and had struggled for weeks to find regular employment after aborting her prestigious job with the orchestra in Paris. She hadn't dared to settle in London, by far the most likely place for her to secure work, for fear her tracks would be followed. Neither had she dared to take a job on the performing circuit, for fear of reprisal and recognition, dutifully shunning orchestral openings in preference for a part-time post at the university, in a town where she knew no one and no one knew her. This had provided her the perfect anonymity needed, if not the necessary income to exist safely. Her working contract was only for a year, which had also suited her, so she had persuaded herself that a few pupils would only constitute a short-term arrangement, a fact she would have to conceal for now.

Outside, Tess hesitated before ringing the bell. She deliberated whether to ring the bell or bang the large tarnished door knocker, deciding she didn't want to sound like an unwelcome bailiff. She was aware that her first impact was going to have to go a long way to compensate for the disastrous musical impression she felt sure she was about to make. Looking through the long window to the right of the door, she had noticed a sparsely furnished room, a small tiled fireplace, and long blue velvet curtains, which hung from the below the high ceiling in a rather imposing if antiquated fashion, thanks to the bronze tassels clipping them back neatly to the wall. She rang the doorbell, pressing it long enough to ensure it was heard. Her mouth had gone dry, and she gulped nervously.

A few seconds later, she heard the sound of footsteps rapidly descending the stairs from inside, and the next thing she knew, the door had opened, and on the other side stood a tall and willowy figure, much younger than Tess had imagined, smiling and extending a long and slender right arm.

'Tess. So pleased to meet you. Come in. Please.'

Giselle's voice was gentle, and her soft French accent unmistakable.

'*Alors*. Let me help you with that,' she said, motioning to the weight on Tess's shoulder.

Tess lugged her culprit companion over the doorstep. Trying

not to be intimidated by Giselle's height, Tess looked up, grinning weakly.

'Thank you,' she said. 'At least this is one way to keep fit!' she quipped nervously.

Giselle smiled back. She was beguilingly beautiful, in a distant and understated way. Her smile was one of those that invaded her whole face, teeth beautifully uniform and clean and surrounded by thin milky translucent skin, on which there was not a splash of make-up, but what struck Tess the most were her opal-shaped hazel-green eyes, which now looked down at her appraisingly. Her long, silky, nut-coloured hair was ruler straight and fell obediently over delicate shoulders. Tess realised they must be of a similar age, and for no particular reason, this comforted her a little. Giselle beckoned for her to go through to the lounge.

'Alors,' she said again. 'This is where we will be, and please. Have a seat.'

She pointed to one wooden-backed chair, next to which was another one, with her own 'cello propped up against it. In between both chairs were a music stand, a book of blank manuscript paper, and a pencil already placed on it. Tess sat down cautiously and decided to come clean.

'I'm afraid I must explain why I am here,' she began and thereupon proceeded to tell her of the unlikely gift from Great-Aunt Con, the music on the radio, and the coincidence of seeing Giselle's advert a few days later.

'I confess, I can't really believe I am doing this,' she said apologetically. 'It's not as if I've ever done any music before, and I feel a bit of a fraud, actually. So please don't let me waste your time.' *Or mine*, she added silently to herself.

'Nonsense,' Giselle said, still smiling that smile. It really did have a hypnotising effect. 'You must know that there is music in everyone. Some hide theirs more than others, but it is my job to let it out. Besides, if you never try, you will never find out, *mais non?*'

Tess was impressed by her English and then immediately

crippled by the reminder of her own appalling French and swallowed again.

'Yes, well, I suppose that is why I wanted to come,' she found herself saying, unconvincingly. 'Maybe we should have a trial lesson, just to see perhaps?' she added.

'Bien. Of course,' Giselle agreed. 'I understand entirely. I was a beginner once too, you know.'

Her eyes, laughing with reassurance, made Tess want to relax. This might not be so bad after all.

'Now, shall we begin?' said Giselle. 'Bring your 'cello case over here, and let's see what's inside.'

Chapter 14

David sped up, arriving at his front gate the same time that two paramedics were wheeling Brian out the front door on a trolley. He lay motionless and ashen. Maureen stood behind them in the doorway, her face in turmoil. She looked up and saw David with a degree of relief, but she was blocked behind the ambulance men and couldn't move. David waited as they lifted his father down the path and through the gate, until their faces were in alignment. Brian's eyes were closed. He looked pale, and David wasn't even sure if he was conscious.

'*Dad*?' he whispered.

Brian's head turned slightly towards him, his heavy eyelids struggling to respond.

'Dad, are you alright?' he said, regretting the words as he said them.

For Brian clearly wasn't alright, that was much was clear. David reached down to touch Brian's hand, but it felt limp and clammy. Brian wasn't immediately recognising him, and David's medical instincts were working rapidly. He glanced at the paramedics, who were attaching leads to his chest with deft expertise and hurrying to get him into the open ambulance.

'I'm Brian's s-son,' he stuttered. 'What's happening? I'm a doctor, for what it's worth,' he added, with no discernible degree of confidence.

'Hello, sir,' one of the paramedics said. 'Looks like your

father's had a heart attack. We need to get him down to the hospital straightaway. We picked up an emergency call from your mum. He fell and lost consciousness. Vital signs weak when we arrived, no cardiac arrest, as yet.'

They lifted Brian past the gate, over the pavement, and quickly brought him up to the waiting ambulance.

David nodded, knowing only too well that the next few moments were critical. He looked on hopelessly. In slow motion, David looked on at his father, seeing instead a man who looked old and weak. It was not an image he would easily forget. Behind him, he could Maureen's footsteps drew near. His mum; not hardly. He turned his head to look at her and saw her tears mounting up. He instinctively put his arm around her. She was shaking and seemed so small and vulnerable. Clearly in shock too, as David realised that she was probably nearly eighty herself. She wasn't perhaps as strong as he had assumed.

'I'm so sorry I wasn't here,' he offered, feeling wretched for the distress Maureen must have suffered in his absence.

'I stupidly left my phone behind,' he explained, lamenting this fact entirely. The thought of not being there when his father most needed him was acutely distressing.

'Oh, David,' Maureen began, her lip quivering. 'It happened so quickly. You had only been gone about ten minutes, when I heard him fall in the hall. I was in the kitchen preparing the lunch; he didn't cry out or anything. I just heard a crash, and there he was, collapsed on the floor. I, I thought he was … *dead.*'

She started to sob quietly.

'I didn't know what to do. He wasn't responding, so I just grabbed the phone and called the ambulance. Waiting for them to arrive was terrible; he was only just breathing, but he looked so … grey. He couldn't talk to me.'

She sniffed again, clutching a handkerchief to her nose.

'I didn't know your phone number anyway,' she added, which only marginally comforted David. 'I kept thinking of you, with losing your mum and all. I haven't known Brian that long really, you know. He's just been such a good friend to me since my Ken passed away.'

David suddenly felt very guilty. Why Maureen's past had never occurred to him before filled him with shame. He was filled with remorse for casting her in semi-adulterous light, when all along, they had filled a void for each other with a companionship that was both necessary and healing. Immediately, his feelings for her were transformed, and he gave her another squeeze.

'Listen, Maureen,' he heard himself saying. 'Dad's a strong man.'

He tried to say this reassuringly, although at this precise point in time, he had never been less convinced. He needed to bluff, however, for his own sake as much as hers.

'He will be in the best of hands. I know you did all the right things.'

He noted with some reassurance that there were advantages of living near a teaching hospital.

'C'mon, let's go and grab some things and follow him down there,' he said, starting to steer Maureen back up the path to the house.

David drove as fast as discretion would allow. Fortunately, the roads were not impeded by rush hour traffic, although, being a city, they were never empty. Buses were the most infuriating. He wanted to slap a siren on top of his roof and be able to weave freely in and out of the lanes, but conscious that he must remain calm for Maureen, he bit his lip and tried not to think what was happening to Brian right now in the ambulance. He would need to call Richard. His brother would no doubt be at work in his smart London office, dealing with multiple important things simultaneously, or worse, be conducting a board meeting from which he couldn't be extracted. As brothers, they had become a little closer in recent years, especially since David's divorce and the death of their mother. Their natural competitiveness had probably played a healthy part in the development of two undeniably successful careers, a competition that was salvaged from any malady by the very contrasting paths they had chosen. Richard, the oldest, was married to the suave and upwardly mobile Olivia, and both seemed ostensibly happy together, although in truth, they were both as wedded to their jobs as they were to each other, hence ruling any children out of the equation for now. David wished Richard was here now. He knew Brian privately adored them both, and they him. Especially now.

David swung into the hospital car park, and hopped out to open the door for Maureen, who he quickly realised with frustration wouldn't exactly be able to run to the A&E department. Mustering all the patience he could, they linked arms together and accelerated towards the row of ambulances that lined up outside the casualty department doors. David ushered her in and made a beeline for the reception desk. His heart sank. The waiting room was full and busy. He spoke to an officious-looking receptionist and gave her the details. Next, they were told to take a seat; fatal instructions, David knew. They found themselves sandwiched between a sixteen-year-old clad in rugby kit and more covered in mud and blood than injury, and a pink febrile toddler who had fallen asleep in her young mother's balloon-sized arms. David sat for a few minutes, but waiting was not something he was inclined to do; neither was playing by hospital rules. Maureen touched his arm, sensing his awkwardness.

'Perhaps they will let us see him soon?' she suggested. 'It all looks horribly busy today.'

The child next to them started to wake and cough, her cheeks turning from a rosy to blackcurrant colour with every spasm. David tried to ignore her.

'Knowing these places, we could sit here for hours,' he said grimly. 'They told me he's in Resus, so I'll give 'em ten minutes, then I will start jumping up and down.'

It was at that moment that the doors swung open and a young

nurse came into view, pushing an unwieldy wheelchair in which sat a middle-aged man in grubby pyjamas. She rolled it next to David and Maureen, parked the chair alongside them, and applied the brakes.

'Just leaving you here for a few minutes, Mr Taylor, whilst I go and chase this X-ray form,' she explained politely to her patient, who looked tired and uncomfortable.

She looked down at David and Maureen and smiled. David glanced up at her, distracted. But what he found looking at him were two arrestingly deep blue eyes, and a face that seemed familiar yet unknown all at once. A face which interrupted him, and yet in seconds, had left an imprint that was indelible.

Chapter 15

Kitty yawned and rolled over. She put out a leaden arm to reach her phone and stuck an exploratory leg diagonally across the bed to wake Nick. But he was already up. The sheets were still warm where he had been, and Kitty smiled. She knew he would be busy shaving in the bathroom and then on his dutiful way to bring up her morning cup of tea, which she realised tenderly, she was more grateful for than she had ever really told him. Twenty years of morning tea.

I am a lucky one, she thought. It really does pay to be a sleepaholic, she realised astutely.

For Nick slept as lightly as a feather, always had done, and probably always would. And as far as she could detect, he hadn't suffered any serious consequences to date, yet now, for the first time, Kitty considered how different her life would be if she had to coax a snoring, reluctant husband out of bed each morning, rather than the other way round. It was not a pleasant thought. Sam was bad enough. He had inherited her propensity for sleepy hibernation, and she knew that her morning drink was essential before daring to tackle Sam and goad him out of oblivion.

Her mind paused as she thought of him, and she let out a heavy maternal sigh. Right now, he resembled a gigantic ball of wool with which she was trying to knit a lovely jumper, hugely impeded by the big knots she had to keep unpicking, with varying degrees of patience. Patience was not one of Kitty's virtues. It was a weakness which only seemed to justify itself when trying to shoo five children out of the house every morning. Kitty's brood had learned from painful experience that if they hadn't prepared themselves the night before, they would receive only milliseconds of assistance before Kitty's emotional whistle blew and the whole military operation of leaving the house by 8.05 would crumble. And each of them, in their own secret way, treasured leaving the house as calmly as possible without having ruffled Kitty's feathers.

Yet Sam seemed to test her to her very limits of endurance. If left to his own devices, she felt sure he would morph into a hapless delinquent who spent the day under covers, superglued to headphones and devoid of all necessity for speech. It wasn't that she knew he didn't care about college and his exams, but much to her extreme irritation, he seemed to cope with all deadlines by complete denial, which only increased both her impatience and her blood pressure. She knew it was a vicious circle, and she needed to stand back. Yet somehow, in a process that was both wordless and undefined, the pattern had become such a process of habit that neither of them knew quite how to extract themselves from the battle without redefining the entire rules. But there it was. The daily conflict was as unavoidable as the school run itself.

Today would be no exception, she thought wearily. Sam was going for some work experience in London, which she had somehow engineered through vastly complicated efforts via a colleague of Nick's cousin. The link and favour was tenuous, at best, and was quite possibly going to end in disaster if Sam decided, as he most often did, that any form of communication was unnecessary, and he was simply going to grunt his way through the day. The reality of a grown-up employment world still seemed light-years away from her firstborn, but this was only conjecture on her part. She had washed and put out a clean pair of trousers and freshly pressed shirt in his room by way of enticement, hoping against hope that he might wake up with a fresh and supernatural injection of enthusiasm, and a desire to be compliant with the dress code.

Downstairs, she could hear Basil barking at the back door. His bladder was full, and recently, he had taken to making a canine point of emptying it against the kitchen dresser if he was required to wait too long in the morning. She heaved herself out of bed with some urgency. Tilly was calling from downstairs in the utility room, something about no tights, and Angus was banging his football boots together in the hall, which she now realised would mean clods of earth scattered everywhere. She made a mental note to self to hoover up later, before the mud had time to become embedded in the faded Kilim, a present from Nick which he had bought her on a package tour to Turkey in those prehistoric days before the children arrived, when they had had absolutely no idea it would have to compete with muddy football boots for preservation.

As she entered the kitchen, Tilly's voice was rising to a shriek.

'Muuuuuuum!' she wailed. 'I told you I needed more tights.'

The fact that Kitty had bought a pack of five two weeks ago seemed to have escaped Tilly's notice. *Does she deliberately sit in lessons snipping holes in them?* Kitty wondered. Deciding the fight was not worth it, she scooted back upstairs to extract a pair of her own and collided with Nick on his way down. He was frowning.

'Kit, let the dog out, will you? I haven't got time to clear him up this morning.'

He sounded hassled, and he still looked tired. Before she could answer, Sam's rap alarm started to waft down the stairs, and Lucy's hair dryer started going off simultaneously. Nick looked thunderously in the direction of her bedroom. As both twins and the eldest, they had the least of their father's tenacity at this hour of the day, expecting, as he did, that they would somehow set a good example to the younger ones. In this, he consistently felt varying degrees of disappointment.

'How many times have I told her not to wash her hair in the morning?' he asked, groaning in despair.

Kitty wisely decided not to engage in the controversial subject of teenage female coiffure.

'Don't worry, love,' she said flatly. 'We'll all be out in a jiffy.'

She bounded across to Lucy's room, knocked loudly a couple of times, and yelled up to Sam that he had ten minutes. Then she grabbed a pair of black tights from her own drawer and scurried downstairs to appease both Basil and Tilly, hoping that the latter wouldn't notice that the tights weren't hers. Angus looked up, smiling.

'Good day for my match, Mum,' he said, grinning. 'And thanks for washing my kit.'

Kitty felt her heart doing flip-flops. In one sentence, he had absolved himself of all blame for the chaos that littered the hall floor, with his usual panache and precision. He was simply the most infuriatingly charming child she had ever met. It worked every time.

Toby sauntered out of the study, looking serious. His Thunderbird glasses framed a pale eleven-year-old face with sonority and weight.

'Mum, I've lost my history prep. I know it was on Dad's desk last night. Has Angus moved it? Mrs Thompson will *kill* me. Why does everyone move my things?' he asked, in consternation.

Kitty looked sympathetically at her youngest child. *He bears the whole world on his scrawny shoulders*, she acknowledged to herself. Knowing that anxiety would be spreading at metastatic speed, and that her resilience to help him more than the others was impartially based on his age, she darted back into the study and began sifting her way through the paper mountain that was Nick's desk. Fortunately, the said culprit was only hidden under three letters, and she wondered, not for the first time that week, if she should take Toby for another eye check-up.

'Here you are, sweetie,' she said, handing him his prize. 'I'm sure Mrs Thompson will love it.'

Toby looked at her adoringly.

The kettle was boiling. Every morning, Kitty wished that she could somehow split herself into six or more pieces and attend to them all concurrently. She swept a hand through her tangled curls, where isolated silver threads were beginning to make filigree patterns around her face, and hurriedly poured water into the tea that Nick had started to make, popping four slices of bread into the toaster.

Sam unexpectedly appeared in the kitchen, looking alarmingly dishevelled. He was wearing an old pair of jeans with rips across the knees and a black T-shirt on which was emblazoned the words 'Unusual Genius.' He looked vacantly in the direction of the toast. Kitty steeled herself. In a voice both artificial and controlled, she spoke to him with a deliberately blank face.

'We've got to be at the station in twenty minutes, love,' she began, hoping the connection would fall into place. Silence.

'Will you be going like that?' Her voice rose suspiciously.

Sam looked at her in disbelief. Then, thinking better of the unwanted combat, he turned and set off up the stairs again.

Kitty was momentarily engulfed by mild relief. Consoling herself that he'd bought his train ticket in advance, which now saved them valuable minutes, she started squeezing the tea bags against the mugs. She felt Nick come up behind her and, in an impulsive gesture of solidarity, turned to give him a squeeze. He was her staunch ally throughout the daily morning war zone. And she was grateful. The toast popped up.

Miraculously and almost to Kitty's disbelief, everyone except Sam was in the car within the next ten minutes. Nick had made a run for the main road, where a colleague picked him up religiously at eight o'clock. Tilly was bundled up in a snood, which covered most of her face, and Angus and Toby had for once got into the back without arguing about seats. Lucy was sitting looking every bit the prima donna for having beaten Sam to the passenger seat, her rapidly ironed hair pinned up elaborately with black sequined slides, and a disturbing amount of mascara adorning her pretty green eyes, which Kitty was inclined to think leant more cartoon than artistic impression. Thoughts of Minnie Mouse came to mind. She pipped the horn twice and started to turn the car round in the drive. Glancing up in her mirror, she was pleased to see Sam coming out of the back door, dressed almost respectably in her chosen clothes, but his straight black hair still slanting in opposing horizontal lines, and forming a jagged screen across his eyes. To her chagrin, he was still wearing his favourite scruffy vans and a jacket, which although dark, could hardly be described as office appropriate.

Never mind, she told herself. No one will have to see his mother today, unlike those ghastly parents' evenings where she felt sure that she, Kitty, was under grave suspicion every attendance, rather than Sam, who perhaps should be. The thought of today's obscurity raised her spirits somewhat. No. All she needed to do was drop the kids within walking distance of school, leave Lucy in a road near college, and deposit Sam safely at the station, complete with ticket and a map to the offices, and a reminder to buy some sandwiches for lunch.

She circled into the station forecourt, having mostly emptied the car of its cargo. No noise from Sam in the back made her suspect that he was still half-asleep.

'Okay then, love?'

She glanced over her shoulder at him, which simply confirmed her suspicions.

'Hope it goes well today, then, and remember to say huge thanks when you're done. They are doing you a big favour today. Oh, and don't get lost getting there; I've given you the map. I'll be back here at six. Ta-ta.'

He looked impassively at her, though his lips gave the tiniest smirk.

With a nod, he opened the car door and raised his arm half-heartedly in a wave. Then he was gone, neatly sidestepping the parked parallel vehicles with remarkable ease until he was blocked from sight by a van.

Kitty paused, took a long deep breath, and glanced in her rear mirror. The commuter rush was thinning, and she allowed herself the luxury of just sitting still as she began to make a mental list for the day. It had been hectic since the concert a week ago, and the memory of it often caught her off-guard in moments like these. For it had been a resounding and jubilant success for the senior citizens, who were already plotting their next adventure. Kitty marvelled at their grateful enthusiasm. Yes, it had certainly been worth it. She started to twiddle an obstinate curl round her finger as she stared out at the passing pedestrians.

For her, an attic window long closed had now, somehow and surprisingly, been unlatched. She had sat throughout the performance, captivated and entranced. Something had creaked open, leaking its contents silently yet profoundly into the days that had followed. A deep sense of frustration had since engulfed her. She wanted more, more of the fresh air that had wafted into her soul without warning. Music that was an unexpected yet utterly welcome trespasser. How could she have forgotten? This sense of anticlimax, combined with a gnawing anxiety about ever finding David again, had resulted in a clinging heaviness and despondency which she was finding very hard to shake off.

She stared out at the sad little petrol station opposite the station, which mirrored her gloom with its dreary exterior and sullen grey pumps. The sheer monotony of having to fill up the car again was too much. She glanced over at the adjacent coffee shop and, in a moment of impulse, swung the car into gear and drove over, parking swiftly outside. Robotically, she clicked the car lock and wandered inside. The tables were mostly full, mothers with laden buggies, old men quietly alone with their newspapers, and a couple of truant children in school uniform, giggling over their steaming cardboard cups. Kitty felt suddenly conspicuous, when all she wanted was to become invisible. She ordered a flat white, grabbed a paper from the rack, and found a free table at the back of the shop, where she decided to maximise all anonymity by opening up her smartphone to check her mail. In the corner of her eye, a passer-by walked in front of the shop window and flicked his hair. The action of it jarred in her memory, and she looked up. He had paused hesitantly outside the entrance. Kitty looked again. Dull familiarity rose within her. She stared in bewilderment, struggling to retrieve an archive that she recognised but yet did not. Then the door opened, and the tall man flicked back his tousled long hair again as he entered and made his way to the counter.

Kitty froze. In an instant, her memory fused, bringing clarity. She looked over at him, studying his face intensely. For the man who had just walked into the coffee shop, she *had* certainly seen before. As if he had been reading her thoughts five minutes earlier. For the man ordering his drink with his back to her now was Yani Belushi himself.

Chapter 16

In the seconds of suspended time before he would turn back towards her, Kitty made her decision. With split-second intuition and transcending any chance for nerves, her eyes looked up at him, smiling, as he swung round to face her, tray in hand, eyes roaming for a seat. He stared blankly at her, awkwardly trying to avoid her gaze. Kitty instinctively half-rose out of her seat— grinning—and beckoned to the only empty chair opposite, whilst he, feigning recognition, moved slowly yet without expression towards her, sensing a snare but with no recourse but to oblige. The other tables were full.

His heart sank; he was used to these bizarre connections. He knew full well that his face could spark a reaction from the thousands of anonymous people who had sat through his concerts made invisible by the blackness, night after night. They would glance knowingly at him on trains, in shops, and in the park, prolonged stares at the oddest of moments—just like the one he found himself in now. An unsettling sense of nakedness accompanied him as he slowly arrived at her table, waiting her cue. The solitude he had craved before an important rehearsal would now be squandered.

Kitty held her smile and sat back down in her chair. Yani slowly placed his tray on the table and pulled out a seat. Kitty dove in quickly to rescue his embarrassment.

'I, er, hope you don't mind. I mean, I'm so sorry because

I know you don't have a clue who I am, but I came to your concert recently and suddenly recognised you. I mean, you *are* Yani Belushi, aren't you?' she spluttered, tripping over her words.

Yani paused. Now it was his turn to make her squirm. He looked at the comically haphazard and freckled face which stared back at him with such charming inquisitiveness and reconsidered. Her stubborn curls were making an untidy exit from a hair comb, her make-up was carelessly applied, and she looked distinctly windswept as a matter of design rather than accident. There was a welcome in her face which was irrepressible, and Yani was a great connoisseur of faces, having made a lifetime of studying them.

'Yez. I am he,' he said, still allowing no hint of a grin to form in the corners of his mouth.

His Slavic accent was heavy and undisguised, Kitty noticed, quickly trying to dispel any thoughts that she might be about to suddenly swerve dangerously outside predictable social zones. For he was certainly several years younger than her and looked every bit as if he had stepped out of a vastly different planet and culture. He even *looked* like Beethoven, or at least as she had always imagined him, from the faded framed prints of famous composers which had adorned the walls of the music department she remembered at school. For the briefest of seconds, she regretted her impulsiveness but decided to plough bravely on.

'I, um, really enjoyed your concert, I mean *really* enjoyed it. It was incredible. I'm afraid I don't get out to concerts much,' she added as an afterthought.

It was a vague attempt to elicit a sympathetic response, realising instantly that it would only seal her own naïveté. But she needn't have worried.

'Well zen, I am honoured,' Yani countered politely.

Their eyes held each other in scrutiny, as they both paused for direction.

'I mean, I do *love* classical music. And I used to play the piano a little bit,' Kitty went on, groaning as the words tumbled out uncensored.

She took a long gaze down into her cup and waited for his response. She felt convinced that her brazenness would make him flinch, when in fact, it was a clumsy attempt to place a stepping stone across a decidedly murky river of conversation. With that, she partially succeeded.

'Oh really?' he said, half-amused.

Musical interest came from the most unexpected sources, as he had frequently discovered.

'Yes. Well, nothing serious, really, just something I loved to do as a child,' she explained. 'I wish I was able to play more, really, but sadly, my children don't allow me the time.'

Yani looked at her. She seemed past the age of pregnancy and preschoolers, so he guessed her children were older, but you could never be entirely sure.

'Well, maybe za door will open for you again soon,' he said. 'It's never too late to start again, you know.'

Kitty stared at him questioningly.

'Do you think so?' she asked. 'I reckon my fingers are too stiff now. Anyway, I don't really have much spare time.'

She stirred her coffee spoon round and round in circles in her cup, till the foam started to avalanche down the sides.

'Oh no, I 'ave to keep playing to stop my fingers getting stiff,' he said reassuringly. 'But pliz, whatever you do, keep going; otherwise, all those lessons will be wasted. Find one new piece you like and learn it. It will all come back, I assure you.'

Kitty considered. She hesitated.

'Do you teach?' she ventured nervously.

He laughed. 'No. Not really,' he said. "I don't 'ave za time, either. You don't need lessons; it will all be still there. Trust me.'

Kitty was flattered by his confidence but recognised the caution in his response. *Don't go there*, he was saying, so Kitty decided to change tack.

'I think all children should learn the piano, at least have a go,' she suggested boldly. 'I mean, the trouble is persuading them. I have that very problem with my own son.'

Yani looked up, intrigued. A mother with her assertiveness would surely have insisted.

Kitty continued, 'When they are nineteen, they cannot be told anything, but you live and learn, don't you, with your first?'

She knew this was going to be rhetorical, but she blundered on.

'He had lessons years ago, and I could have made him continue, but as a youngster, he was just intent on playing his guitar, so now it's probably too late. He thinks piano is for, well ... fossils,' she said matter-of-factly. 'He really is very musical,' she added, realising that she must sound like some ghastly mother extolling a dormant prodigy.

She looked up at Yani for a response. His face was now gently smiling, although she had a vague sense the smile was aimed at, rather than with, her.

'I think, madam, you should perhaps return to the guitar teacher,' he said professionally.

Kitty liked being called 'madam.' It gave her a false but definite sense of identity, and she wondered nonchalantly if Sam would ever address a female stranger by the same term. He is probably only about ten years older than Sam, Kitty thought with consternation. The quantum difference in maturity between them was simply immeasurable. Kitty wondered in that moment what this dark-haired man must have been like at nineteen. It was impossible to hazard a guess.

'Sadly, he sold his guitar not long ago to buy a laptop,' Kitty confessed.

It had been yet more fuel for a heated argument at the time, which she had squarely lost.

'Do you have children?' she quickly deflected, already knowing the answer.

'No indeed, madam. Not yet.'

71

He looked away awkwardly, and Kitty wondered if she had touched a nerve, never quite trusting herself in these situations; she realised that perhaps he was older than he looked, although she found men curiously impossible to age.

Internally, Kitty stepped up onto her maternal podium. It was always extremely difficult to summarise Sam to anyone, let alone a foreigner, but she felt she must offer an explanation.

'To be honest,' she started, 'I feel a bit of a failure. I think boys are harder than girls when it comes to these things,' realising as she said so that Yani almost certainly would have no reason to agree.

'He is a lovely lad, mostly, but I can't seem to motivate him with anything. Teenage boys don't seem to notice their mothers,' she added wistfully.

She went on, 'If only he could find someone to inspire him with music, I'm sure he would do well. I just need to find the key … but it isn't that easy.'

She looked down at her cup again, hoping she wasn't sounding too pathetic. Yani cleared his throat and looked at her thoughtfully. Kitty was utterly oblivious to the fact that she now had his full attention.

In his mind, he remembers a day in his youth, a day when he gave his first real concert, aged only twelve. He is playing for them now, these kindly old men, his saviours and angels, being all the fathers and mothers he has never known, and his young heart bursts with pride. His childish thank offering receives a rapturous response, in the dusty sparse school hall which has become his first recital room. He can see the moisture in their eyes as he takes a shy bow, can feel their joy and hear their applause, and looks out at them unsteadily and uncertain, his eyes seeking the one face he adores above all others. For Viktor Papadasi is gazing radiantly back at him, clapping thunderously, his worn and leathered face creased into myriad smiles. He thinks his whole being will burst in gratitude for this open window he has been given, the key to his soul. He feels for the first time the thrill of giving so much pleasure. In this moment, he thinks, I know true happiness. For this reason, I was born.

Kitty looked up, expecting Yani to offer a helpful platitude, but saw instead two dark eyes looking intently at her or, more correctly, staring through her. It was as if he was in another world, oblivious to the conversation they had just had and to the drab cafe atmosphere, where condensation was pooling on the window frames and slowly ascending up the glass walls. She suddenly felt really small and stupid, wishing she had not made a spectacle of herself by saying hello, for she could see that he wasn't really listening, that courtesy was constraining him, and a forced politeness was making him stay, measured, yet reluctant.

Yani jerked back to the reality of the woman sitting opposite him and blinked himself back into the present. A shot of pity suddenly surged from him towards this woman, clearly perplexed by her son. An ache of infinite familiarity rose within him every time he considered either motherhood or troubled children. A thousand pictures ran through his mind, unbidden and tormenting, and he fought to quell them. The deep irony wasn't lost on him between his situation and hers. He considered, and then he placed his cup slowly back on its saucer and looked squarely at her. Before he had a chance to think further, an unexpected and virtually unorthodox impulsiveness overcame his natural reserve.

'It might not be too late, you know,' he said quietly.

Kitty raised an eyebrow.

'If you'd like, I would like to meet your Sam.'

Chapter 17

He awakes warily in his little wooden bunk, apprehensive not to make a sound. The other children are still sleeping, and the orphanage's morning bell has not yet rung. He must be quiet now, and yet, all at once, the silence terrifies him. Like a shroud concealing unknown fear, this quietness is not a friend. He remembers again. Sounds which no child should have to hear, mysterious screams and cries muffled through floor and wall. He lies in the stillness, hearing his heartbeat thudding softly against the mattress. He is only nine years old but carries the suspicion of a detective, his childish trust long diminished. For he has been here too many years, his childhood years stolen. A small boy who has learned to cower and fear, his young and tender heart enclosed by an impenetrable steel shell.

But it is no good. He must reach the bathroom, and urgently. For if he wets the bed again, he will face another beating, and his small buttocks are only just healing over from the last punishment. He thinks for the millionth time of his mother, an imaginary person whom he idolises in his dreams but who has no face. He has forgotten how to cry. All he can hope for is to survive another day, to speed through the weeks of childhood as fast as he can so that he may be free to leave this place of incarceration.

He quietly sits up, trying not to make a sound and disturb the boy sleeping beneath him. If only he were underneath, it would be easier to slide out unnoticed, but his pleas to change places have gone unheeded. The warden of his dormitory is a man of abstract age who has a constant wheeze from years of cheap cigarettes and a wet cough which makes his breath reek. He carries a bunch of keys in his pockets which jangle as he walks, a sound which raises terror in this young child's heart. Yani has never known him to smile. His bedroom is at the end of the door, stationed between two large dormitories sleeping twenty boys each. The boys range from five years old to eighteen, the younger ones sleeping in another nursery block, and the older ones at the back of the orphanage. Korce lies to the east of Albania on a hilly slope which has been cut out to insert the terracotta painted building. A state-funded enterprise and flagship of communist endeavour, craftily engineered to sit a kilometre above the town. Safety in isolation for the villagers, but hardly so for the orphans. The windows are barred and pitched high, so the children cannot see the farmers and women working their soil below or the dusty road which snakes up in front of the orphanage, transporting vehicles up to the mountain villages behind. All they can hear is the sound of occasional traffic, bleating horns, and distant cowbells. Cockerels crow loudly from the farms below, and Yani often is woken by them first, as has happened today.

He surveys the distance to the door at the other end of the long room. The morning light is starting to change the colour of the tall blinds above from blackness to pale grey, heralding a new day that does not hold any promise for Yani. He glances down again to the bunk below. Lorik is deeply asleep, and he is grateful for that. The toilet is situated at the far end of the room, a row of porcelain urinals and square china slabs with an oily hole in the middle, the showers also without curtains or privacy. Yani gingerly swings his legs over the side of his bunk and noiselessly slithers down to the wooden floor, taking care to land without a thud by holding tight to the iron bed frame. He pauses. The floorboards creak constantly, so he will have to sidestep the culprits like hidden landmines, but experience has served him well. He tiptoes very slowly across the room, taking extreme care with each footstep, looking around him at each sleeping body he passes. A stir from any of them could be treacherous. For the children have been trained to report each other, knowing that an even worse fate befalls those not sounding the alarm. As he nears the bathroom door, he looks warily down at Agim, the eldest boy in the room and the cruellest. Given the job of patrolling the younger boys, his betrayals are universally feared. Yani stares down at him, his bullish features still for now, but ugly even in sleep. He glances up at the window at a rodent sunbeam which is casting a torchlight through the blind from outside down onto the floor. Dust sprinkles and dances within it. Agim stirs and turns over. Yani freezes, holding his breath. He waits before taking another footstep. Then he edges towards the bathroom door.

Suddenly, from nowhere, a foot flies out and trips him up. He lands with a loud crash on the floor, knocking a chair down before he can reach the bathroom. Agim is on his feet, his dark eyes glinting with a menacing, sickly glee. Yani is trapped. Down the corridor, he can hear a door slam and the sound of jangling footsteps coming nearer as the warden has heard the noise. He knows his punishment will be terrible if at the mercy of them both. He feels a sharp blow strike his face, and his hands reach up to touch a wet cheek. The older boy then pushes him roughly into the bathroom, knowing punishment meted out behind closed doors will only serve to terrify the rest. In seconds, the warden is with them, angry to be roused so early. There is raw fury in his eyes. He hasn't slept well, again. A relentless run of early-morning misdemeanours has exhausted his patience in recent days. Yesterday, he had beaten a boy so hard from behind that the blood had soaked through his trousers. Yani is quivering from head to toe. He is defenceless against the two of them. The warden slams the bathroom door behind him, with every intention of waking the sleeping dormitory.

He strides towards Yani, who is cowering in the corner shower. Agim circles towards him too, their fists raised, their faces black. Yani looks at the door, which is agonisingly out of reach. Adrenaline surges through him. He is by far the smallest, yet the most nimble. He has no time to think. They step towards him, and in a flash, he ducks sideways. They collide with each other, the warden hitting his head against the metal shower butt and tiled wall. In the seconds it takes them to stand up, Yani slips around them and runs for the door. He grabs a big china *pitcher on the side by the door filled with water for morning ablutions. As they run towards him, he throws the water in their faces and then drops the jug on the cold concrete floor; it breaks with a loud crash into a hundred jagged pieces. He reaches down quickly and grabs the biggest piece, which he holds as a dagger towards them. Swiftly, he backs towards the door. His young eyes are an inferno of anger and hatred. Momentarily stunned, the two attackers pause for just enough time to allow Yani to dart out of the door and run across the dormitory, where heads are now raised in alarm, watching him. He must reach the main corridor. Youthful speed is his only hope.*

Out of the dormitory, he runs for his life, faster and faster until he reaches the main foyer. Behind him, he can hear shouts and footsteps. Already he has a plan. He has formed it in his mind a thousand times and in a thousand ways. It is actually so rehearsed that its execution seems strangely automatic. He must get to the laundry room and then hide. But first, he must get them off his scent. He darts towards the main entrance and slams a door behind him. They must believe he is outside and making for the road.

Without shoes, the ground is harsh and painful, but he barely notices. He makes an immediate right turn back around the orphanage wall, running for all he's worth, panting like a fevered bloodhound. Round another wall he charges, until he is at the back of the building. There is a drop over some railings about ten feet to the cellar rooms, where he must get back in unnoticed. His hands are bleeding slightly from the broken china, but to drop it would leave evidence, so he clutches it firmly, the sharp edges cutting into his small palms. Without hesitation, he leaps onto the sandy floor below and lands with a roll near some old sacks. The dagger scatters underneath him. Looking up, he notices a small open window grate into the laundry rooms. Somehow, he must scale the wall. He looks back at the sacks. He needs to act quickly. Dragging one over, he hauls himself up like a chimpanzee, grabbing both the drainpipe and an overhanging branch. He can hear distant shouting, but they still seem to be round the front. It won't be long until they finish searching the back; he must be inside by then.

With a superhuman and desperate strength, he catches hold of the open window ledge and pulls himself up. Yani is lithe and underweight, so his body weight is no opposition. Somehow, he lurches himself over and in, falling several feet onto a wicker linen basket in a darkened room. He looks back at the window and reaches from the inside to pull the lid shut. He stops breathlessly, orientating himself. In the darkness, he can make out several other large baskets, each containing the weekly laundry. There is a sink against one wall. He goes over quietly and turns the tap. Water comes easily out, and he thirstily cups his reddened hands to drink. His ears are still straining. It is silent and eerie in this room, and the walls are thick. It is hard to know if they are still in pursuit. Instinct tells him to hide. Without further ado, he turns the water off, lifts the lid of the nearest basket, and clambers in, concealing himself under the dirty sheets. There in the dark and malodorous softness, he trembles, awaiting his fate.

Chapter 18

No one was more surprised than Tess at how much had enjoyed her first lesson with Giselle. A week had passed, and still she was trying to get her head round it all. It had been the most unusual experience. She had felt an instant bonding with Giselle, whose warmth and encouragement had done more than just feed her musical confidence. Of equal significance was the discovery that once again, she had been mesmerised by the sheer sound of bow on string which even she, after only an hour, had been able to achieve.

Of course, Giselle had demonstrated magnificently, drawing deep, sonorous tones from her darkened instrument, which Tess noticed seemed more of an extension of Giselle's own body than a separate entity. The first part of the lesson had been entirely taken up learning how to hold the bow, placing her fingers correctly round the hardened end and aligning her fingers to an unfamiliar position. She had wished that her fingers were as long and slender as Giselle's. She noticed how clean and undamaged they were by contrast to her own worn nursing hands, made depressingly old by constant scrubbing. Giselle's fingers, in harmony with the rest of her, were tidy, sensitive, yet quite acrobatic, distinct in their paleness, with her creamy skin contrasting sharply with the dark of the wood. She listened and observed, awed by the ease with which those fingers darted up the shaft with intention, control, and accuracy. But the sound which string and bow made when fused startled her most of all. She was totally lured by the rich booming sound which reverberated around the room, convincing Tess that the noise must surely be seeping through all the walls and into neighbouring houses. Combined with Giselle's delightful lilt which totally becalmed her, Tess was, within an hour, completely hooked.

After that, the lessons proceeded (for Tess, at least) with enthusiasm and relish. She began to look forward to this weekly oasis, so alien to anything she had hitherto known. Little by little, she began to coax her fingers around the bow, which was becoming more familiar every time she picked it up. She learned to play a simple ditty based on four notes and was entranced by Giselle's harmonising as they played together. The age-old wonder of making music was taking hold, even of the most unlikely of pupils. Giselle, too, had secretly warmed to Tess, an easy and willing student from her perspective, and her enjoyment of sharing a passion overflowed effortlessly into her teaching. If only Tess had known that pupil was feeding teacher just as much as in reverse. They were a similar age and both eager to respect each other's mutual achievements, although Giselle had her own reasons for wanting to learn about Tess's life as a nurse.

The truth revealed itself naturally enough. Tess had been intrigued by Giselle's story and hesitantly asked as much as she dared without prying about her reason for being in Sheffield. She learned that she had been a conservatoire prize winner and had travelled across Europe with prestigious orchestras, so it baffled Tess why Giselle was seemingly content to be quietly living here with no obvious commitments, other than to her occasional pupils. One week, she had observed, somewhat clinically, that Giselle's pallor did seem a little surreal, her milky skin more than translucent and unable to mask heavy rings which sat like grey boats under her huge eyes. It tumbled out one day, when Giselle had suddenly put her 'cello aside and wiped her forehead, laying the bow carefully down beside her.

'Tess, please forgive me,' she began. 'I'm afraid I will have to stop. I have a migraine coming on, I fear. I do apologise.'

Tess looked closely at her. She did seem even paler than usual.

'Oh dear, of course. I'm so sorry. Please don't worry a bit. Um, can I fetch you anything?' She rose to go in search of some water.

'No. Thank you. I think I just need to go and lie down before it kicks in. I will be okay. I'm afraid this is, well ... a weakness,' she said, smiling limply.

But as she turned to stand up and walk to the door, she suddenly stumbled, catching the chair as she did, which toppled over and crashed to the floor. Tess was by her side in a flash, placing an arm underneath her shoulder to steady her. She helped to ease her onto the sofa, lifting up her weightless legs and placing a cushion under her head. She could sense that Giselle seemed dizzy and disorientated. A sense of unease crept over her.

'Are you sure I can't get you some water and some tablets?' she asked again.

Giselle was lying back with her eyes closed but seemed all of a sudden incapable of speech, with only a gentle murmuring coming out of her lips.

Out of habit, Tess reached to feel for a pulse. It was rapid and weak. Her thoughts raced. Was this merely a simple faint?

After some minutes, Giselle opened her eyes slowly and pointed with an arm towards the hall. She still did not seem able to form words but was clearly trying.

'Giselle,' Tess began, trying to sound reassuring, 'it's okay. I am here. I'm going stay with you. I'll call a doctor if necessary.'

Already consequences were forming in her mind.

'I am just going to fetch some water,' she added. 'I will be straight back.'

After she returned from the kitchen, Giselle had lifted her head and was coming round. To Tess's huge relief, she began to talk, in a whisper but conscious, nonetheless.

'Tess, please don't worry. I will be alright. I should have told you before. I 'ave a condition I should have told you about.'

Her face was pale and expressionless.

'I'm afraid…well, it's just that I 'ave… a brain tumour.'

There was a stunned silence, as Tess's heart sank in disbelief.

'They call it an astrocytoma. I've 'ad it for two years.' She looked up regretfully, as if in some ridiculous way she was responsible.

Tess stared at Giselle carefully. For a timeless moment, she held the diagnostic word in suspense. Then clarity began to bring some welcome revelation as she started to piece it together, knowing what this might mean. Despite the shock, she found herself strangely unsurprised. It was rather like finding a missing jigsaw piece which slotted neatly into place, making sense of the whole.

Giselle went on, 'This happens often, I'm afraid. I get so dizzy. Sometimes, I 'ave seizures. The doctors cannot operate but gave me radiotherapy. This is why I can't work in an orchestra just now; it is just, well, too much of a risk.'

Tess looked down at her in sympathy and dismay. Still so young and beautiful, yet so fragile. This must cast such a shadow over her life and career, Tess recognised. So hard to bear. Her vocational manners surfacing, she intuitively reached for Giselle's hand and gave it a squeeze.

'It's okay. I do understand. I'm just so glad I was here today, and if you don't mind, I *am* going to make us both a drink so I can stay with you until I am sure that you are alright. You can sleep if you want,' she added. 'I don't want to leave you alone.'

Giselle looked up, relieved. She was feeling exhausted and certainly grateful for Tess's clearly experienced ability to comfort and reassure. There had been so many awful times when she had fainted and collapsed, having seizures in public places. The shame and embarrassment of it constantly haunted her and made her increasingly nervous to venture out alone. But being alone still unnerved her; if only *he* had still been here. The thought was crippling her, and her mind began to wander. She abruptly shook it off.

An hour or so later, after Giselle had dozed off for a short while, Tess had found tea bags and sugar in her scant little galley kitchen, and the two women sat quietly in the lounge, sipping tea. The afternoon sun was starting to slip beyond reach of the windowsill, and the golden chrysanthemums in a vase on the coffee table were trying to lift their chins and catch its final rays. Tess heard more. She learned about her illness and how she had collapsed during a performance. Then as a result how she had been politely evicted from the orchestra, a position she had fought hard to attain and which had exhilarated her beyond all imagination. A prized career suddenly snatched away, but worse still was the deep wound of loss she carried. Giselle had hardly told anyone about this. Even now she was wary to divulge, but recently, loneliness had taken a toll, and somehow she just felt safe with her new companion. She felt fairly certain there was safety in telling Tess, so far removed was she from any repercussions. She went on.

'You see, the worst part of it was that I 'ad to leave behind the man I loved.'

Tess waited, sensing that this was painful, so she listened patiently, unsure of what was coming. Giselle went on.

'When I found out the truth, I just couldn't tell him. The prognosis is so unclear. I, well, I just couldn't put him through the uncertainty and the trauma. He has already 'ad so much hardship in his life, you see.'

She sighed, looking out of the window with a fixed gaze.

'I just 'ad to leave, to get away. I couldn't be a burden to him with this.' She pointed at her head. 'And so,' she said slowly and deliberately, 'I just ran away.'

Tess blinked. Time stood still.

'So where is he now?' she found herself asking, incredulously.

'Alors. I don't know.'

Water was forming a dewy seal under Giselle's eyelids.

'I left him in Paris, and I never went back.'

Chapter 19

It was unpleasantly stuffy and noisy in the waiting area, and David and Maureen were trying unsuccessfully to contain their anxiety. The pretty nurse had returned to her duties on the ward, to David's mild regret. The impact of her face had been disarming, yet he could not think why. He wondered if he'd seen her before. She seemed strangely familiar, but no immediate recall offered any explanation. Her charge was now in the supervision of a male casualty nurse, who seemed determined to be as vague as he possibly could every time David tried to ask where Brian was. He was getting visibly annoyed. Finally, he stood up.

'Stay here, Maureen,' he said. 'I will go and find a doctor. Someone must know where he is.'

He set off to the nurse's station, where a group of staff in scrubs and crocs were standing around, examining an X-ray. It was hard to break in, and David knew well the strain of interruption. He coughed.

'Excuse me, does anyone know where my father is, Brian Simpson? He was rushed in by ambulance, and we've been waiting here for half an hour.'

His eyes wandered searchingly to a board of names scribbled on the wall. An older-looking senior nurse appraised him through rectangular red glasses. She looked terrifying, even to David.

'He's in cubicle four and is just having another ECG, but you must please wait until I can accompany you.'

It wasn't an option. David sighed and smiled at her through clenched teeth. At least his father was alive. The relief was palpable. He learned to play the game of acquiescence with some of these nurses, but their abruptness never failed to catch him off guard.

'Thank you, I'll wait,' he said, standing back to take a seat propped up against the desk.

He was not going to let this nurse out of his sight and return to Maureen just yet. He knew he must hover, for she was bound to get distracted in the next few minutes, which sure enough, she did. He watched as she was called to help a student nurse check a blood pressure in the adjacent cubicle, speak to another doctor about a ward transfer, and answer the telephone in the space of minutes. This deft sweep of multitasking did perhaps explain a lot. It was hard to maintain a degree of graciousness when being called in all directions.

However, he continued to stand his ground. He was thinking apprehensively about his dad, now weak and vulnerable on a hospital trolley, and of his impotence to help. This was not a state of affairs David ever endured easily. Years of hospital autonomy had shaped an identity in him which had become second nature, and he was struggling in no small degree to remain patient with this officious nurse in charge. He was also feeling in some unidentifiable way responsible for what had happened. If only he hadn't gone out to post that letter when he did. If only he had taken a closer observation of Brian that morning, for surely there would have been tell-tale signs. And with a sudden stab of pain, he thought of his mother; without her here, Brian was now, in some finite and indefinable way, his responsibility.

At last, Mother Superior glanced at him and jerked her head down the corridor.

'Come on, then,' she said briskly, leading him away. 'Let's go and see how your father is. They should have finished his tracing by now.'

Turning round with a slight rustle, she set off at a pace David knew he would be well advised to match.

They drew near to a cubicle at the end of the corridor, the curtains still drawn.

Next thing David knew, she had swept them aside, and he was face-to-face with his father. Quickly rushing over to embrace him, he hugged awkwardly around the wires and leads stuck to his bare chest.

'Grief, Dad,' he said, trying to sound jocular. 'I thought I told you I was on holiday from work.'

Brian managed a grin. He still looked clammy but certainly more alert than he had been on the paramedic's trolley.

'I'm sorry, son,' he said hoarsely. 'Couldn't get you too relaxed. I'm so … sorry.'

He looked up at his son appreciatively.

David winced at this unnecessary apology. With a sudden clarity, he knew he simply wasn't ready to lose his father. The delicate thread of his life was much too dear and monumental to snap yet. A protective urge swelled up inside of him. He leaned down again and clumsily tousled Brian's silver hair, still in disarray. Brian grinned again. Words weren't necessary to define the strength of emotion that hovered between them. Brian had never been more relieved to see his son. Suddenly, he looked startled.

'*Maureen!* Where is Maureen?' he asked anxiously.

Somehow in the drama of it all, they had both forgotten where she was, indeed had forgotten her altogether. David quickly explained and cursed himself that yet another half-hour had probably passed since he had left her alone in the reception area. Determined to make amends for his brusqueness, he told his father he'd be back and went off to find her.

He found her sitting quietly where he had left her. She looked exhausted. With a big smile born out of relief, he explained the good news that Brian was making a recovery, although it was too early to tell much more. Together, they returned to find Brian talking to yet more doctors but were soon ushered aside by two nurses, telling them he would be transferred to a ward as soon as a bed had been found.

David suddenly felt hungry. He remembered the bread and olives he had bought that had been abandoned on seeing the ambulance. Lunch had evaded them all. An inner radar told him that a canteen wouldn't be too far away. Maureen declined to accompany him, preferring to sit quietly with Brian and wait. He excused himself and quickly followed directions in search of food. Two floors down, he found himself queuing up outside a dining room that smelt of gravy and greasy chips. It was crowded and busy. Filling up a tray with an unappetising plate and grabbing a disposable cup of coffee, he made his way over to the nearest table that had a space. It seemed strange not to be wearing hospital rags, yet sitting amongst those who did. Putting his tray down at the end of a table, he sat down and stopped. Sitting directly opposite him was the nurse with the denim eyes. David held her gaze. Inside, something stirred which he knew shouldn't.

'Hello again,' he said, hesitantly.

Chapter 20

After two nights and one long day spent cowering in the cool, dark laundry room, and only coming out with trepidation to drink, Yani dozes again, until his senses are suddenly alerted by the sound of banging doors on the ground floor. He hears women chattering and clattering footsteps approaching. Nearer and near they come, and then he hears the door to his room open noisily, his heart now beating as thunderously as an African drum in the cage of his thorax. He holds his breath in sheer terror.

Suddenly, he feels a lurch, as the basket is roughly jerked on its wheels and squeaks towards the door. It is large and well filled with sheets to provide good camouflage, but Yani hardly dares to breathe lest a fraction of movement betray him. But the women are conversing loudly enough to mask his breathing, and he is aware of other baskets being assembled for dispatch. His tummy has been gurgling and aching in hunger for hours, and he begs it to be silent now. His mind works quickly as to where they might be heading. He knows the laundry is sent into the villages to provide menial labour for some of the village women, but beyond that, he is clueless. The baskets start to rumble down the corridor, and Yani curls up foetally by instinct, willing the smelly sheets to render him invisible. After a few jolts and turns, he hears the sound of the big wooden outside doors being heaved open. He senses the daylight invade his tomb of white, although he is fairly sure he still cannot be seen.

Down the path they move, and he can hear the voice of his porter agonisingly close. She is breathless and cursing, coarse exchanges bouncing between the women following the descending basket train, as it bumps its way out and down into the main road below the orphanage. He is thinking fast. In a matter of moments, the basket may stop and the lid lifted off. His mind goes blank. He has no idea where he is going.

His little heart is still trembling, and by instinct, he prays silently, Please, God, save me. *It is a raw whisper of a prayer.*

After about half an hour of trundling, the basket suddenly stops. He hears a man's voice shouting to his pusher. Then all goes quiet for several minutes. He can no longer hear the laundry women. The eerie silence unnerves him. Where is he? He hears a dog bark nearby, and this causes his heart to start beating hard again. For surely the dog will smell him. The barking becomes louder and nearer. Then, he feels himself being pushed into a yard and hears another woman's voice calling to the man, a softer, gentler sound. He waits for the sound of a sniffing dog, but it doesn't come. The basket wheels are lifted over a ledge, and Yani realises he is being transported into someone's house. He lies motionless. Suddenly, a baby starts to cry very loudly nearby, and like a blind man relying heavily on his ears to paint a scene, Yani imagines that he is in a poor peasant house somewhere in the Albanian village he has always lived, yet never seen. The unfamiliarity is overwhelming.

The mother softly coos to her infant as Yani deciphers he is being picked up. The basket is momentarily forgotten. He hears the woman leave the room, then all is silent again. He waits for a few minutes to assess his options. He must escape from the basket before he is seen. He waits some more. Every second seems like torture, as indecision paralyses him. Then, abruptly, the desire to escape trumping risk, he wriggles up to the top of the basket and very cautiously lifts the lid.

The room is small and sparsely furnished, with a metal grated window looking out onto a vegetable garden beyond. He guesses the kitchen is next door, where the mother may be feeding her baby. This doesn't give him much time. He quietly lifts the lid higher and, seeing no one, slithers out and onto the cold stone floor. He darts to the window to survey his exit path. The coast seems clear. The man doesn't seem to be there, and he slides behind the door, waiting to sprint. Still no noise from within or outside, other than the buc–buc sound of a few chickens pecking in the yard. Ahead, he can see other small houses and vegetable plots adjoining this one, and the sandy August fields ahead. If he can only get to the fields, he will be safe. He looks down the garden. There is a barbed wire fence at the end, but no tree cover between the garden and the field. He is going to have to make it across that golden expanse, and fast. He slips outside the door, pausing only for a second, before making a dash across the garden. He leaps over the bristling potato and tomato plants and reaches the fence, panting and breathless. Squeezing through the sharp fence, he rips the worn cloth shirt on his back, but he doesn't care. Only the large field before him lies between him and freedom.

Out of nowhere, he hears a man suddenly shout. He looks back. The man has seen him. In tandem, the dog starts barking, and the man's hollering crescendos. Without a second to lose, he runs for his life into a shimmering horizon of wheat.

Chapter 21

Kitty shot a glance in the hall mirror and steadied her rebellious hair with one hand, taking a deep breath of disapproval at her visage. She was expecting Yani any minute now and suddenly felt apprehensive. Sam was playing *Chopsticks* loudly on the lounge piano; he had argued violently with Kitty for having arranged a morning lesson in the school holidays, when he was surely entitled to be asleep.

The gate creaked open, and Kitty wiped two sticky hands down her skirt. A few footsteps, and the doorbell rang. She walked towards it courageously and opened the door. On the other side stood Yani, smiling and dressed in a dark suit, which was flapping loosely off his bony shoulders, which for some unfathomable reason, with his windswept locks, reminded her of a scarecrow.

'Mrs Morgan, good afternoon,' he began politely.

'Oh, call me Kitty, please,' she said, grinning.

His smile was warm and expansive, and she felt slightly at ease.

'Please, do come in. Sam is warming up, as you can hear.'

She straightened her lips horizontally whilst raising her eyebrows at the same time.

From the next room, she could hear Sam's version of *Chopsticks* getting faster and faster and completely out of control. She suddenly heard him slam on the bass notes and start to play the *Pink Panther* theme. He obviously hadn't heard the doorbell. Kitty winced.

Yani stepped into the hallway. He surveyed the scene before him with some amusement. Coats were spilling off a coat rack, which was shuddering under its colossal weight, and various shoes and handbags were strewn along the hall, which Kitty simply kicked out of the way with expert panache. She was so accustomed to the clutter of her household that she was now oblivious of its effects on newcomers. A skateboard was teasingly poised to take the ground from under his feet, and Yani nervously stepped round it. This was an alien environment to him, having lived his entire life in sparsity. His possessions, now as always, were few and far between.

Kitty gallantly thrust the lounge door open to reveal Sam, hunched barefoot over the keyboard, hammering away. His faded jeans seemed to have parted company from his T-shirt, his hairy back revealing more flesh than Kitty considered decent. He startled when Kitty tapped him on the shoulder and leapt up with a growl, halted only by seeing Yani standing behind his mother. Kitty eased in quickly to puncture the awkwardness.

'Sam, this is Yani,' she announced with artificial brightness. Turning to Yani, she simply said, 'Yani, please meet my son, Sam. He has been *really* looking forward to this.'

Sam looked unconvincingly at Yani, and not for the first time, Kitty wondered why it was that the adolescent brain often seemed incapable of persuading any facial muscles to smile. But her thoughts changed nothing. Sam was staring blankly at Yani, without a blink. All Kitty could do was to hope that Yani possessed a certain degree of kindness and patience in the face of her surly ingrate.

Determined to aid Yani as much as she could across this rickety bridge of communication, Kitty prattled on. She told Yani about Sam's musical exploits thus far, explaining how he had always wanted piano lessons, though intentionally avoiding eye contact with Sam as she said this. She then offered Yani some coffee and hastily retreated to the sanctuary of the kitchen.

When she returned a few minutes later with a hot mug, she was pleasantly surprised to discover Sam was grinning, and Yani seemed relaxed too. She slipped out quickly. A few minutes later, as she was lifting a basket of laundry upstairs, she was momentarily transfixed to hear the most beautiful sounds coming from her tired old piano, wafting up the stairs and throughout the house. It was extraordinary, and to Kitty's surprise, she felt a burning coal warm in her throat. She had somehow stumbled in some inexplicable way onto holy ground. She stopped midstair to listen. It was simply exquisite, whatever it was. Surely Sam would have to be inhuman not to appreciate this. She gave a little self-congratulatory smirk. Perhaps just for once, she had done something right? *Maybe this would mark a turning point in Sam's life.* She surely hoped so. So far, all attempts to find the 'on' button in Sam's life had failed majestically, but out of nowhere, she suddenly felt a steam of rising hope begin to stir.

For Sam's part, something remarkable really was happening downstairs. He couldn't fail to be impressed by Yani's immediate transformation of the old wooden piano. He was embarrassed now to have been plonking around on it when Yani had arrived. The instrument quite literally had undergone a resurrection and come to life. Sam sat and watched, entranced. If only he could play like that. He stared at Yani's busy fingers with incredulity.

Yani was enjoying himself. He hadn't taught for a while, and this was something new and invigorating. He knew he must command Sam's respect above all else in this first lesson. The music must be caught, not simply taught. For no apparent reason, he instinctively liked Sam. For Yani, music was simply a key, opening doors beyond which the room was impossible to predict. His mind started to drift as he skipped through long memorised favourites, his fingers obediently performing the notes so deeply etched into his very core.

For this I was born, he thought again. He felt himself being pulled back, far back into another place to where the music was taking him. A surge of wordless recognition and compassion rose within him, as he glanced sideways at his dazed pupil. He knew he had Sam's full attention now, and his thoughts started to digress.

The small boy runs for all his life through the jostling sheaves, carving a blunt and jagged slice through a virgin harvest. He can hear more shouts and barking, fearing the dog most of all. He daren't look back. His feet are broken and hurting, but he must go on. At the end of the field, he can see woodland beckoning, and he must reach its canopy fast. He clambers over a small stone wall and hurtles into the undergrowth. The tall pine trees crowd around him, but he darts between the slender pillars as he makes his way up the side of a hill. He can still hear barking in the distance behind. He scrambles up to the top, where the treeline breaks before a road. Beyond lies more woodland. Yani considers. The road will expose him, but the woodland may go on forever, and its towering darkness frightens him. He decides to cross over and remain hidden. Without slowing down, he leaps further and further into the undergrowth, panting and breathless. Sharp twigs crack as stones stab into his soles, and his legs are scored with scratches, but he cannot focus on the pain. He keeps running and running until he realises he can no longer hear the dog. Or the man. He slows down slightly and listens again. Where are they? He stops, panting hard.

Back in the field, the man pauses. He didn't see Yani slip out the side door of his house, only catching him in the corner of his eye as he had run towards the fence at the end of his garden. Wretched village kids, he groans. Stealing again, no doubt, although he is relieved to see that his chickens are safe. The boy is too far away for him to recognise, and he knows better than to run through his unharvested field. That is probably the worst damage, he thinks, ruefully looking at the field beyond him. At least the boy is young and small. Beside him, his dog barks incessantly, eager for the chase, but the man bids the reluctant beast to stay.

Yani pauses for breath. He must have run for over a mile now. Maybe two. His throat is dry and parched, and his legs start to feel weak. He hasn't eaten for nearly two days. Dare he sit down? He listens for sounds and clues but can only hear birds high above him in branches ten times his height. The cool damp of moss and twigs beneath him and the sunless air above him make him feel pitifully small. He looks at his torn legs and feet. Somehow, he must go on and find some water, then he can wash them and drink. He gets up and slowly starts to pick his way through the trees, walking on and on until eventually, the trees break again, and he finds himself at the edge of another sloping field. Far away in the distance, he can see a cluster of houses, with several fields first. He wonders if he can risk walking across them; instead, he walks stealthily along the edges, looking behind him constantly, as if at any moment expecting to see either the man or dog. But it is all quiet. He can see no one.

An hour later, he approaches the village and holds back, pondering his course. He stops at a small stream at the bottom of one field to splash his legs and cups his hands thirstily. The water is cold and refreshing. He cannot think about his hunger, but he knows he must find food before nightfall. He knows that he will have to enter the village in order to find it, however risky that might be.

Slowly, he circles the houses to plot his next move. If he is caught, he will likely be returned to the orphanage. He knows his coarse flaxen uniform will give him away. He looks at the houses ahead of them and their flat russet roofs. He stares again. In the middle of them and rising above them, he sees a steeple. And then, as if reading his thoughts, a bell rings out five times. Answering him. A thought comes to his mind: maybe he can sleep in that building; he would prefer that to the fear of the outdoors. Gingerly, he approaches and then stops. A couple of young girls are running in play between two houses, and the sound of their happy laughter strikes a strange discordant note in his ears. He cannot cross into the street yet; he must wait until dusk. His stomach aches for attention. Instinct drives him to notice the fruit trees in the small gardens. Like a worn and hunted animal, he creeps nearer and watches *for a chance to pick an unripened apple from a low branch. He can hear the sound of voices in the distance, but he is too far away to see anyone. He slips into the nearest garden and tugs on a branch, releasing two unwilling victims. They taste sour and hard, but he eats hungrily and takes a third. Then he slips out of sight and hides under an overhanging tree to wait for the shadows.*

Chapter 22

David shifted in his seat uneasily. Across the table, the attractive nurse was tearing open a sugar sachet and looking at him quizzically. Her eyes were sparkling with interest, dancing Mediterranean pools of blue. David was finding it hard to resist their appeal. Her straw blonde hair was tailored neatly and compliantly around her small, heart-shaped face. He still had an uncanny sense that he already knew her. Except that he didn't. He looked down at his plate and stirred the unappetising contents round in clockwise circles with his fork.

She broke the silence.

'So…we meet again,' she said, teasingly.

'Yes,' he began, warily. 'I'm, er, just grabbing a bite. It's been a long day, one way and another.' He sighed, his lips tightening.

'I'm sorry,' she replied, shooting him a look of mild concern. 'Are you visiting, then?'

It was more of a standard response, although not without interest. Since the demise of the staff canteen, patients, staff, and visitors all shared this place, which generally forced an unwelcome alliance, especially for nurses on their tea break, wishing to escape from the ward. David understood instantly, without her even realising.

'Yeah. My father was rushed in with an M.I.' He regretted the words as soon as he'd said them, realising he had exposed himself too soon.

'An M.I.?' she replied. It wasn't a question so much as a check.

David played it cool, holding his cards for a bit longer. He wanted stay professionally anonymous for now.

'I mean, a heart attack, is what, um, they think,' he said, trying to sound vague.

'I'm sorry,' she said, her aquatic eyes staring at him, focused. 'I hope he's okay?'

'Yes. I think so,' he replied, pausing and holding her gaze for a second longer than he ought.

It was becoming an automatic conversation, less about Brian than it should, as he was quite simply bewitched by her eyes. David tried to steer it back on course. He had rarely, if ever, found himself so immediately attracted to a girl, and he felt uncomfortable. He wondered if she felt this invisible chemistry too. He rapidly assembled himself and, like a cloud passing in front of the sun, thought of Evie. Enough. He cleared his throat and tried to feign disinterest, in the nurse at least. He concentrated on Brian and told her briefly about the events of the day.

'Woah. Sounds like you've had a bit of a day,' she said sympathetically.

She took long sips from her cup, over which she continued to dismantle him with her stare. He started to eat hungrily by way of distraction, when he felt his phone vibrate in his jacket.

'Excuse me,' he said, delving into his breast pocket.

He glanced down at the screen. A message from Evie. *How timely*, he thought.

'Oh, don't worry,' she said politely, rising out of her chair. 'I'm just going to grab some more tea. Can I get you some too?'

'No, um, no thanks,' David said as he watched her walk back across the room to the serving hatch, her trim figure complimenting the whole. He looked down at his phone and opened the text.

What he read next didn't seem to make any sense. He read it again.

David, I'm so sorry to do it this way, but there's no easy way to tell you that it's over between us. I have met someone else. Please don't chase me back, because I won't be coming. It's over, David, and I'm just so sorry. I hope you will find it in your heart to forgive me, if not just yet.

He stared at the message in disbelief. He couldn't fathom it. *What on earth?*

Whilst he was still staring at the screen, he felt the nurse return to her seat with her tea. He couldn't look up at her, so he continued to stare at his phone. She respected his interruption and said nothing. David looked at his phone implacably and at length. In his mind, ludicrous synaptic decisions were gathering at such speed that they seemed to bypass consciousness. He looked up at the nurse and, slowly, without stumbling or faltering, heard the words exit his mouth, before he'd even had time to think:

'This probably sounds crazy, but do you fancy a drink after work?'

Chapter 23

Tess stared at him. Then she broke into an awkward giggle.

'I'm sorry. *Seriously?*'

David wasn't sure whether to take this as a good sign or not. 'One hundred percent.'

He didn't flinch. A loaded pause hung between them as they locked eyes.

He continued, 'I mean, as long as you're not married or something?' he said half-jokingly, having already scanned her bare fingers.

Tess looked at him closely. She had simply rushed down for a hurried break and bumped into a stranger, someone she had fleetingly seen earlier, and now he was asking her out for a drink. It was madness. And yet. She looked at him intently. His watery brown eyes hid behind them certain mystery, framed by dark brows and a strong masculine chin, forked with gravitas. His healthy front teeth were separated by a minuscule crevice. She couldn't deny his good looks, even despite some early signs of weathering, which somehow seemed to play in his favour. His rolled-up sleeves revealed dark-haired and muscular forearms, and his hands were large but tidy and well-manicured. Clinical sort of hands, perhaps, certainly experienced. Tess considered. She judged a lot about people by their hands; it was just a nursey phenomenon. She thought about Giselle's long, delicate fingers and her own shorter but neat ones, worn down by incessant hand-washing. *Who are you?* she thought. She realised this was all a bit surreal. He certainly was beguiling. But she had been caught unawares. She looked at him as he awaited her response.

'Well,' she began, hesitating. 'What can I say? Hmm, a bit sudden, don't you think? I mean, you know nothing about me,' she reminded him, as if that fact wasn't obvious enough.

Another scrutinising pause followed, whilst David could hardly believe his own impetuousness.

'Like absolutely *nothing*,' she repeated, as if to wedge it home.

'Perhaps a drink is a good way to start, then?' David said, still grinning. 'I'm not as bad as I look, and I promise: no strings.'

He tried to sound convincing.

'Tell you what. Why don't you finish your shift? I'll go back and see my dad, get a taxi for his girlfriend home, and then wait downstairs till you've finished. You can think it over, and if you believe that I'm some evil predator, you can say no and call security before you go home. If, on the other hand, you think a glass of sauvignon with a tall, dark, and not-so-handsome stranger is what you need after work, I can happily oblige. It's a win-win.'

Tess laughed at his teasing and wondered how he knew she liked sauvignon. Was he some flirtatious parasite? Her instincts said no. She continued her appraisal, liking the more she looked. There did seem something intriguing about him. She paused for a final verdict.

'Okay, then, deal. But not for long; I'm back here early in the morning. Wait for me downstairs in an hour.'

During the next hour, David checked in on his father and was relieved to get some reassurance from the registrar. He had suggested tactfully to Maureen that he would order a taxi for her to get home, as she must be tired. He, untruthfully, had said he wanted to stay a bit longer at the hospital. Maureen needed little persuading. She had become almost phobic of hospitals since her husband had died there nearly two years ago. Memories had come flooding back to her today, and none of them good ones. She was absolutely done in. She excused herself and went to the waiting taxi. David sat with Brian for a little while longer, pleased that he now seemed sleepy and reassured by his presence. He had no energy to talk, but it suited them both. Strangely, David didn't feel guilty about Tess. On the contrary, he felt as though he'd just stumbled across a winning lottery ticket. Perhaps it was just the shock, or a knee-jerk response to Evie's bombshell, but he simply just felt numb.

What a difference a day makes, he thought once again, looking at the clock impatiently. Ten more minutes, and then he rose noiselessly, softly putting a hand on Brian's sleeping shoulder and slipping downstairs.

Tess was sitting waiting for him, to his immense relief. His stomach lurched a little on seeing her. She rose as she saw him coming, her uniform now submerged in a long woollen cardigan, a leather tote bag slung casually over her shoulder. She looked mildly bemused.

'Guess you will have to choose. The watering holes have changed a bit since I was last here. Any ideas?' he said, hopefully.

Tess looked up, still trying to work him out. The pub opposite the hospital was too noisy and certainly not safe from inquisitive eyes. She did not relish having to explain herself at work the next day.

'There's a nice wine bar a couple of streets away.' she suggested. 'Ten-minute walk.'

'Sounds good,' David replied. He was not remotely bothered.

They walked out of the hospital entrance and turned into a road leading behind A&E. The evening street lights were supplementing the fading light, and traffic was busy in both directions. Headlights shone in their faces as they both walked in parallel, neither looking at each other. David tried to pace himself with her brisk walking, feeling both nervous and victorious in equal quantities. But still, no guilt. Tess was easy company, and he felt relaxed. The sheer novelty of her presence energised him.

They crossed over a couple of streets, and she slowed up in front of a dark-glassed bistro called Edelweiss. Inside, small candles flickered on tables next to tiny vases of single carnations. Inside was pleasantly full, and as she pushed open the door, he followed her in.

Two hours later, David found himself outside, hailing a taxi and in triumphant possession of Tess's mobile number. She had chatted amicably and comfortably over a couple of drinks and then had abruptly risen and explained she must go. Outside, they had lingered a moment before she deftly leant up to peck him on the cheek and thank him again. He stood and watched her retreat under the lamplight. There was simply something irresistible about her, something he had not ever really felt so instantaneously, either with his wife-or Evie, for that matter. He wanted to bottle it. Or pinch himself. Did she feel it too? He wondered if he was dreaming, as she disappeared round the corner out of sight. He looked down at the drinks receipt in his hand. There were eleven digits scribbled hastily in biro, staring victoriously back at him. He carefully tucked it in his wallet and walked towards the waiting cab.

Chapter 24

After darkness descended over the village, Yani creeps nearer. Lights can be seen inside houses, but shutters are being drawn. A few stray dogs are barking in the distance, but the roads are empty now and deserted.

He crosses quickly down two streets to the main square, acutely conscious of his bare feet. The cobbles beneath him are still warm from a dying sunset. Opposite, a church building rises before him, with a black hat of a steeple on top, which has been smashed and broken. A town clock hangs conspicuously above the main wooden doors. He looks right and left before crossing over them; very warily and with some difficulty, he lifts the iron latch off its hook. It is almost as tall as he is and heavy. He pushes his whole lean body against it. With a hesitant welcome, it slowly swings open with a creak.

Inside, all is dark and cold. There is no light to illumine the shadows. He has never been inside a church before, if that is what it is. Feeling strange and mysterious, his eyes widen to survey. He can barely make out the dark wooden benches on either side, and he tiptoes slowly down the cool tiled floor to the front. Behind it, barely visible, he can see a painted statue recessed into the thick stone wall, but he is not sure; he can't quite see. It is too dark. He turns away and looks around for a hiding place, a sleeping nook where he can lie down. He chooses a bench about halfway down and curls up beneath it, on the unforgiving slate floor. His feet touch a strange leather cushion, hard and worn. He swivels round and puts his head on it. Within minutes, concealed under the wooden slat, he shuts his eyes. He is cold and hungry but, above all, frightened. Images of the orphanage chase and haunt him, but the unknown is more terrifying still. Sleep doesn't provide a quick escape, as his mind wanders over the fearful day's events. He has no energy to plan his next move, weakened by hunger and fatigue. Hope is fleeing his young heart. Perhaps he will die, after all. He curls up tighter and thinks of the only thing which ever brings him comfort: his mother. Tears spill unforbidden down his dirty cheeks, giving rise to painful sobs. He is so alone. Eventually, and when they finally subside, he drifts into a flighty slumber as the darkness wraps him deeper into the night.

In his dreams, where he has been so many times before, she comes to him, her warm arms outstretched and her face beaming. He runs to her in the sunlight, and she lifts him high in the air before enfolding him in her embrace. Her hair is dark and silky smooth, and he can feel her breath on his cheek and smell her warmth, as he nestles into her soft neck. Her arms enclose him, and he holds tightly. She is here, and he is safe.

A few hours later, he stirs, still in the twilight zone between sleep and wakefulness, his dream not yet erased. His eyes half open, and he sees her again, holding him, but this time as an infant. She is now grey and still, and he is held on her knee in solid drapes … of marble. The arm holding him has been broken off at the elbow. His eyes startle open. He is staring up at a statue, carved into the wall and washed clean by the morning sun, which has broken through from the windows high above him. He begins to remember. But his dream hasn't left him yet, for she is still there. And now he looks up in wonder at the Madonna and child, seeing only himself. And her. As his consciousness returns, he still can't take his eye off her, clinging desperately to his dream, which is already starting to fragment and disperse into oblivion. He sits up stiffly and peers over the edge of the pew.

He can now see clearly what was veiled last night. The vacant altar space gleams before him in a pool of sunlight, and above the pillar, he sees another statue. But in contrast, this one puzzles and disturbs him, and he frowns. A man is standing outstretched against a wooden beam. He is wearing little, but as Yani looks closer, it appears the man's arms and feet are secured against the beams by nails, from which ooze drops of red paint. His head is hung low, and his eyes are shut, and Yani shudders. One of his feet has been broken off too. It is grotesque, and he recoils from wanting to look at it, but just then, his heart stops and freezes. He can hear the church doors creaking as the latch is turned open. He is not alone.

In an instant, he ducks down under the bench, hoping his peeping head hasn't been seen. He hears footsteps shuffling down the aisle and the sound of an older man clearing his throat. He is coming nearer. Yani presses himself in desperation against the back of the pew, seeking invisibility, his eyes tightly shut, but in vain. The footsteps stop beside him, and he knows he has been seen. A voice finally breaks the silence.

'Hello, little one.'

The voice is kind and gentle. Yani opens his eyes in dread.

But what he sees looking down at him are the softest and most twinkling brown eyes he has ever seen, set amidst a worn face of cobwebbed wrinkles. The old man stoops towards him and holds out his hand, smiling.

Chapter 25

A week had passed since Sam's first lesson. His second one was due this afternoon. Kitty could barely conceal her delight and anticipation. It was hard to summarise the effect Yani had had on Sam. He had been busy all week, shutting himself industriously in the lounge and practising hard. Surfacing for food and drink, he had retreated time and again to the keyboard and had even neglected his laptop for days on end. It was little short of astonishing.

As she let Yani in, she was simply glowing and displayed the widest of grins, which accentuated the needle-thin gap between her incisors. Lipstick seemed to have been added as an afterthought. Yani found her both amusing and welcoming. He had found himself surprisingly eager to return to No. 6 Aston Gardens. It was quite unlike any other home he had visited, although in reality, English homes were still foreign territory to him. He tried to pretend otherwise. It was as if this house added a splash of colour and vitality to his intense routine, leasing both salve and energy in abundance.

Today, the noise levels were bordering critical as his sensitive ears tried to compartmentalise each source. Angus and Toby were engaged in a rugby tackle under the dining room table, with Toby, as the smallest, clearly faring worst. He was yelling furiously as Angus pinned him to the floor, and Kitty was ineffectively remonstrating with both of them to stop, whilst trying to talk to

Yani at the same time. The radio was competing unsuccessfully from the kitchen, whilst upstairs, Yani could hear a squall of girls' high-pitched laughter. Tilly had three friends over, and they were painting their toenails lime green on the faded honey-coloured landing carpet. Outside, the dogs were barking wildly at two fat pigeons who were taunting them from the washing line. Suddenly, the kitchen door slammed shut, and Lucy stormed through, clearly in protest about something, stopping midsentence when she saw Yani standing awkwardly in the hall. Kitty ushered him hurriedly into the lounge and towards a victorious-looking Sam.

The hour passed quickly. Yani was delighted with Sam's progress. To him, it was always the litmus test of good teaching if he was rewarded on return. Sam seemed to have mysteriously discovered the power of speech and chatted happily to Yani throughout, peppering him with questions and marvelled by his demonstrations. Kitty was humming in the kitchen as she stirred spaghetti in a gigantic pot. Onions and basil, chopped deftly from years of experience, flew into the mix. Kitty always enjoyed creating these concoctions, whilst her untidy rows of unopened recipe books adorning the kitchen shelves looked on with disapproval. She always improvised with whatever happened to be left in the fridge. Meals had to be produced in minutes and for the masses (she always had to assume a minimum of two extras), so pasta was always the safe option. She had long ceased to worry whether her food was especially appetising or ever to pander to the children's whims. It was quite simply eat or starve. She had absolutely no patience with picky eaters. Fortunately, complaints were few and far between, and she hummed smugly to herself whilst stirring the glutinous ingredients with a large wooden spoon. She eyed the half-open remains of last night's Rioja beside the hob and impulsively sloshed it all in.

From the lounge, Yani began to smell the winning combination of fried garlic and onions. This had the combined effect of making him both inexplicably happy and hungry. He tried to analyse it to himself whilst demonstrating a chromatic scale to Sam. There was something alluringly secure about Kitty. She was, from all appearances and despite the chaos, just simply *there*. There, and for everyone. He felt relaxed and devoid of any need for pretension. Not only that, he was relishing most of all the very real sense of being wanted. Needed, even. He realised this wasn't just about piano lessons. This was something more, something deeper and more meaningful perhaps, than even the music. It took a lot for Yani to ever think that. But he was grateful to oblige, happy to in some intangible way return the favour that had been once been bestowed on him. That's what music was: a rich gift, and not just for the student, but for teacher and listener alike. It had to be excavated and then shared. And multiplied. A language that must be spoken, not merely thought. Sam was looking across at him gleefully, and Yani sighed with warmth and fulfilment.

Suddenly, he is back in their little modest apartment. The memory of it is still so clear, achingly tender. The shutters are open to the street, and he can hear the noise from below ascending softly through the open window. Her fresh clean sheets sway prettily on the tiny balcony. The small table is laid in simple style. He remembers the glass carafe, the faded embroidered tablecloth, the old painting of St Nicholas Bridge looking down on him from the wall opposite. He hears plates clatter in the kitchen, metal on china, glasses clinking. Adile is singing quietly, absorbed. He can smell the bean goulash announcing its arrival, and he is hungry. In the corner of the room, Pjeter sits patiently, absorbed by his paper, eyes squinting through outdated lenses. And there in the corner, he sees an old ebony piano, his music stacked neatly beside it.

Yani jolted himself back to the present. A wedding photo of Kitty and Nick was staring back at him for the mantelpiece. Thinner, younger versions of themselves, full of hope, promise, and unlocked dreams. They seemed diminished without their children, just a fraction of the whole. How lucky these kids are, he mused, hearing the loud shrieks of giggles coming from upstairs. They have absolutely no idea, but they are unutterably and indisputably fortunate. And yet oblivious. He knew he was glad to be here, to be in this house, to have met these people. Another chance encounter. Life was surprisingly full of them.

'I tell you what, Mr Sam,' he deflected.

Sam liked the quirky, broken way he spoke.

'When I come back next week, I think you will 'ave it, ziss page. Remember, fingers like ziss,' he said, fisting a ball with his left hand and holding his right hand floppily over it, his wrist still straight. With the palm of his right hand secure, his fingers wiggled easily. 'Keep zem loose.'

'Yeah. Okay,' Sam said happily.

He looked down at his large palms and stretched his fingers out flat. What had last week seemed to represent large and impotent Cumberland sausages were now transformed agents, possessing unlimited artistic potential. *Funny what fingers can do,* he thought obliquely.

Chapter 26

Giselle put down the bow and wiped her brow with the back of her hand. Her head was starting to spin again. Popov would have to wait. It was certainly a difficult passage. She steadied the 'cello on its stand and made for the bedroom. She felt frustration rising with the likely outcome of another migraine. She hoped fervently it wouldn't lead to a seizure. She must lie down. It seemed such a tiresome waste, these hours spent languishing when she couldn't concentrate, when even thinking hurt. She knocked back two tablets with a glass of water and lay down on her side with feline suppleness, pulling her slender knees up under her chin and shutting her eyes.

Unbidden, his face suddenly appeared behind her lids, stooping tenderly towards her, his hand caressing her cheek. She felt a defiant tear escape and fall down the slope of her nose until it stopped on the ridge of her lip. She silenced it with her tongue. She had cried so often for him that now, even the taste of her tears mingled their saltiness with grief. This was the only place she could reach him now: in her dreams. And this was where he would forever be, for he was never lost to her there. Within minutes, she drifted off to sleep, in desperate search of reunion.

Meanwhile, at the same time, Tess was sitting with her 'cello case opened at home, her new wooden friend balanced stoutly between her knees, her toes barefoot on the carpet. She was growing more addicted to its sound every time she played. She tried to play long and slow drawn-out bows, like Giselle had showed her. Don't rush, she had said. The minutes passed by unnoticed. It was her day off again, and she hoped the elderly couple who lived below were agreeably deaf to her practising. She wanted to impress Giselle today with her progress. There was no denying that she was concerned for her. She had researched astrocytoma and discovered to her dismay that the outlook was uncertain, but she certainly didn't want to ask too many questions. All she could hope was that the tumour type was not aggressive. The alternative was unthinkable.

She started to think of Giselle's lost love, the man she had abandoned and from whom she did not seem able to recover. It was all unbearably sad. Tess wished she could help in some way, but all she could think of was to come prepared for lessons and offer her companionship in some meagre and small way. She felt a twinge of guilt when she thought about David. It seemed wholly unfair for her to be both healthy *and* have David to think about. Somehow, he had occupied her thoughts quite a lot in the few days since she had seen him. It was odd. She was most surprised at how he had literally popped out of nowhere, for she certainly hadn't been looking for *him*. Tess's two former relationships of any significance had been short but nonetheless real, but as each one ended, she had grown more independent. Men were at best good company, at worst unreliable wasters. This wariness had been confirmed after watching Sylvia and Lizzie fail to secure elusive happiness with any man to date. Plus, most of her colleagues seemed to be trapped in stale, miserable marriages. No, she had absolutely no desire to join them.

She put the 'cello to one side and reached for her phone on the table, which was now flashing. Two new messages. Both from David. He had texted her the following morning after their drink, and she had kept respectable distance by replying politely, but only after a few hours. She swiped them open.

'Hey. Guess who. I'm coming over to the hospital to visit

Dad again. Any chance of a nurse called Tess on duty today? If so, perhaps she would like dinner afterwards with Dr Simpson?' No kiss.

Tess smiled. *Doctor?* She was intrigued. He certainly wasn't familiar at the hospital, and he hadn't mentioned he was a doctor over their drink. Just that he was over from Australia visiting his father, who just happened to have had a heart attack. *Good timing, that, if you had a son abroad*, she thought. *If you were going to have a heart attack*. He certainly seemed devoted to his father. And she liked that. She had no real concept of fathers, her own having been conspicuously absent for most of her life. Maybe that was another reason she kept men at arm's length too, which she had to confess was true. However, she was enjoying his humour and even the chase, she had to admit. But she needed to keep one foot on the brake. Just for now.

She glanced at her watch and jumped up. Time to go. She quickly tapped a reply:

'Nurse Tess is not on duty today but yes, she would like dinner tonight. 8pm? Your choice.' No kiss.

Chapter 27

She hurriedly dressed and raked a brush through her flaxen bob. No time for make-up today, but she didn't care. Placing the 'cello carefully in its battered case, she grabbed her bag and keys and set off towards the bus stop. Outside, opaque skies and the last autumnal vestiges had surrendered to a monotonous November. The trees had shed their vibrant hues and were now uniformly bare, more bronzed leaves lying beneath her feet than above her, as she crunched through them briskly. On the bus, she looked out at the rows and rows of flint-coloured terraced houses, as the bus strained its ascent up the steep hill. She reached the nearest stop to Giselle's and alighted, lugging her cargo carefully and not a little intimidated by the odd stare from passengers.

If only they knew, she thought. *If only they knew that a few weeks ago, I'd never, ever believe I'd be here now.*

She reached Giselle's house, slightly breathless, and rang the bell. She was a few minutes early and hoped that wasn't a problem. For Tess was nothing if not punctual. *Time*, she thought, *was like an unwilling child who needed to be coaxed and controlled. If you gave an inch, you lost a mile.*

Giselle had woken half an hour earlier and was feeling a little stronger. Her throbbing head had subsided, but she knew teaching would demand more concentration, which she wasn't sure she had too much of. But quite apart from wanting to see Tess, she knew she had to work. Things were so tight financially. She had no support from anyone; her mother was a chronic alcoholic who she was barely in touch with now, and her father had died in a motoring accident when she was twelve. She had no siblings, either. Her entire world had been her 'cello. And him.

'Hi,' Tess said brightly after Giselle opened the door.

She stepped into the hall, looking closely at Giselle for clues. She appeared ashen and thinner than ever. Tess wondered if she ate much at all.

'Is this okay, I mean, are you feeling up to teaching today?' she began.

The last thing she wished was to be a burden.

'*Mais oui, bien sur.* Yes, yes, of course. Please. Come in.'

She extended an arm into the house. Tess followed her through. The curtains were drawn in the lounge, and Giselle went to open them. Tess noticed afresh how shabby this room was; it was hard to imagine it ever having been loved. Now the only remnants of any habitation were a worn sofa and tired drapes, plus two pieces of old dark furniture, which no doubt belonged to an abstract landlord. On one, Giselle's music was piled high. On the other, there was a distinct absence of photographs or anything personal. Tess began to realise how little she knew about her teacher. She waited until after the lesson before probing a little.

'I'm guessing you won't be staying here forever?' she ventured.

'Ah, *Non, j'espère que non*. No, I 'ope not, but for now, I 'ave no choice. I must be near a good hospital, so the oncologists can keep a close eye on me. So. 'Ere I am for now.'

'So will you ever go back, to France, I mean?' she continued. A subtle cue.

'Well, *peut-être*. Maybe I will. It's just …'

Her face turned towards the window, and Tess saw a shadow flit across her eyes.

'It's just … I need to let him go,' she said finally. 'He deserves more than this. I couldn't do this to him. It's not fair, after all, I 'ave no, how do you say, a life on the shelf?'

'A shelf life,' Tess corrected. 'Maybe he would disagree?' she suggested cautiously.

Giselle grimaced and looked closely at Tess. *What would she know?* she wondered.

She stared at Tess's face, dominated by two dazzling blue eyes. *Those eyes would make any face beautiful*, Giselle thought. Faint freckles had been sprinkled like demerara sugar over her nose, whilst her white skin contrasted heavily with Giselle's own olive complexion. Giselle surmised that Tess's face would most likely fry like bacon rashers in the sun. She abruptly changed the subject.

'So how about you? Do you 'ave a young man in your life?' she asked teasingly, her eyes dancing a little.

Tess hesitated, taken slightly off guard. 'Not exactly,' she said.

There was another pause, whilst Giselle waited expectantly for an explanation.

'Well… I did meet someone last week, actually,' she confessed. 'But we are hardly in a relationship, yet.'

She tried to sound vague, but Giselle was fishing.

'Let's just say it's early. I'm actually meeting him for dinner this evening, I hope,' she added, blushing slightly. This conversation wasn't supposed to be about her.

'Well, that sounds good,' Giselle replied. 'Who's the lucky chap, then?'

'Hah! Good question. He's just someone I met at the hospital; he's called David, and he's a doctor, funnily enough. But I met him when he was visiting his father, who had a heart attack. I dunno, he just seems really nice, but I hardly know him. We'll see.'

'*D'accord.* Well, good luck. I hope you 'ave a lovely evening,' Giselle said quietly.

Tess cringed.

'Thanks,' she said, determined to move on. 'I'll see myself out, don't worry,' she said, rising to her feet. 'And thanks so much for the lesson. It was really great.'

'I hope I haven't tired you out too much,' she added, 'and please, *do* call me anytime if you need anything.'

She looked concerned. The offer was genuine, and Giselle was touched.

'Thank you, Tess,' she said. 'It was lovely to see you again. *À bientôt.*'

As Tess walked down the hill to the bus stop, she glanced back at the house and saw the bedroom net curtains moving. Giselle, who had been staring down at her, disappeared immediately behind them.

Chapter 28

David was in the shower. He scrubbed shower gel vigorously all over his body, relishing the warm suds and familiarity of his childhood bathroom. He had the house to himself. Brian was still in hospital for another few days, and he felt like a fifteen-year-old again, about to go on a date. He stopped to correct himself. He *was* going on a date. He wrapped the towel sound his middle and tucked it in, sucking in breath as if to remind him of once-impressive abs. Well, perhaps. He deliberated about a shirt and realised the choice was limited. *If only Mum was here*, he thought with regret. His shirts would have been washed and ironed almost before they had left his back. *I wonder what she would have made of all this*, he thought, chuckling to himself. She had never known Evie, so he felt she was already being left behind. Yet he had the distinct feeling that she would approve of Tess. They both were so practical, so caring. Yes, he was sure Mum would be happy. He slapped some aftershave round his neck. He didn't want to come on too strong, but the synergy was there; he knew it intuitively.

He dressed methodically and came downstairs. He thought about his letter again and wondered how it had been received. It had been nearly two weeks now, and he didn't know what to expect. He had checked his email several times a day, half-expecting a reply, but so far, nothing. He didn't know what to do next, as there was nothing he really could do. He would just have to wait, infuriating as it was. He would give it another fortnight, and if she hadn't responded, he would write again. Just to check she had got it. He thought about how much had happened since he had landed in the UK. *You just never could tell what was round the next corner*, he thought, soberly.

He recollected the many chance encounters which had determined his life so far. Meeting Laura, his first wife, at a dinner party, which he almost didn't go to. Then he met Evie one evening, when they were both jogging along Brighton Beach; he was going to run with his squash partner, only he had pulled a hamstring. So he ended up running alone that night and found himself running alongside her. She had started talking to him, and by the end, after they had stopped breathlessly to do their stretches, they collapsed without thinking into the bar behind them for some liquid refreshment, and the rest was history. And now Tess. If Brian hadn't been taken to hospital, he would not be slicking his hair back now, feeling an adrenaline rush of archived teenage excitement.

After much deliberation, he had not bothered to respond to Evie. In any case, he would have to fly back to work in a few weeks, having exhausted his compassionate leave. He would face the music then. Right now, he was undeniably distracted.

He walked through into the kitchen to grab a cold drink and flicked on the television. He poured a long glass of Evian and clinked some ice cubes into the tumbler from the fridge, remembering how ecstatic Mum had been when Brian had bought it for her, one of his last gifts. Modern living, she had mused, incredulous at having a fridge which could produce ice cubes. David patted the fridge door affectionately. Her joy was his too. The cold water tasted good. Distracted, he heard the news being read: more immigrant problems, Middle Eastern conflicts, cabinet spats, and something about finding the body of the well-known French cellist Sabine Dubois, her body too badly decomposed to easily identify. *Poor sod*, he thought.

He slipped on his dark blue linen jacket and glanced at his

reflection in the hall mirror on the way out of the door. Not bad for the wrong side of forty, he persuaded himself. Maybe. He hoped Tess would agree. The thought of her quickened his pace, and he drove impatiently into town, to the Italian restaurant he had told her to find him at. There was no sign of her as he entered, and he was momentarily thwarted. Was he hoping for too much, that she would be there? He chose a table in the corner and sat with his back to the door. As if reading his thoughts, he had barely sat down when he felt a tap on his shoulder, and before he knew it, he was rising again to greet her, planting a fleeting kiss on both of her cheeks. She smelt divine. And she was smiling. David looked at her appreciatively. She radiated youth and vitality, a smattering of make-up, but it was almost imperceptible. A splash of pink lipstick was enough. She had on a flattering short navy dress which accentuated her twisted pearl necklace and studs. Chiselled knees and calves descended into some classy heels. Small and chic. Nurse Tess seemed to have vanished; she had made an effort, he could see. He wondered if she thought the same about him.

They ordered drinks and stared at the menu, feigning interest. When the waiter arrived to take their order, Tess was busy telling David about her day off and the music lesson. David was bemused. Music was one of the rare skills he had little aptitude for, being practically tone deaf. She told him about Giselle and her illness, her broken heart, and asked David's opinion on her prognosis.

'Not really my field,' he admitted, 'but I'm guessing it depends on how successful her radiotherapy has been. Tough one, though. Not nice symptoms to live with. Didn't her man try and chase her? I don't think I would have let someone slip through my fingers *that* easily.'

He played the bravado card without disguise. Tess looked at him thoughtfully.

'It appears not,' she replied, 'although it does seem strange. She says she left no trace, but she could certainly do with him right now. I find myself worrying about her, all alone. Anyway, tell me about yourself,' she modulated. 'When will you be going back to Australia?'

It was an open-ended question. She assumed that work would make a claim on him before too long, but she was simultaneously apprehensive of his answer. She was warming to his charm, and she knew it.

David tried to sound as vague as possible. He didn't want to think about it, either.

'I've taken a month's compassionate leave,' he explained. 'Initially, I came home for a fortnight but extended it when Dad got sick. They were okay about it; anyway, these things happen. I'm just glad I was here when it happened. I keep replaying over in my mind what might have happened. Honestly. *If he had died …*' His voice drifted off, his eyes lowering.

'Hey. Don't go there,' Tess said softly. 'I think you were *meant* to be here. Don't you believe that some things are supposed to happen?'

He raised his eyes at her question.

'Yes, I certainly do,' David replied, not taking his gaze off her for a second.

Neither of them needed words in that moment. David's heart had decided instinctively. Eventually, he broke the pause, sipping his wine. He cleared his throat, because what he wanted to tell her wasn't easy to talk about, and he hadn't even felt able to share it fully with Evie.

'Losing Mum was the hardest thing that's ever happened to me,' he began, telling her a potted version of what had happened.

Tess listened patiently.

'So I just don't think I was ready to lose Dad yet too. We've become surprisingly close since all this,' he admitted.

It was something else he couldn't quite put into words, but it was true nonetheless.

'Well, that's a good thing,' Tess said. 'I wish I had a dad like yours,' she added wistfully. 'I never really knew mine. He disappeared when I was a kid, and that was it. Not that I've ever really been that bothered,' she lied, unconvincingly. 'But it would have been nice to have a good dad. Yeah. I think you're lucky.'

'Thanks. I do too. I'm certainly lucky this evening,' he said, grinning.

Tess's heart skipped a beat. There was something so winsome about him, and she ached too, thinking about his grief. She felt a twinge of guilt, thinking about her own mother, who she hadn't contacted for a few weeks. Her passive, sad mother, whose life had never really launched, Tess sometimes thought. She just seemed to exist. Tess felt powerless to make it otherwise. She made a mental note to ring her and suggest an outing. Something, anything, although right now, imagination eluded her.

David then told her about his unknown sister, about his mother's letter and Brian's summons home. And the letter he had just posted a fortnight ago. Tess was utterly transfixed. It sounded like something out of a magazine.

'So how do you feel now?' Tess asked with concern. 'What will you do when she responds?'

'*If* she responds,' David said grimly. 'She may run a mile.'

'I don't think so, somehow,' Tess said hopefully. 'Maybe this is another thing that was meant to happen.' She smiled slyly.

'Maybe,' David replied, finding it hard to disagree.

He had never really thought much about fate, choosing rather to dissect life's events in hindsight. Again, he pondered on those extra little things which seemed, mysteriously and recently often, to evolve into matters of great substance. He certainly had an eye for detail, and that much had made a surgeon of him. Those observation skills had also made him notice Tess's eyes the first time he saw her.

They ate dessert and lingered over coffee. Neither of them wanted the evening to end or were sure how it would. After David called the waiter and settled up, he suggested they walk along the river. As they sauntered down the hill, the night air was pleasantly cool but not cold. David reached for her hand. Then as they came to the river's sidewalk, he stopped to face her, took her face very gently in his hands, and kissed her.

Later on that night, when he lay sleepily in his bed, musing over the events of a magical evening, he remembered the softness of her skin, her face, and her lips. She had felt it too. Of that, he felt certain. It was intoxicating. She had not asked him back, yet even that felt special, sacred even. His desire for her was unquestionable, her denial tantalising. He thought about her life, about her work, her kindness, and her simple and unalloyed care. A true nurse, he conjectured impressively. There was a freshness and honesty about her that made him want to confide in her. He shut his eyes and started to drift off to sleep. One thought mingled with the next, and something jarred in his memory, but he couldn't immediately place it. Then he remembered. A 'cello. A 'cello lesson, and a murdered cellist.

Sleep consumed him before he could think anymore.

Chapter 29

Reluctantly, Yani holds out his hand, and the old man lifts him to his feet, still beaming at him. Yani is perturbed and terrified. He is unfamiliar with kindness and has no idea how to respond.

'Who are you hiding from, my boy?' the man asks. And as if guessing his thoughts, he adds, 'Don't worry; I won't tell.'

Yani still cannot speak. He is convinced that if he says anything, he will be exposed and condemned, so he remains silent, numb with fear. The priest seems to understand his paralysis and doesn't repeat himself.

'Perhaps you are hungry?' he suggests. 'I can give you some food if you would like. My house is only across the street.'

Silence. Yani stares at him, tight-lipped, but his hunger is overwhelming.

'Come. I promise I won't hurt you. I won't tell a soul.'

He leads Yani to the door of the church, and the boy follows, instinct telling him to make a dash for it at the entrance. But there is something benign and harmless about this old man, which steadies him. He has never seen anyone look so old. Should he follow?

He thinks again. If he can only get food inside his clawing stomach, then he can plot his next move, another escape. He decides to take the risk. Outside, the street is quiet; it is still early in the morning, and the working day has not fully begun. The golden morning sun is still busy painting the cobbled square. Yani is unaware that he has interrupted his secret morning prayer. He follows him across the street. Viktor Papadasi unlocks a door and takes the boy inside.

'Here we are,' he says, looking around a cool but tidy little room, which contains only a table, two chairs, a wooden bed, and a small desk in the corner. The old man walks through to a tiny kitchen out the back.

'I will fetch you some food, eh? And then you can tell me who you are. If you want,' he adds hastily.

Yani waits cautiously in the main room. Anxiety still pulsates through him. He hears the man open a cupboard and recognises the sound of pouring water. He looks around the room before he notices it. Above the desk, on which several books are sitting next to a big opened book, is a picture of the tortured man again. It stands out against the whitewashed wall. He is smaller here, but Yani is puzzled. Why is he hanging like that here too? It is a horrible thing, and fuels his already heightened fears.

His thoughts are interrupted by the priest's return, who is holding a plate of bread and some cheese, some fruit, and a tomato. In his other hand, he carries a glass of water. He looks at the boy, who is still staring at the wall. The priest hovers, realising with a jolt what the boy is looking at.

'So you like my picture, then?' he asks slowly, curiously.

Yani is too frightened to respond. Wide eyes which resemble two large conkers transmit an answer. Slowly, it dawns on the priest that perhaps an explanation is needed.

'That man is Jesus,' he begins but then remembers he is holding food before a famished boy. 'I will tell you about him, but first, have some food. Come. Sit down over here. You look very hungry.'

He motions towards the table and chair, and Yani obediently sits down. The plate is set before him, and Yani looks up for final confirmation. The old man nods.

'Eat,' he says emphatically.

The boy grabs the bread with both hands and tears into it with his teeth. The old man watches on, alarmed. The child clearly hasn't eaten for ages. He is so thin and clearly panic stricken. Viktor Papadasi is guessing he has run away. But from whom? He doesn't want to frighten him with further questions, knowing he must build trust.

But what to do with him? The day begins to unfold worryingly before him. He cannot conceal a young child here for long. Even the walls have ears, he thinks. The Sigurimi, or secret police, have their spies in every community, family, and room. He begins to suspect that the boy may have escaped from the orphanage. He thinks he would most likely have recognised a local child, who he imagines wouldn't be so gaunt and clearly traumatised. He has heard such terrible stories of that institution that he has no desire whatsoever to return the child to the authorities. No, it is better that he asks no one and knows nothing. But he must act quickly. Already, an idea starts to form in his mind.

Yani finishes the contents of the plate quickly. Fruit is smeared all over his face. He wants to say thank you, but he still daren't speak. Instead, he smiles weakly at the old man.

'More?' Viktor asks kindly.

Yani nods vigorously. The old man returns from the kitchen with more bread, a napkin, and this time some bananas too.

Once he is finished, the priest looks back up at the picture again. He doesn't want to scare the child, but he is conscious of needing to keep a one-way conversation running. He is desperately trying to think of something to say. He begins hesitantly, picking his words carefully. He points up at the crucifix.

'You don't need to be afraid of Jesus,' he says comfortingly, as Yani looks up too, nonplussed. 'He was being punished for something he didn't do. He was killed, but ...' He paused, trying to wrap sense around his words. 'That wasn't the end, because you see, he didn't stay dead.'

The priest looks at Yani's puzzled face and realises he is talking in riddles; the boy doesn't see at all. He prays inwardly for illumination and gives a little cough.

'Jesus is God's Son,' he begins, 'who simply asks us to believe that. And he is always here to help us,' he adds, trying to sound reassuring. 'So that is why I hang this picture here, not to remember his death, but to remember that he still lives. And it reminds me who is going to help me when I pray. Because he loves to answer our prayers, little one.'

His face reflects that sincere belief, but he decides to leave it there. He is aware he has probably already confused the boy enough.

Yani stares at the twisted figure. God has a son? He has never thought of that, and Yani wonders how old he is. But why would God let his son get killed? And how can he be both dead and alive? It doesn't make any sense. But something is ignited in his young heart. For he has always prayed, every long day of his short life. In this most intensely atheistic nation, no one has ever told him about a God and church, but he just knows that when he lies awake through the long and lonely nights, he has never been completely alone. Whoever and wherever God is, Yani has had nowhere else to turn. So has this Jesus been listening all along? He is amazed to be told that, because he has always believed deep down that someone was listening. He has no concept of faith, but this knowledge from Viktor Papadasi resonates powerfully with him. And now it seems that Jesus is answering at long last. He has prayed for rescue more times than he can remember, and it dawns on him slowly and euphorically that he is now indeed being rescued. He looks up at the dying man and, in a moment of direct clarity, receives an epiphany.

'Thank you, Jesus,' Viktor hears the young boy say.

Looking down at him, he sees that there are tears cascading down from the child's eyes.

Chapter 30

Seconds pass, and Viktor Papadasi has to masquerade his own weeping. He moves forward and places a grandfatherly arm on his shoulder. He is deeply moved. But before he can say another word, two skinny brown arms have been flung round his waist, and the child buries himself against his cassock, heaving great sobs against the priest's portly girth. When the child's cries finally subside, Viktor knows what he has to do.

'I promised I wouldn't ask where you have come from, little one,' he says, 'but if it is somewhere that you don't wish to return, ... where maybe people have mistreated you?'

He pauses, looking down at the boy carefully as a slow nod confirms his fears.

'Then I want you to tell me absolutely nothing, and I will help you. But we need to hurry. I have somewhere I can take you, which is completely safe. No one will know you there. For it is not safe to stay here.'

He is thinking apprehensively of the Sigurimi, who even now, after Enver Hoxha's demise, retain active cells throughout the region. Even in his own village, he has his own suspicions. Bribery is a fluent language in this poor rural community. He knows his own safety will be compromised if he is found contravening the authorities, but his moral conscience takes precedence, and not for the first time either. He clears his throat.

'But first, my child, I must make a telephone call. I will not be long, and I will come back. I need you to promise me that you will stay here

if you want me to help you. But if you do not, then I will not lock the door. You are free to go. The choice is yours, but please, I beg you, let me help you, because I do believe I can. Out there,' he explains, beckoning to the courtyard, 'is not safe for you. Not safe at all.'

Yani looks up at him, bewildered. He has never seen a face with so many lines on it or one that radiates such love. It is a feeling he has never experienced before, and it envelopes him completely. Childhood prohibits much analysis, but he simply knows that he feels no fear with this old man. There is no decision to be made, yet what he says next become the four most significant words of his life.

'I will stay here,' Yani says quietly.

Viktor nods, pleased. 'I will be back soon,' he repeats. 'Stay here, and perhaps you want to lie down?'

He looks across at his neatly made bed.

'You can rest if you want.'

With a final smile, the priest takes a small shoulder bag from a peg on the wall and slips out of the door.

When he returns an hour later, he finds the boy fast asleep on his bed. Relief washes over him. He had sincerely hoped he would still be here, especially after the conversation he had just had with his niece, but he wasn't absolutely sure that he would be. He has been to the house of his old friend, Dr Kapllani, and asked to borrow his telephone. He is the one person who can be trusted, and he was right. No questions asked, the doctor discreetly took him into his house, straight to the telephone, and shut the door behind him in privacy. It is a friendship that has long stood the test of time.

His niece, Adile, his sister's daughter, lives several hours away in Durres, by the coast. Her husband, Pjeter, has a small shop in the town centre. She is in her midforties; they have struggled without success for nearly twenty years to have a child. It has been the ultimate trial for poor Adile, surrounded as she is locally by her three sisters and their multiple progeny. Viktor tells her about Yani, his conjecture about the orphanage, and his dilemma. Adile listened patiently and, to his immense delight, agreed to take him in for now. She will speak with

Pjeter this evening, and tomorrow, they will bring the car over to collect him. That way, no one will think anything strange. They will simply be visiting her elderly uncle.

For Adile and Viktor Papadasi have a special bond, both adoring the other. She is the eldest child of Viktor's only sister, ten years his junior, his brother having died at a young age from tuberculosis. Recognising his vocation to the priesthood lay ahead, he had known from the day she was born that this child would be the nearest thing to his own. Her sisters followed in rapid succession, and he is deeply fond of them all, but Adile has a claim on his affections which he cannot quite verbalise. Especially on account of all that she has suffered. But for nature's cruelty, he knows that Adile would have made the perfect mother, and it has long been a source of spiritual frustration to Viktor that his prayers for her child have so far gone unheeded. Pjeter is an older man who is quiet and studious, a musician in his spare time; when he is not checking accounts and ledger books in poor light late into the night, his eyesight sacrificed on the altar of necessity.

Yani sleeps solidly for a couple of hours, and when he wakes, Viktor Papadasi is still there beside him, reading quietly from the big book on his desk. The priest knows that he has less than a day to conceal the young boy and win him over to his plan. He senses that both Adile and the child deserve nothing less. He senses certain fingerprints of a divine orchestration. Perhaps God is answering his prayers, after all.

Chapter 31

Adile and Pjeter had been as good as their word. After Adile had hung up on the phone from Viktor, she had wiped bulbous tears away from weary eyes. The grief of unfulfilled longing had been carried by them both through long and dogged years, a silent amputation whose phantom pains they experienced by day and whose ghostly spikes tormented their dreams at night. Adile's sisters, though kind and well meaning, faced the opposing dictate of parental exhaustion. Adile would have given an entire limb to face their burgeoning responsibilities and fatigue, but it seemed there was no middle ground. Their baby's ever-present absence was now an unspoken and buried family secret, whilst life carried on as it always had. Birthdays, anniversaries, and family gatherings fused them all together, whilst the sisters assumed Aunt Adile had reconciled herself to the situation, surrounded by the children she genuinely loved, yet in reality maimed by the loss they massaged.

For Pjeter, there was no decision to be made. He had taken Adile's sobbing frame in his arms and softly kissed the top of her head. His loss was as acute, only plagued by a compounded sense of failure at his inability to give her the child she had so desperately wanted. All medical tests had proved inconclusive and fruitless, limited as such options had been for them. Now that she was well into her forties, time was a fiendish thief, determined to steal their dwindling hope. Not that taking this child would be without risk. To bring an unknown child into their familiar community would doubtless cause suspicion. They would need to get the family on their side, yet even that may not be easy or safe. Complicated for them all, let alone the boy. Pjeter had conjectured that adoption would be the only route to satisfy the authorities, but he knew that the bureaucracy would be fraught with obstacles. He brushed the thought aside. This may be their only chance, but one they had to grasp with both hands. About the boy himself, he realised, they knew absolutely nothing.

They had left Durres early the next morning for Viktor's mountain village of Voskopoya on the eastern border. It was going to take them several hours, and Adile had carefully packed up some food, a large bottle of water, and a blanket. As a large coastal town with an important historical port, Durres had once been a vital thread of the Via Egnatia from Rome to Constantinople, and despite widespread communistic ravaging of virtually all its ancient church buildings, it retained an impressive amphitheatre and archeological museum. Pjeter was lucky enough to have access to an old Fiat; so far, the car had defied age and calamity, even though the potholed and animal-strewn roads proved a constant hazard for both driver and vehicle. Viktor had clearly thought quickly. The luxury of an automobile was in no small part going to determine the success of this mission. Getting the boy to anonymity so far away quickly was only possible by car. The buses were not safe, and speed was of the essence.

As Adile stared at the bumpy road ahead of her, thoughts began darting from her mind like pieces of exploding popcorn. Viktor had been brief. There had been no time for questions; telephone calls were always kept discreetly short. As they drove on together, fevered excitement and apprehension waged war in silent anticipation. Eventually, Adile could bear it no longer.

'What are we doing, Pjeter?' she had blurted out anxiously.

'I wish I knew,' he had replied, his lips trying to form a smile, his hands gripping the wheel tightly.

The reality that their whole life was about to be upturned now confronted them both. After a long pause, Pjeter looked across at her worried face and softened.

'It will be okay, my love,' he said tenderly, patting her arm.

'Oh, Pjeter, I hope so,' she had said. *I really hope so.*

Leaving the city traffic behind, they were soon winding along the hillside route, flanked by the long arms of craggy mountain ranges on either side and slowing frequently for shepherd boys with long sticks to beat their crowded flocks of brown and white sheep across the road. Donkey-drawn carts bound with firewood bundles impeded them too, cumbrous and speed-defying. While Adile tried to quell her impatience, Pjeter narrowed his eyes in deep concentration, his thoughts racing as fast as hers at what they were about to do. There was no going back now.

Beside them, men with rolled-up sleeves pedalled overladen bicycles, whilst daring motorcycles bipped at the occasional antiquated bus, chasing each other back and forth around the jagged hairpin bends. Alongside the dusty road, nutmeg-faced children chased the traffic happily. Adile watched old women carrying their wicker baskets, shuffling slowly, headscarves knotted securely behind their heads and aprons encircling full black skirts, despite the oppressive midday heat. In the fields, golden cones of dried maize were stacked, tied together like bobble hats. *How different the journey home will be,* she thought pensively. She looked across at the folded blanket, soon to be filled, and felt herself shivering.

They arrived shortly after midday, knowing that this clandestine salvage needed to be both swift and unnoticed. It was necessary to be back home by dark, so they wouldn't be missed. Inside his little hut, Viktor Papadasi sat with the boy patiently, trying not to transmit any consternation about the future, either to him or Adile and Pjeter. He willed his fears into a prayer, in between popping up and down to look out of the window, and hoped that his absence from cleaning earlier that morning hadn't been spotted. He had told the boy he was a *prifti*, or priest, but he was almost sure the boy would have no clue what that meant.

Truthfully, it was a title that he'd held dormant for more years than he cared to remember. He had been on the cusp of priesthood and taken his vows of celibacy in 1945, only months before communism had slammed an iron fist on the table, determined to extinguish all trace of religion in whatever guise or form, sparing no clerics either, whether prifti or iman. As if the declaration of an atheistic state could obliterate his internal faith, he had often thought. *What foolishness.*

However, it was a vocation that was to cost him dearly in the years ahead. He was to lose many friends and heard of many more loyal priftis who simply disappeared, never to return. Erased and vanished but never forgotten, this terrifying brutality had, rather than deter, merely forged his resolve to keep the candle of faith alive; a flickering fragment of light in a dark cellar. Along with so many others, he had been forced into menial labour, compelled to take desultory cleaning tasks. St Lucia's Church in Voskopoya had been one of only a handful in Albania that hadn't been totally razed or converted into a storage room or sports hall. It had certainly been vandalised, but less savagely than most. He guarded it jealously, lovingly sweeping the cold floors each day, yet only able to gaze out upon an imaginary congregation. Like an athlete's baton, he guarded his beliefs fiercely, though the responsibility weighed heavy on him. He carried in his ageing body the hopes and prayers of all his spiritual ancestors, and he had determined that whilst there was still breath in his lungs, he must embody a human temple for this sacred flame until such time as he was able to pass it on. Enforced silence for so many years had deepened the mystery of earthly pilgrimage to him, but where human words may have been rendered impotent, he knew that prayer was certainly not. He had spent many long hours on his knees in a divine communion that he could not really explain, even to himself. Whether he lived to see the answers to those prayers or not was immaterial. He knew they would outlive him, and from that assurance, he derived his greatest comfort.

He glanced at the crucifix again on the wall and frowned. Normally, he never left his house without covering it with an innocuous water-coloured painting, left to him by his mother. It was his own personal defiance of state censorship, but he never underestimated the risk, which could even now cost his life. It was a routine so layered in habit that its ritual was indelibly ingrained. However, yesterday morning, he had uncharacteristically forgotten to cover it.

Strange, he thought. A small but significant oversight, *almost as if the child was meant to see it.*

His thoughts were interrupted by the sound of an engine labouring up the cobbled hill. He heard the engine stop and the doors creak open. He had explained as little as he dared to the young child, who was now looking anxiously up at him.

'They are safe people, my child, loving people. They will look after you. Please trust me,' Viktor had told him, with as much reassurance as he could muster.

The child only stared at him, unable to speak. He hadn't even asked the child his name. It was safer not to know.

A knock at the door later, he rose and, opening it, fell into Adile's embrace. She stood before him, her face awash, as he held her for the longest time.

Chapter 32

Looking back, whenever Yani thought of those early years in Durres, he only remembered raw happiness. Despite that era being full of turbulence and instability, he had found peace in the eye of the storm. Times were indeed changing, as the walls of communism crumpled untidily before them, leaving a pile of political rubble and mess. Anarchy, even. But nothing could detract from the profound sense of security which now enfolded him between the walls of his new home. His love for Adile and Pjeter had been instant, and vice versa. Somehow, the three of them would face the world together, and never for one moment had he ached for anything more, save his own mother. Adile had just intuitively known this, never asking out of turn, never trying to usurp the place in his heart reserved only for her.

Their humble apartment was a palace in comparison to all he had ever known at the orphanage. Adile kept it pristine and spotless, even though their possessions were few. Having the sole attention of two adoring parents, and now reams of new cousins (mostly his own age) who welcomed him instantly, were riches beyond his imagination. Days were spent at school with them all, where suddenly, he had become absorbed into a large and loving family by benevolent osmosis. Summers fused in childhood bliss along the long sandy Golem beach, chasing waves and each other. He had felt strangely oblivious to the constant swirl of fretful adults around him, murmuring constantly about the unrest and violence. At the old port, emigration queues of thousands had formed, each person desperately attempting to escape to a new life in Italy and beyond. But there on the endless stretch of sandy shores, they could play and swim to their hearts' content, once Yani had learned how. It was on those long beaches that he truly tasted unalloyed freedom for the first time: in his heart, in the vastness of the ocean, and in the ubiquity of the sand between his toes. He would lie on his back, looking up at the vast expanse of sky above, basking in the warm kiss of the sunshine, and never more convinced that his heavenly Babi was smiling down at him.

His adoption had been easier to approve than Pjeter at first had supposed. Papers had eventually been released from Korce, legislative bureaucracy being recently relaxed, and Yani instantly found himself the bona fide son of his overjoyed parents. Adile and Yani were both transformed overnight, leaving Pjeter soaking in the radiance of a resurrected wife and a young son who simply worshipped his every move. Adile's sisters had embraced Yani as one of their own too, each delighted by the sheer joy that his arrival had brought to their older sister. Years fell off her like a snake shedding skin, and having a youngster around the house had forced Pjeter to rewind into a long-forgotten youth, leaving Adile dizzy with happiness to see Pjeter and Yani roll around like puppies as they tumbled together, arm wrestled, and learned to juggle.

Pjeter became the finest teacher. From him, Yani learned to read, to write, and to do his sums, but most exciting of all, he learned to play the accordion. In his youth, Pjeter had played *muzike* in part of a folk band, starting with the lute-like *cifteli*, which resembled an enormously long wooden spoon with only two strings, but quickly preferring the scope of the accordion, which he produced at every wedding and celebration thereafter. He would help little Yani place the large musical box on his lap and show him how to coordinate the treble keys at the front and the bass keys at the back, all the while using the bellows to emit its inimitable sound. The boy learned so quickly that Pjeter was astonished. Yani would race home from school each day, begging and imploring to be allowed to practice, such that after a few months, Pjeter and Adile began to hold many late-night conversations as to how they could possibly assist his progress. There was no spare money for lessons, and Pjeter already was stretching his evenings too late in order to spend time with Yani. In the end, the answer came quite unexpectedly.

Pjeter had seen a classical concert advertised in the Aleksander Moisiu Theatre Hall, a glassy grey building in the town centre, and had managed to get tickets to hear the Symphony Orchestra of Galicia and a renowned violinist, amongst other things. However, it was not the violin which had captivated young Yani. To the surprise of them both, Yani had come home clutching Pjeter's large hand, stunned into complete silence by the wonder of what he had just heard.

'Did you like that, my son?' Pjeter had nervously asked Yani as they walked home together, along the broad pavement lined with palm trees, which swayed gently above them in the warm evening air. He had never seen Yani so quiet. The boy had sat throughout the entire concert, frozen faced.

'Oh yes, Babi!' Yani had replied, as if that was the strangest question to be asked.

For in that one evening, Yani had decided without any doubt what he was going to do with the rest of his life. He had never heard it before, or the beautiful sounds it made, but when the orchestra ushered in the man who sat before the giant black instrument, Yani knew he had finally found the key to his very own heart.

From now on, and however hard it would be, he would chase this dream until he caught it.

One day, it would be *him* sitting on that stage. One day, it would be Yani who could play the piano like that.

Chapter 33

Ten years and a lifetime later, Yani had indeed caught his dream. His vocation had welcomed him with open arms, as if it had been simply waiting for him to arrive. Pjeter had, through an extraordinary sequence of fortunate events, secured the services of a distinguished piano teacher, Zonje Goga, who had taken on Adile as a cleaner in return for lessons. It was a small sacrifice for Adile, overjoyed as they both were with the child's prodigious progress. For it really did seem that Yani had exceptional talent. The teacher was more excited about her new pupil than anyone she had ever taught before. From then on, the doors swung open easily. Yani had done his part through sheer willpower and determination, but practice was never a struggle for him, merely a glorious and defining addiction which he was simply unable to stop. It was an extension of himself—and just meant to be.

Viktor Papadasi had visited regularly over the years and was more delighted by the outcome than anyone. He was also experiencing his own rebirth, as now, after so many long years, churches were once again being rebuilt, and he found himself officially known as the prifti he believed God had called him to be. He wore his black clerical gown with more joy and fulfillment than it was possible to measure. It was nothing short of a miracle, but then that didn't surprise him, either. He had ample reason to believe that God was quite good at those.

Before long, Yani was being paraded around at small

gatherings and school concerts, and then, gradually, the audiences just grew bigger and bigger. Word got around quickly, as mothers whispered to each other on cafe corners about the extraordinary achievements of Adile's precious orphan. Listeners tossed him shiny lek coins, and his noisy cousins made a highly successful job of trumpeting him around town. Both Yani and his teacher knew that the only route ahead for him now lay in Tirana at the Academy of Arts, but to do that, he would need to successfully audition.

In the weeks leading up to it, he had barely been at home, spending long days at Zonje Goga's house; she had kindly offered her piano for him to practice on. She knew that Yani had far exceeded what she could honestly teach him now, and his dream for success was as much her own. He had come home tired and exhausted each night, hungrily grateful for the meal of fish and *patate* which Adile had carefully prepared, but barely noticing her slight pallor and drawn face. He knew she was anxious for him, as indeed she was, but privately, she was concealing another disquiet. A couple of times in recent weeks, she had fainted for no apparent reason, and she couldn't shake off a morbid premonition that she was unable to explain to Pjeter. Nor did she want to try. In the small hours of the morning, she would stare at the comforting silhouette of his back and listen to the rhythmic sound of his gentle snoring, willing herself to believe it was a soothing lullaby before finally falling, as the dawn began to creep under their curtains, into a superficial and ineffective sleep.

Yani wasn't unduly concerned about the audition. Performing made him feel fully alive, and he had memorised his pieces fastidiously. His teacher had also prepared him for the accompanying *solfège* and harmony tests, so it was just a matter of willing the intervening days away, which he did impatiently, oblivious to any strain Adile was shadowing.

When the day came, Pjeter had taken him by bus to Tirana, just under an hour away. Yani was mesmorised by the hubbub of the noisy city. The streets were busy and wide, and several times, Pjeter had to grab an arm to stop Yani walking into oncoming traffic, which swerved and hooted obdurately around them. Walking swiftly across Skandenburg Square, where only a few years earlier, Hoxha's thirty-foot statue had been toppled by a feverish crowd, they finally came to a square fronted concrete building, which greeted them implacably. They climbed the steps together. Once inside the vast hall, they were greeted rather coldly by an officious, thin-lipped woman, who ignored Pjeter's nervous smile and ushered Yani away from him, heels clicking, to a room beyond, before shutting the door firmly behind them.

Two hours later, after Pjeter had paced up and down the long avenues of Tirana, he returned to find Yani standing on the steps, waving a letter triumphantly. He had been told his performance was outstanding and had been offered a place on the spot.

Chapter 34

'I did it, Babi!' Yani had cried, as Pjeter's long arms embraced him euphorically.

'My son. My *son*,' Pjeter had repeated, feeling his eyes well up without warning.

He held the boy tight and then looked at Yani with unbridled love and astonishment. This was surely one of the proudest days of his life. He instantly wished Adile was there to share it with him.

Thinking of her, he exclaimed ecstatically, '*Mami*! We must get back and tell her.'

He tugged Yani's arm in the opposite direction of the academy. Both of them tumbled down the steps, laughing and whooping as they went. Yani could only imagine her face when she heard the news. They couldn't get home quickly enough.

When Yani thought about that day ever after, he was never sure if he could fully describe the antithesis of emotions that came with it.

They had finally reached Durres as the sun was setting over a breezeless, calm Adriatic. Yani had remembered in slow motion ever since, from the time they stepped off the bus. Racing back to the apartment, they had half-run, half-chased each other home, both determined to reach Adile first. Bounding up the outside steps, they had reached the front door, Pjeter only noticing fleetingly that the lights weren't on. The house seemed eerily still.

Bursting through the front door, they had bounded into the

hall, before something stopped them, almost tripping them up. Pjeter snapped on a light, seeing before his brain could catch up, what his eyes couldn't believe: In front of them, motionless, Adile lay in a twisted bundle on the floor. Her eyes were open, staring glassily straight ahead.

In that instant, they both knew what it wasn't possible to absorb. It was too late; Adile was gone.

***

She was only fifty-seven. It had been a brain haemorrhage, the doctors said. Nothing less than a massive bleed, which would have killed her instantly. Emptily, they tried to comfort Pjeter and Yani that she probably wouldn't have known much, except a blinding headache. Even that knowledge was unbearable, and Yani had felt tortured by an irrational guilt. If only they had been there, rather than chasing his selfish dream. In the weeks that followed, it had been impossible to overestimate the tidal wave of grief that drowned them both. Yani had simply shut down, the earlier triumph of the day completely evaporated, and Pjeter had never recovered. Even now.

They had been inconsolable. Neither had been able to comfort the other, and the shock lived on, for many months and years afterwards. Finally, Yani had decided that, abstractedly, the only escape from his desolation was to move to Tirana anyway, even though his motivation to go had completely run dry. What use was it if she wasn't there to share it with him?

Viktor Papadasi had come to conduct the funeral, throughout which he wept openly. His grief was as raw and bloody as theirs. Adile had been like a daughter to him, his loss gaping and profound. Whenever he had tried to talk with Yani, both came to abrupt and choking stops.

'I don't think I can do it,' Yani had wailed to him on more than one occasion, when talking about moving to Tirana.

Viktor had looked at him tenderly, agonised.

'We often don't think we can do things,' he had answered, willing himself to believe it.

Then, mustering strength from an inner reservoir, he had tried to gently coax him.

'She would want you to be going forward, Yani; you *know* that.'

He coughed awkwardly, and there was a long silence.

Yani looked down at his shoes, unable to disagree. He had nothing left to fight with. He couldn't play the piano at all just now.

Zonje Goga had come and offered unexpected help in that regard.

'Here you are, Yani,' she had said rather abruptly, handing him an unfamiliar score.

He had stared at her, weary and irritated.

'This will help give your grief a voice, a language.' It was a copy of Ravel's *Sonatine.*

Now he could never play that piece without thinking of Adile and all that she had meant. As time slowly and eventually delivered a modicum of anaesthetic to his broken heart, he had travelled to the academy bravely, but very much alone. Zonje Goga was right. The music was a balm. He had forgotten how to pray or even what to say. Yet it was here, as a fledgling student, that he discovered something quite remarkable. He realised that his fingers were praying for him. Bit by bit, and piece by piece, he began to touch heaven with his soul and, in doing so, found heaven waiting in return.

Chapter 35

David brought a breakfast tray up to his father's room, hoping it would suffice. He had been home from hospital for almost a week and was making steady progress. Automatically, he placed the morning paper on top, just as his mother would have done. It was strange, he thought. He recognised the predictable pattern of bereavement, mimicking actions of the deceased until they now had become part of his daily routine too, as each little task brought a peculiar comfort. He knew Brian would feel the same.

Maureen had visited almost daily, but as she lived in a different neighbourhood, visits necessitated a bus journey, which David could see was taking its toll. She couldn't disguise her relief that David was around to look after Brian, but between them all, an invisible anxiety was brewing as to what would happen when David returned to Melbourne. David's concern was also compounded. He had seen Tess three times now, and each occasion had surpassed the last in his estimation. He was falling unashamedly in love and increasingly believed that Tess felt the same. It was more wonderful than he could have imagined, yet so completely unexpected. He still hadn't told Brian but knew it was only a matter of time before his father would guess. He couldn't keep pretending he was out visiting old friends, as most of them had long since left Sheffield. Today, he wanted to conceal his secret for a little longer. He wasn't quite ready to share this new-found happiness, especially as the thought of Australia loomed like a black thundercloud on the horizon.

Richard and Olivia had driven up to visit twice, and it had been good to see his brother again. Olivia, however, seemed more of a social parasite than ever, and David found her increasingly crass and patronising. In his estimation, she contrasted violently with Tess, who was refreshingly unconcerned about either her appearance or her achievements. In short, Olivia was as ambitious as Tess was not. He had even less inclination to tell them about her and felt fairly convinced there wouldn't be an automatic connection. Olivia had never really approved of either his marriage or, illogically, his divorce. He surmised that their relationship had fallen prey to busy careers, two lives lived in parallel, but without real emotional depth. Yet it seemed to suit them in a mundane kind of way. It depressed him. David was glad they didn't have any children, suspecting they would be a total inconvenience. Such was the overriding debt he owed to his mother. She had sacrificed so much for them, and now he began to understand why. He realised that any guilt she might have carried had been masterfully concealed. It had never occurred to him to question her unswerving maternal loyalty, and it distressed him to recall their frequent episodes of boyish insensitivity. She had deserved more from them both. There were now so many questions he wanted to ask her but would never be able to. He sighed. He must not dwell on regrets.

He had also decided to send another letter to Kitty. The disappointment at her lack of response had been rather eclipsed by Tess, who nevertheless had lent some useful moral support, seeming as eager as he to discover her whereabouts. Again, he shielded this from his father. He had no desire to involve him in any emotional trauma, but he did feel uncomfortable at what felt like a minor conspiracy. He had typed out the letter and slipped it into his breast pocket the last evening he had been with Tess. He pulled it out to show her, and she had immediately offered to post it, as her flat was minutes from the central sorting office. He handed it over readily. It felt good to have an accomplice, an ally even.

Tess was, in truth, as keen as David to solve this mystery. She had always had a penchant for the unresolved and unusual, as her wobbly pile of crime paperbacks at home testified. It bordered on an addiction, her interest in forensics. Only this time, there was no crime, just a mystery, and even more enticing, it was real. She was spellbound.

She popped the letter into the anonymity of her bottomless bag and, after a protracted and reluctant goodbye to David, determined to walk home via the postbox and aim for an early night, rueing the fact that she had to be up early for work the next day. She was becoming increasingly tired from squeezing the two new passions into her life alongside work: David and the 'cello. Both required her to burn the midnight oil, even if it was undeniably worth it.

She hurried along the busy streets, lit well now it was dark, whilst a swell of thinning rush hour traffic hummed beside her, wafting unwelcome fumes onto the pavement. She never liked walking out alone after dark, but it would only take an extra few minutes to detour round the block and catch the last post of the day. She waited at the red lights to cross and pressed the top button. A cyclist on a fold-up bike pulled up next to her, his suited leg clipped neatly at the ankle. His helmet and backpack neatly in position, she identified with his desire to scurry home.

Great design, those bikes, Tess thought. He looked across at her and smiled beneath heavy dark eyebrows, just as the orange lights started to flash. *Off you go*, she thought, willing his acceleration.

As the cyclist lurched forward, the next few seconds happened in a blur. A lorry came at speed round the corner, into the oncoming traffic. The cyclist stood no chance. In a haze of screeched brakes and horns, crumpled metal and twisted flesh collided. The man's torso disappeared under the belly of the lorry, leaving two long and lifeless legs protruding and crumpled between the wheels.

Chapter 36

Tess looked on, stunned. Her heart rate exploded. Suddenly, a man ran across the road and began attending to the cyclist. Another joined him. And then another. With no time to consider her response, she knew she must call an ambulance. She fumbled in her bag, hands trembling wildly, and felt the familiar solidity of her phone. She wrapped her fingers round it and dialled 999, checking her watch on instinct and summoning emergency help.

Then, with a sickening feeling in her stomach, she looked on at the people attending the crash scene, only they didn't seem to be doing much. She looked on, poised to join them, but unable to move. She noticed that the lorry driver had opened his door and jumped down to join them. Head in hands, he dropped to his knees, distraught. In slow motion, she knew that their inactivity told her what she intuitively already knew.

Time suspended itself as she remembered hearing the blare of sirens and blue flashing lights puncture the night sky. She still remained frozen, rooted to the kerb. What else could she do? A small crowd had gathered around the lorry, trying in some way to shield the still man, who only seconds earlier had grinned at her. *I was the last face he saw*, she realised in disbelief. *Good God*.

No, this wasn't good at all.

She wanted to sit down; her legs felt weak, but she knew she must stay to give a statement. To help. To do something. She walked over the road, traffic now halted on all sides. She lowered

149

her eyes in disbelief as she got nearer, seeing for the first time the expanding crimson puddle which was spreading over the grey tarmac from beneath the lorry. Only in the dark it resembled a slick of shiny treacle. She daren't look, yet had no option. As the paramedics lifted him onto the trolley, she saw a disfigured head and neck still helmeted, but impotent, his scarlet face crushed to a pulp. His neon hi-viz jacket still clung to him stubbornly. She stared in disbelief and then had to look away. In all her years at hospital, she had never witnessed first-hand an accident at such close quarters. She wanted to cry, but all tears had stalled.

An hour or so later, when she had finally extracted herself from the gruesome scene, given her eyewitness account, and done all that she knew to do, she reached for her phone again. This time to call David.

Within minutes, he was there, leaping out of his car and running towards her, consternation riven on his face. She collapsed into his arms, and only then did a rumble of sobs well up from within. Fatigue and exhaustion accompanied them. She shook violently and uncontrollably, and David just held her, his strong shoulders encompassing her shock and trauma as best he could. And in that most terrible of moments, she knew without any shadow of doubt that in his arms, there was nowhere else she would rather be.

Chapter 37

Kitty had taken the liberty of inviting Yani to dinner. Weeks had passed in blissful anticipation of Sam's weekly and undeniable metamorphic transformation, and it was spilling over infectiously to her too. Balanced, as her whole life was, on the psychological health of her children, Kitty was enjoying the current and somewhat rare ride of well-being. It was as if a pilot light which had long simmered, hidden in the bowels of a boiler, had suddenly whooshed into a roar. For both mother and son. Nick had listened patiently as, evening after evening, Kitty had regaled him of Sam's latest accomplishment, trying not to exaggerate the progression of his achievements, but it was evident to Nick that nothing else seemed to be dominating Kitty's thoughts these days. He was trying with differing degrees of success not to get annoyed with Sam's incessant piano practise, which now seemed to preoccupy every evening. He would have to get some headphones. However, he listened to Kitty's wittering with seasoned bemusement. He never tired of her enthusiasm, so often humorously expressed in ways Kitty was mostly unaware of.

But for all that, he was quite mistaken. Kitty had, and very uncharacteristically, buried the secret of David's letter with no small degree of success. Quite why she had decided not to tell Nick yet, she wasn't even sure herself. It was just too … private. For now. She would certainly tell him when the time was right. But in this, too, she felt a pang of guilt, as there was very little that

Kitty was ever able to hide from Nick, intended or not. Secrecy was a virtual impossibility for Kitty. Yani had certainly provided a welcome distraction from her gnawing frustration and deep fear that she would never hear from David again.

Yani's cultural reserve was fast thawing in Kitty's company, as he too discovered with rising amusement her quirky, frenetic, and amiable chaos, which seemed to follow her everywhere. She was as transparent as he was self-contained. She represented the antithesis of so much he had ever known, and he felt drawn, warming his hands by the fire of a family cohesion which he had never really experienced since those brief happy years growing up alongside his cousins. Kitty, meanwhile, was oblivious to his observations. Her incessant chatter didn't leave much time for personal questions, although whilst stirring the stew that evening, as Yani sat leaning back on a chair watching her multitask with some incredulity, it occurred to Kitty that she really knew nothing about him.

'So,' she began, 'where *was* it you said you came come from again, Yani? I'm really very ignorant about Eastern European geography. Have you been here for long?'

It was an abrupt question, clumsy even. But she ploughed on, before Yani could answer.

'I think travelling is just *so* fantastically healthy, don't you? I do wish we Brits weren't such abysmal linguists.'

She said this with a sweep of her wooden spoon and an air of ridiculous and unfounded superiority. Gravy sauce dripped onto the floor, unnoticed, as the spoon dangled precariously. Roger dutifully obliged by trotting over to lick it up. Yani smiled.

'Albania. That's where I come from,' he replied. 'Although it's been a long while.'

In the lounge, wafting sounds of Sam's minor scales were being hammered with brutal ferocity, as Yani tried to ignore his ill-disguised attempts to show off. Sam had been delighted that Kitty's irrepressible hospitality had extended towards a supper invitation. Yani smiled again, invisibly communicating with Sam, who he could hear had just successfully mastered what he hadn't been able to do five minutes earlier. Satisfaction washed over him. Kitty was looking at him inquisitively. She didn't want to reveal further ignorance, but almost for the first time, it occurred to her that there was a definite past to this man's life that she had never quite considered before.

'So, er, do you have a family back there? I mean, do you get back there often?'

Yani quickly donned a mask of indifference with impressive aplomb.

'No, no, not now, sadly,' he said, lying as expertly as he could against Kitty's stare. 'I don't 'ave much time to visit these days,' he added, this time more truthfully.

'Hmm. What about a girlfriend, then?' she tossed saucily.

Kitty was nothing if not pathologically nosy. Plus, she felt there was a healthy enough age gap between them to protect her, even though she looked up slightly warily as Nick came into the kitchen.

Yani was cornered but rose to greet Nick with his customary courtesy, but also by way of distraction. They had been waiting for Nick to arrive home, and he looked predictably weary and clearly in need of some food.

'I was just asking Yani if he had a girlfriend,' Kitty explained, grinning sheepishly whilst the wooden spoon still hung suspended. Roger sat transfixed beneath.

Now Yani paused. Her frankness had caught him off guard, and Nick seemed also to be waiting with humorous intrigue, amused as ever by Kitty's forthright indiscretion. Yani felt his heart beating a little faster. He looked at them both. What came out of his lips next bypassed his brain.

'Yes. Well, I do... I mean, I did,' he fumbled. 'It's hard to explain.'

Inside, he was choking. He had never divulged this to anyone, least of all relative strangers, but he had been ambushed by Kitty's disarming ease. Now the silence hung between them, hovering.

She is teasing him now, her head swung back in laughter as her hair swishes to reveal a sinewy neck. Pjeter is shuffling awkwardly and bustles into the room, carrying a tray of glasses and iced lemonade.

'So Yani didn't tell you about me?' she asks incredulously.

She laughs again, a tinkling cascade which energises and relaxes them all.

'Then I don't think perhaps you know this boy very well, after all?! I'm so very pleased to meet you.' *She plants a firm but delicate hand into Pjeter's worn one.*

Pjeter looks down at her warmly, aching for Adile to be able to share this joyful introduction.

Back in the kitchen, the words just seemed to flow out of Yani's mouth, unchecked.

'I do love a woman very, very much,' he admitted.

The pause lengthened. Kitty and Nick waited patiently, as Yani garnered it to dramatic effect.

'The only problem is, I 'ave absolutely no idea where she is now. Because two years ago,' he said, staring at them without flinching, *'she simply vanished.'*

Chapter 38

Stupor suspended over the table. Nick cleared his throat anxiously. Kitty's eyes remained transfixed on Yani's face for a second and then snapped back into the moment and returned to the stove. She started ladling warm rice onto plates and topping them with the bubbling stew. Nick grabbed the wine bottle and began to tear off the seal.

Yani hadn't felt able to say much more, other than muttering he didn't know what had happened. Yes, the police had been involved, but no, nothing had as yet been forthcoming from their enquiries, although the case remained open. She had simply been there one day, full of life and vigour, then gone the next. Her flat had been left untouched, her clothes and belongings as she had left them; the only thing missing had been her phone and purse. Even the flat had been left open and her laptop neatly stowed on top of her bedside table. It was all highly unusual, unexpected, and sinister. No history of psychological disturbance or trauma, no letter, nothing on her emails. Why, they had only celebrated his birthday the night before at a nearby restaurant. She had oozed joy and optimism about the week ahead, he remembered. She had finally decided to have a makeover and get six inches of her long hair cut off. All these details he seemed to remember with precise clarity, even though the mention of them elicited noticeable anguish.

This had all happened two years ago, but it was fairly clear to Nick and Kitty that the wound was still dangerously raw. Yani was visibly shaken, even talking about it. Still, questions dangled in the air for them both, some they didn't even dare to formulate, and the conversation became stuck. Uncharacteristically, Kitty decided not to prod any further that evening, sensing a rather urgent need to return to terra firma whilst her swirling thoughts calmed down.

The meal passed rather uneventfully after that, as one by one the children trooped in, nose first, in search of the aroma emanating out of the kitchen. A welcome distraction, Nick and Kitty both thought.

Not exactly saved by the bell, but saved by the kids, Kitty thought with relief.

In the days that followed, she berated herself that she hadn't even asked her name, but she decided to google his. Nothing there, though. His personal history read much as it did inside his concert programme: a pianist of high acclaim, educated in Tirana, then Paris. A list of prestigious concerts performed throughout Europe in recent years, and a year's scholarship in America.

It was inconceivable to Kitty that Yani was in any way linked to her disappearance, and yet she seemed to recall thinking in these cases that the most likely suspect was often the person closest to them. Was that true? Kitty shuddered. That she had taken him in so unsuspectingly and readily entrusted her son to him was indeed a little disquieting.

Nick too had his concerns, which naturally didn't alleviate hers. Neither of them had any reason to distrust Yani, but yet. There was something missing here, something unresolved, and Kitty was at a loss to know what. Or how to proceed. To take Yani out of the equation for Sam now would be simply catastrophic. Plus, she had no reason that she could give Yani to discontinue lessons which he would believe or that would not make him suspicious of her thoughts. No, they must sit tight for now. Nick agreed that lesson times must be in the evening, when he was home from work and the rest of the family were around. Kitty chided herself for her suspicions, remembering the raw pain Yani had shown as he talked. She willed herself to believe the best of him, which her very nature usually dictated towards everyone, but this time, she had to admit, she was struggling.

She felt slightly untwined again. Piano lessons had certainly interrupted her from thinking about David, but now, she began to think of him more and more, yet without any reasonable solution. Her frustration grew daily, yet there was simply nothing she could do. She had no possible means of contact and chided herself for the hundredth time for not storing the letter safely out of reach from mongrel jaws. Basil certainly had an odd penchant for chewing the post, especially important bits. Invoices often didn't stand a chance. She hadn't wanted Sam to see it for sure, but she had hurried, and perilously so. She found it difficult to even stroke Basil these days, desperate as he always was for her oft-distracted attention. A massive part of her life had made its way through his intestines. Somehow, through his dark and muddy colon had passed the name of a brother who she was now incapable of ever discovering. Basil just looked up at her innocently, head cocked to one side, more puzzled than Kitty by the disdain of his mistress. He sensed it, and she did too. Guilt and anger simmered away inside of her, and the little dog knew it. She just had to turn away whenever he looked up at her.

One evening, when her stress levels had reached a somewhat irrational crescendo, she told Nick she was going out for a quick walk. Yani was due that evening to teach Sam, but she had a short window to get some fresh air, and she set off briskly up to the top of the road, which was punctuated at the end by a large old church on the corner. She fairly stormed past it and then stopped. It was starting to drizzle, and she had come unprepared. Lights were on inside. It was evensong. A faint sound of organ playing could be heard from outside, its familiar whine and wheeze somehow distinctly reassuring. Kitty walked nearer. The service had only just begun. *Why not?*, she thought. *It's warmer in there than out here, and I can afford a few minutes.*

In some indefinable way, church had always calmed her, providing a sanctuary of mysterious security on the sporadic occasions she stepped inside. She gently opened the big oak door and slipped in unnoticed.

The service had begun, and the sparse, mostly elderly congregants were warbling with impressive conviction the last verse of the hymn she had heard outside. She grabbed a hymn book and looked up at the number on the board. Fumbling quickly to find the page, she joined in quietly, already smiling at herself for being there so unexpectedly. The thought of the chaos she had left behind was now rather pleasing, as an internally smugness began to germinate.

An elderly gentleman stood up to give the lesson, and her mind wandered again to David.

Where are you? she wondered. *Who are you,* and come to think of it, *who am I?* She looked up at the rather well-preserved and ornate ceiling and imagined God to be hovering up there somewhere, like Aladdin on his carpet, surveying the scene below, which included her. With a sudden gust of desire for some spiritual dialogue, she decided to challenge the Almighty.

'So then, Mr God. What now?' she asked, a tad irreverently. 'Helloo? Seriously, I need to find my brother, and it's over to you because I am a bit stuck. I just wish he would write to me again. Urm, could you possibly fix that, *please?*'

She looked up to the dark, high ceiling. With her prayer thus candidly ascended, she looked down again and stared at the grey heads in front of her. *Oh, come all ye faithful,* she thought, as her eyes strayed up towards the lectern.

The old man was now reading very slowly and deliberately, peering over the large black Bible before him through thick lenses, as if to prevent verbal stumbling. He seemed of amorphous age, perhaps between seventy-five and ninety-five, but Kitty wasn't really listening. She was waiting for an answer. Then as he straightened his back a little, he suddenly raised his voice, and to her genuine astonishment, Kitty found her ears hearing his voice issue the command:

'*Though it linger, wait for it.*'

Kitty glanced up at him, incredulous, as if a thunderbolt from heaven had just coshed her on the head. Wait, *what*? Was that a coincidence? She glanced at the service sheet. The reading was from Habakkuk. She made a mental note. Did she *really* just have to wait? Could she? It was a frustratingly unsatisfactory answer, on the one hand. But feeling strangely invigorated by this most unexpected and, she felt, near certain divine intervention, she assembled herself. Halfway during the next hymn, she turned and slipped out, just as impulsively as she had slipped in.

Back home, Nick was trying unsuccessfully to persuade Lucy to help with supper, and Sam was warming up by trampolining on the piano keys in the lounge with unbroken fortissimo. *I must ask Yani to teach him a new piece,* Kitty noted, *or we are all going to go insane.*

Toby and Angus were wrapped in duvets and playing a game of dive bombs down the main stairs. *Why is it,* she thought, *the minute my back is turned, all thoughts of homework are abandoned?*

She quelled a venomous thought towards Nick who, to be fair, was completely distracted in heated remonstration with Lucy, who was now shouting back. Tilly had entered the arena, and she could hear it was now turning into a cat fight. *Why does he rise to the bait every time?* she wailed internally. Best just to leave them. Then she felt guilty. Two premenstrual teenagers for him to deal with after a long day at work. Poor Nick. She switched her allegiance. *This family is so crazy,* she thought wearily. Suddenly, she didn't want Yani to come, after all. She always felt she had to pretend that they were all vaguely under control, when she knew full well this was complete rubbish. This was arsenic hour.

But when the doorbell rang, she let Yani in, simulating her

usual welcome. His hair was damp from the rain, and she thought too that he seemed drawn and a little pale. Maybe effort was required on both their parts, after all. She knew his rehearsal schedules were inclined to be intense and unrelenting, and that he really was doing her a favour, which he possibly would rather not. She ushered him into the lounge, where a beaming Sam awaited. His monstrous energy was overwhelming. Yani took a deep breath. Kitty retreated to the war zone of the kitchen and steeled herself.

Half an hour later, Yani appeared at the kitchen door, where by some sprinkling of magic dust, Lucy and Tilly were sitting, heads down in homework and scribbling furiously, oblivious to the TV still on up in the corner, which Nick had failed to turn off. He had retreated to his study, tired but dutifully dispatched. The boys upstairs had gone ominously quiet, but right now, Kitty couldn't be bothered to investigate.

"E is doing well, your Sam,' Yani said politely.

The shadow of a weak smile passed over his face. Was it her imagination, thought Kitty, or did he look exhausted? Or was he suspicious of her suspicion? She felt on edge but desperately didn't want to be—or even to show it. She reached to the fridge for her giant monthly planner, pimpled by stickers, to arrange the next lesson. But she never got any further.

When she turned round, Yani was staring at the TV screen, his face now an ivory shade as she followed his gaze. For there, on the screen, was a picture of a river near Paris, and underneath, she read the subtitles, as she heard the same words being spoken:

'Police have today discovered the body of a woman thought to be drowned some while ago. She is possibly believed to be the missing cellist Sabine Dubois, who mysteriously vanished without trace two years ago from a nearby suburb. Identification has not yet been confirmed, and the death is still being treated as suspicious.'

She looked carefully at Yani's face. But very abruptly, without a word, he started up, grabbed his bag, and ran for the front door. It slammed behind him. Kitty didn't try to stop him. She wasn't sure if she was now witness to some sort of murder scene by association. She stared at the screen in disbelief as Lucy and Tilly carried on writing obliviously.

Chapter 39

Yani had both run and stumbled back to his apartment. He was still quivering, even once he had got inside. Blinded by shock and numb from disbelief, he barely had strength to check the newsfeed again. But there it was, an hour later: an unidentified woman's body dragged from a river in Paris. It couldn't be.

He found himself reaching for an unopened bottle of whiskey, which had been given to him months ago as a gift. He actually loathed the stuff, but tonight was an exception. He looked reluctantly at the amber fluid and took a large gulp, choking as it hit the back of his throat. Adding some water, he lay down on his couch and stared up at the ceiling. *No, no,* no. *This wasn't happening. Please, Babi,* no. He closed his eyes.

In his mind, he can still remember the first day they met. He had just returned from his year at Juilliard, and she had recently graduated from the Paris Conservatoire; he had seen her face advertised on a hall corridor for a debut concert. He had stopped to stare at her delicately attractive features, noticing that her eyes seemed to be smiling even though her mouth wasn't. She had intrigued him even before they met. He had noted the date, wondering whether he might just go along. Which he had.

'Enchanté,' he had said to her when introduced by a friend afterwards.

'De même,' she had quietly replied, locking eyes on him warily. She

was even more beautiful than her photograph had hinted. And her eyes really did sparkle all by themselves.

'C'etais magnifique,' he simply said, not knowing what else to say. Her playing had bewitched him.

'Merci, merci,' she had said again and then giggled. He had grinned back, the ice broken. He couldn't stop staring at those eyes. She had blushed but held his gaze teasingly.

'Maybe ... um, I could have the honour of accompanying you sometime?' he had heard himself say, before his brain had a chance to reason.

'OK,' she had said, laughing easily. It was the best deal he had ever made.

And that was that. Afterwards, they had both acknowledged an instant spark, an immediate connection, the stuff of legend. And it had happened to them both. Unprecedented and unexpected, as if they had quite simply found the missing part of themselves.

They had travelled Europe together not long after that, a flurry of concerts in unknown halls and to unknown audiences. The first time they had played together, Yani had experienced a nirvana unlike anything else he had previously encountered. As had she. This artistic zenith had been quite unparalleled, the musical dialogue between them both intoxicating and exquisite. Music had fed their love, and their love had fed their music. Neither of them had been able to describe the sheer force of their feelings for each other; it had been like a dream from which they never wanted to wake up.

He had taken her all the way home to meet Pjeter. It had been the first time since Adile died that he had seen Pjeter smile, but it had also enforced such sadness that she would never meet Adile. But he had told her everything. She had been captivated by his story, with its unembellished drama and trajectory. It was true that she had encountered her own share of youthful unhappiness, but it was nothing compared to his. It made her reel just to think about his time in Korce. For he had taken her back there too, and she had stood above the town, looking out over red-roofed houses below her and the Mordor-like plains beyond. She had marvelled at his childhood escape over and over again, reliving its trauma and implausible adventure.

'My survivor,' she had said quietly, as they stood together, looking across to the khaki mountains on the horizon.

'My darling. It was all for you.'

He had kissed her softly, not wanting to interrupt her reflection.

'Do you think we would always have found each other?' she had asked, looking up quizzically.

He kissed the top of her nose and nodded.

'Without any doubt,' he had said resolutely. He had lifted his chin to the cerulean sky above them. 'I believe there is always a plan.'

Always a plan. Even now?

He sighed just remembering that visit. They had taken the long bus back to the Macedonian border en route for a concert in Skopje, breaking the journey on the shores of Lake Ohrid. On the way, Yani had observed wryly how much had changed in his country over a relatively short time. During the regime, it would have been unthinkable to see flimsy roadside stalls with endless pyramids of tomatoes and potatoes stacked to sell, and bunches of onions fluttering from the straw canopies above. He grimly remembered Adile's food coupons, almost inconceivable now. And littered everywhere, Hoxha's concrete bunkers, which popped up like coconut shells, shelters on a lunar landscape. A defence, against what? Empty and derelict now, but a salutary reminder, nonetheless. He shuddered pensively at the dark secrets they embodied, eager to brush them away.

It had been a breathtakingly dazzling day. The sun had shone on the bluest of waters, diamonds dancing and flickering on the surface. Their hearts had been exploding with happiness, he remembered that acutely. They had sat eating sandwiches by the shore, looking out at the jutting promontory on which the enchantingly small Church of St John of Kaneo stood, proud and timeless. In a moment of sheer impulse, Yani had dropped down on bended knee beside the bench they were sitting on.

'Marry me,' he had said solemnly and fiercely, looking up at her astonished face.

She had nodded her consent with tears, words impossible.

He had grabbed her hand, and they had raced over to the basilica, clambering up the slatted steps in front of the ancient cobbled building. Inside, he had escorted her to the front, where even if there had been bystanders, he would have ignored them. Yet it had been strangely, knowingly, empty. Faded frescoes looked down on them, as together they had stood in the cool beauty of the tiny little church, holding hands tightly. There they had made their vows in a sacred moment both intimate and eternal. Only afterwards did Yani realise Prifti Papadasi should have been there too, but somehow, the moment had overcome them. There would be plenty of time ahead to formalise a wedding, but for him, it was in that place—and in the sight of almighty God—that he had married her.

Chapter 40

David had taken Tess straight home, away from the ambulance and police sirens and hideous accident scene, trying as desperately as he could to shield her from further trauma. He had stayed with her, forging a makeshift bed on the sofa, anxious to get her to sleep, shocked as she was; and he'd left a message for Brian that he was fine but needed to help a friend out overnight. Which was true. He hoped he wouldn't worry or ask too many questions. For nothing in the world seemed more important to him now than to shield her from this pain. But he was hopelessly unable to reverse it and at a loss to know how best to help, for Tess seemed quite frozen, and her pall broke him too.

He found a blanket to put round her shoulders and had offered brandy and tea, but Tess was unable to speak, still shivering intermittently. She sat huddled on her bed, reliving in her mind those last minutes, seconds, before the lorry hit. She just couldn't erase from her memory his face at the red light. One foot suspended on the pedal, ready for the off, helmet down, and yet he had turned to look at her, close as she was, not even a metre away. His expression was etched so clearly on her mind, possibly forever. A kind face and heavy eyebrows, a prominent nose, no doubt nipped cold from the chilly night air. And a half-smile as those eyebrows raised for the very last time at her, as the lights changed to orange. And then. She shut her eyes, trying to erase the image of the large shadow of a big lorry coming from nowhere, obliterating everything.

How infinitesimal the distance is between life and death, she thought. Oh yes, she had seen the face of death many times in hospital, the final curtain anticipated as so often it was by hooks and drips, monitors and beeps, less beeps, the flat line. Even the shocked departures, finding a patient motionless and open-mouthed, but yet still softly warm behind the curtains. The unexplained, the unexpected, all this she knew and had lived. But this was different. She had lived this death alongside him, this complete stranger. She had breathed his last breaths with him; she had literally been with him as he lurched forward full of energy, promise, and eagerness to get home.

And now he was truly home, but where was that? And someone somewhere, possibly multiple someones, were facing a future without him, right now. She was consumed by their grief and her own impotence. *Was he a father?* she agonised. He looked as though he might well have been. Dutiful dad, racing home for bath time, ankle clip tied responsibly to his trousers. A sensible type, briefcase snapped onto pannier. It had all been so dark and fleeting, yet the memory went round and round and round, tormenting her without respite. She wondered why she had been at that traffic light at that moment, the unexplainable questions of probability and chance. Why her? Why *him*? She would never know. It had all seemed so typecast and scripted, so inevitable. And yet. Where was he now? The question haunted her. Gone. In milliseconds. The sense of waste and loss washed over her like a tsunami. *What is this life?* she wondered.

David had stayed with her that evening, and many thereafter. Wisely just listening, and being there. She had never been more grateful for his company, realising with appreciation that this could have all happened before she met him. The deluge of whys pierced her like arrows on a dart board. Each point stuck and embedded in her heart, crippling pains which she was incapable of plucking out. There must be something more, she reasoned. *There has to be something more.* And almost imperceptibly willing it, she wanted there to be something greater than this, greater than this agonising, aching, and inconsolable mess.

She had only taken a week off work, despite David's protestations. Work would provide diversion, which it did, but she was well aware she was only acting, playing out a part which she was not attached to but could automatically fulfil. She knew that deep down, something irrevocable had happened, though she knew not what. She wanted to press a button and snap out of it, but no return to life before this seemed ever likely to come. She buried herself in routine and the familiar, absorbing David's endless supply of company and careful attention with a gratitude she knew she could never adequately express. He had, without her knowledge, contacted work and arranged another six weeks compassionate leave, which had bought some time, but he knew he would soon have to make some decisions about the long term. Australia seemed like another galaxy away. He had left Evie hanging but pushed the thought of that persistently out of reach. He hoped she was happy, but the abrupt and unsatisfactory closure left a dull ache. He had also told Brian about Tess, and he'd reacted well, though with some gentle but undisguised concern. David wasn't ever sure that Brian had really reconciled himself with his son's divorce. But no matter; they both had to look forwards now, to both Maureen and Tess.

Giselle had left a couple of missed calls on Tess's phone before she realised she had missed two lessons. She winced, having always prided herself on being reliable. So she'd left an apologetic text and arranged for another lesson, but as she puffed up the steep hill to her house, she wondered if it was such a good idea after all. But in Giselle, she found a welcome and sensitive listener, who sat appalled to hear the story. Her hazel eyes moistened in sympathy.

'Ah, *non*. I am so sorry,' she said softly.

'Have you ever witnessed an accident?' Tess asked, almost hopefully.

'*Moi*? Non. No, I 'ave not, not yet." She steadied herself.

She looked thoughtfully out the window, as if to consider her response. It was a crisp and windy day, dominated by a rebellious, clear blue sky for early December. She looked back at Tess, her eyes fixed.

'But I 'ave seen other things,' she said slowly, 'things I always want to forget, and yet I can't.'

She looked down at her lap, stroking artistic hands in concentric circles round her kneecaps, whilst Tess waited silently for an explanation. She remembered what Giselle had told her about the man she had left behind. It all seemed so unbearably sad, and Tess felt guilty thinking of her own happiness (and health, for that matter). Giselle looked up at her again. She searched Tess's face carefully, testing those pretty blue eyes, which looked patiently back at her. She had come to trust this pupil of hers and felt fairly sure she could divulge, but even so, she trod cautiously. Loneliness had disquieted her in recent weeks, only her 'cello now offering solace and companionship. This she knew was simply not healthy. Tess waited, whilst on the mantelpiece a little retro forties clock ticked quietly, ushering in reluctant illumination.

'I told you I lost someone once,' Giselle continued eventually, still treading warily whilst Tess looked on. 'Oui, I loved him so very, *very* much. And I love him still.'

Tess said nothing, knowing from experience that listening would extract all she needed to know. Questions weren't necessary at all.

Giselle continued. Somewhere, a window was opening in the recess of her heart. Just talking about him again was fresh air to her soul. She smiled at his remembrance even now. This felt good. She told Tess again, reinforcing what she had already told her.

'You see, I loved him so much, too much... that I 'ad to leave him,' she said, knowing full well the look of confused reaction she would see again in Tess's face.

Tess raised an eyebrow and waited again.

'I am too ill, Tess, for 'im to love me. It is too much. I needed to give 'im freedom to love again, to start afresh. I couldn't give 'im myself with this illness, which may kill me yet. I'm afraid it's true,' she added reluctantly, eyes moistening again. 'I didn't want 'im to see me like this, to care for me and bear those dark memories and grief. And so I 'ad to leave 'im behind.'

The clock continued to tick softly, accompanying her thoughts. She still couldn't tell Tess the full story, but it was enough for now that she had talked of him again. Tess paused, holding the stillness.

'Oh, Giselle, that's *so* hard. So difficult. I'm so sorry. Are you quite sure he wouldn't want to love you through it all? I still can't believe he wouldn't want that.'

'Mais oui, he would want to share it, but I couldn't allow 'im. He has already suffered enough, you see; he has lost so much. His life has been so, well, complicated.'

Her voice trailed, and she hesitated. This was enough for now. Tess seemed to understand.

'I couldn't have survived the last few weeks without someone,' Tess said gently.

This time, it was Giselle who raised an eyebrow.

'You didn't tell me …,' she began and then stopped. 'Oh yes, you did! I'd forgotten. Is that the doctor you told me about?' Her eyes twinkled a little.

'Yep.' Tess grinned. 'Ha! Life is full of these chance encounters, isn't it?' she said slowly, pushing the cyclist firmly to the perimeter of her mind and thinking about David. 'Do you ever wonder about all the people we chance to meet who, well, just end up writing our own story? I sometimes think maybe there *is* a master plan. Not that I'm religious or anything,' she added. But even her doubts about that in recent weeks had taken her by surprise.

Giselle gazed at her in agreement. 'Bien sur, I know this is true,' she replied slowly. 'We have to believe. Otherwise, what is the point?'

It was a statement rather than a question. A rope of optimism they were both offering out to each other across a choppy sea strewn with waves.

'I think we were just meant to meet some people,' she concluded. Picking up her 'cello bow, which she pointed at Tess with a smile, she added, 'That certainly includes you, *mon amie.*'

Tess smiled, warmed by the compliment. A line had been crossed, and it felt good.

As she trotted home, 'cello on her back, she mused about the reason she had got here in the first place. That music in a taxi. How weird, so very strange. Was there someone watching out for her after all?

She saw the bus ahead, coming into its stop, and quickened her step to reach it. She hopped on just in the nick of time, reaching into her tote bag to fish out her phone and text David. Inside, she felt her hand brush against something at the bottom and pulled it out. As she lifted it out, she felt her stomach lurch. For as she withdrew her hand, she realised with incredulous regret that her fingers were clasping the letter she had promised to post for David on that fateful night.

Chapter 41

Kitty had taken the liberty of phoning her younger brother, Max. Another fortnight had passed without either a letter arriving or seeing Yani again. He had postponed the last lesson, which was disquieting in itself. Joining up all these dots was perplexing her, and she reached for the phone at last. She was still in slight paralysis whether or not she should go to the police. Yet something held her back. Initially, she had decided not to tell Max all about the letter and just wait for events to unfold. But it was no good. She needed his nonsensical assurance, so one evening, when Nick had gone to visit Helen, she stole into Nick's study and picked up the phone.

'Hey Max! It's me,' she said brightly, swivelling round to swing two legs up onto Nick's tidy, sacrosanct desk, instantly sensing his gruff disapproval.

'Hey sis,' he replied. She could hear the grin superglued to his face.

Max had always provided Kitty with copious quantities of both security and companionship. She simply adored him. Although four years younger, the gap had evaporated in midlife, and they now remained *meilleurs amis* through thick and thin. After her parents had sought unsuccessfully for nearly a decade to conceive, his unexpected arrival had always been hailed as a supernatural phenomenon, against all credible odds. Yet his being their biological son had obviously done nothing to detract their love from her; if anything, it served to enhance it. Neither had any hidden sense of inferiority jarred her relationship with him. Max had always treated her with truest and unalloyed respect, forged partly through genuine decency, but also their shared love of the ridiculous and absurd. His irrepressible and puckish humour could victoriously salvage nearly every mishap and misdemeanour, and he was about the only person Kitty had ever met who was just incapable of taking life seriously. Even now. She summarised her dilemma in a few short sentences and waited for his response.

'Wow, sis,' he cackled. 'I always knew you were Danish royalty. Or Irish. Or Polish maybe?' he added jocularly.

He had always hypothesised about her sequestered origins, spawned by wild and imaginative childhood games as to whether she had, in fact, with Lady Bracknell postulation, arrived in a handbag.

'No, *seriously*, Max,' she countered, knowing that any sobriety was impossible.

'Always serious, sis. You know me,' he fibbed impudently.

Kitty sighed. Perhaps she would get nowhere with this. She remembered back to her parents' funeral, nearly a decade ago now. Being significantly older than most of her friends' parents, they had passed swiftly and unexpectedly within six weeks of each other, her mother succumbing first. She had always suspected her father had simply expired out of sheer protest. Or logical grief, if such a thing were possible. So they had held a joint memorial service at which Max had succeeded in reducing the entire congregation to helpless and uncontrollable giggles at his rendition of their parents' foibles and exploits. It had been so inappropriately, gloriously appropriate. Tension had popped like balloons, such that the wake afterwards had resembled the Notting Hill Carnival as Max insisted on playing their father's favourite steel band LPs whilst pouring copious quantities of pink cava. She smiled just thinking about it.

'Max. C'mon. Help me out here. I really am having a midlife crisis.'

Max roared a muscular laugh down the other end. He was already visualising front page *Daily Mail* news with a picture of Kit and the Danish royal family.

'*Midlife*?! What about all the rest? You live crisis management every day, sis; you are a white collar CEO of all crises! Seriously. I'm so proud of you. You take cortisol to a whole new level.'

She could hear him pumping up with glee. Nor could she disagree. She could count on one hand the days in her life which hadn't been trounced by some minor catastrophe or other. Or major. She seemed to simply attract stress the way most people attracted the common cold and sometimes wondered if Bridget Jones had stolen her show.

'Okay. Here's the deal,' she said. '*You* will remember that I may have blue blood, and I will try and remember to notify you once I find out.' She laughed, instantly lifted again.

'Yah. Ah wool.'

It was a family joke. Max often slipped into his best Afrikaans accent, which was a hangover from listening to so many cricket commentators over the years. Being a sports teacher was a poor substitute for the glittering international test career he had envisaged for himself every waking day of boyhood. *Still, a man can dream*, he thought, wallowing in the pretence.

Kitty chortled and hung up. The next day, she met Jen for a much-needed conflab. The barista served them steaming and picture-perfect lattes, and they sank down into a rare available sofa in the corner of the store. Kitty relished the chance for some amicable ping-pong to discuss her vexation. There was no one quite like Jen, she realised each and every time they met.

I ought to nominate her for some award, Kitty thought. *The manifold number of extrications she has mounted on my behalf defies belief.*

She launched into a full-scale account of the last few weeks, whilst Jen listened patiently before responding. Kitty gazed at her gratefully. Jen was, as usual, now talking nineteen to the dozen, impervious to the gravity of her friend's dilemma, though not in a negligent way. For Jen, as with Max, obstacles were merely there to be overcome. Her organic self-belief in being able to make this happen was tremendously infectious. By contrast, Kitty knew she was more inclined to wallow in half-hearted despair. She looked up, energised by her friend's optimism.

'Listen, Kit,' Jen said supportively. 'It'll all work out, *I promise*.'

Promises from Jen were nearly always sealed in concrete, and this began to augment Kitty's fragile hope. Jen continued talking about Yani, her black eyes as busy as her lips.

'I mean, if he really loved her, then he's surely not going to *kill* her, is he?' she offered nonchalantly, sipping her coffee with a slow, inspiratory dribble Kitty recognised so well.

'It just wouldn't make sense. So I reckon she was bumped off by someone else,' she added. She seemed determined and quite matter-of-fact.

Kitty frowned. She had considered this too, but why had she suddenly vanished? Maybe she was kidnapped. But why? Sinister ideas transpired as she contemplated from a different angle, the hidden agonies Yani must be experiencing if indeed this were so. She had left several messages on his voicemail, but he had uncharacteristically not responded. She hadn't been able to find out too much more detail about the case, which was now a fortnight old. Only that this cellist had been quite famous, and pitifully young. Such a waste, Kitty sighed. She hoped that Yani would reply soon, as she didn't want to pester him, but Sam was becoming stroppily impatient at having missed two lessons. She feared he might start pedalling backwards. He needed his musical guru just as much as Kitty needed it for him.

The women parted company after another prolonged drink and a disciplined carbohydrate fend-off, by the end of which time, each other's worlds had almost been put to rights. They hugged each other enthusiastically.

'See ya Wednesday!' Jen reminded her. They had both at last taken brave steps to join a Pilates class. 'Booze free till then. Be strict.' It was as much a reminder to herself.

Kitty grinned. She would be going nowhere without her staunch ally against the demons of cellulite. She wondered whether to invest in a sports bra before then. Everything was travelling south these days, she acknowledged despondently. What do you expect if your body has been ravaged by nearly four entire years of being pregnant? It was a bleak thought. Turning towards the direction of the shopping mall, she suddenly heard a text blip from her pocket. Grabbing the phone with her only available hand, she screwed up her eyes. She had forgotten her glasses. Another formidable disadvantage of the fifth decade, she lamented. Squinting down, she saw that it was from Yani. Relief descended as she wondered, and not for the first time, if he was a mind reader.

'Hi Kitty. I hope to see you next Tuesday, as usual. Apologies but I have been away, in France.'

Chapter 42

Fresh skies full of promise greeted Giselle as she drew her curtains. A few undarned clouds scurried high above her, and the sun was making a brave attempt to warm up the sombre slate roofs on the rows of houses opposite. Several monochromed children were starting to trudge towards the school bus at the bottom of the road, rucksacks outsizing their little frames and wobbling precariously on their backs, as they accelerated and chased each other, shrieking, down the road.

Strange to be so mild for this time of year, she thought. Her own childhood in the southern Alps had always been brutally cold, swathes of blanketed snow hugging both mountain and chalets alike in a glacial embrace. Here it was, a few weeks off Christmas, and a topaz sky was greeting her extraneously. She smiled gratefully.

Showering quickly, she slipped into some black jeggings and pulled on a woollen jade jumper, which looked several sizes too big over her slight and delicate chassis. Her bony shoulders stuck out like coat hangers underneath. Surveying the copious number of scarves on a peg behind her bedroom door, she selected her favourite, as she always did, rendering the others obsolete. It was the grey silk dotted one which was the last thing he had given her, bought on a whim in the Marche de Montreuil when she had spotted it fluttering from a stall; she had laughed at it, looking like a cascade of breves. *Snowflakes*, he had insisted, and had bought it for her immediately and impulsively. How she had loved that organic magnanimity about him. She fingered the scarf lovingly, swirling it round her tiny neck, aching to smell him in its folds.

Down in the kitchen, she boiled the kettle and set about making some coffee and rummaging in the fridge for some bread to satisfy the toaster. Eating was always a forced affair these days, former weeks and months of chemotherapy having altered her appetite irreversibly. She would be quite happy not to eat at all, really, but her sheer will to live disagreed. Buttering the toast, she slapped some spread on it and propelled it assiduously into her mouth. She glanced up at the clock. She would have to hurry. Today was her bimonthly check-up at the hospital, and if she didn't hurry, she would miss the next bus.

A few long hours later, she wound her way back up the hill, chastising the weakness in her calves, and stopping at every other lamp post to catch short, raspy breaths. Only on these rare occasions did she indulge in the faintest swell of self-pity. The emptiness of her house would be a yawning hole, waiting for her silently and without consolation. Only this day, as the afternoon clouds now gathered to shroud out the memory of a cobalt dawn, she had reason to combat defeat. The appointment had gone surprisingly well. The consultant had examined her latest MRI scan with barely concealed perplexity. He had expected some deterioration given the acceleration of her recent symptoms, having surmised following her last surgery nearly a year ago such a likely scenario. Unable to extract the tumour in entirety, he had advised Giselle then to watch and wait before further treatment, but her dizziness and infrequent seizures ever since still worried him. Today, however, he was forced to concede that the remaining tumour was curiously shrinking; this news being an extremely pleasant reassurance to them both.

'Come back and see me in two months,' he had said, glasses poised on a curly grey forehead as he scribbled jerkily in her notes, a slanted script which bore no decipherable meaning.

She walked out of the hospital, feeling elated. This was not what she had expected, and unaccustomed as she was to optimism as far as her health was concerned, she was unsure how to handle it. Back home, once she had reheated some unappetising leftovers, she lay down on the sofa and picked up the paper she had bought from the newsagents on her way back. Flicking over the headlines, she turned to the second page, consternation percolating through her as she studied the sub-story incoherently. She stared long and hard at the page in front of her. For there, in black and white small print, with a bold heading, she realised that she was, incredulously, reading an article about her very own death.

Chapter 43

Tess had arranged to meet Sylvia for a long overdue lunch. She had suggested meeting in town, but Sylvia had resisted, citing effort and expense, but Tess knew the real reason was that she wanted to smoke. Increasingly, this was becoming a deplorable irritation to Tess, who wanted to gag every time she entered her mother's dull, airless little house, where walls and furniture seemed cloyed and impregnated with yesterday's cigarettes. The aroma was made worse by Buster's omnipresent dictatorship; the cat's illicit spraying onto sofas and beds equally disgusted her shrewdly aseptic and clinical nose. She had tried with spectacular inefficiency over the years to persuade her mother to stop smoking, but to no avail. Even the e-cigarette she had carefully chosen and wrapped up for her previous birthday present was nowhere in sight. Today, Sylvia sat at her dingy kitchen table, a stubborn fag perched defiantly on an ashtray adjacent to the stove, whilst embers dropped undeterred into the tasteless receptacle beneath. Tess went over to the top window above the kitchen sink and opened it slightly. Sylvia carried on heedlessly, flicking eggs round the frying pan with a worn-out plastic spatula.

'So Ma, how about a walk into the park after lunch?' she suggested hopefully.

Sylvia was still in her dressing gown and slippers at half-past midday, but Tess tried not to despair at such languid existence, energised as she was in comparison by David and Giselle, despite the recent tragedy. Both had provided consolation in unquantifiable and unexpected measure. But Sylvia had no one. It depressed her even more.

She had discovered the funeral date of the cyclist victim and had fully determined to go, but on the day itself, she had stalled pathetically. Just being there, she feared, would have initiated unbidden panic and sadness. She couldn't contemplate seeing either wife or children, if such existed, raw as her own memories still were. She had felt wretched and churlish, but innately knew this was preferable to ripping open a healing wound. Every day, she sought to annihilate that fateful evening from her remembrance, and she was winning, rather slowly, by sheer wilful distraction with the things that brought her joy. This remedial tool was something she sought to impress her mother with, but the older woman seemed either unwilling or unable to grasp the necessary spade with which to dig herself out of life's ditch. Perhaps she should go and see Sylvia's GP? Tess considered, knowing full well her mother's guilt-fuelled aversion to health check-ups.

With the zeal and determination of a personal trainer, she had bullied Sylvia outside after lunch, and they had spent an hour walking slowly round the duck-swarmed pond, encircled by leisurely strollers, buggies, and dawdling pensioners. The weather was not unpleasant, even if the opaque cloud was uninspiring. Tess picked her moment to tell Sylvia about David. This was something she needed to do gingerly, tiptoeing sensitively through her remorse at Sylvia's own solitude. She told her about meeting him, explained about the accident, and downplayed the developing friendship as much as she could. The thought of introducing David to Sylvia rather filled Tess with dread. But to her surprise, Sylvia was unexpectedly positive.

'Well, love,' she said, a rare smile lighting up her crumpled, seared face, 'this calls for a celebration, dunnit? Why don't I get hold of our Lizzie, and you can all come over so we can meet him. Go on, pet, I can cook up something.'

Tess knew this was a grave risk.

She was looking up at her daughter, impressed. Being with Sylvia was the only time Tess felt tall. Tess considered. An evening with Lizzie's dubious maritime tales, an entire packet of fags between them, and Sylvia's signature dish of greasy lasagne was not something she felt she could inflict on David. Just yet.

'Hmm, maybe, Mum. Or you could come to me? Yeah, let's do that, eh? We can drop you back,' she added quickly, recognising her mother's inevitable and likely excuse.

She carried on, gaining momentum before Sylvia had a chance to remonstrate.

'Tell you what, I've got a day off next Wednesday; let's do it then. I will ring Lizzie too,' aware that her sister was unlikely to be either available, or even in England.

Truthfully, their lack of contact was deplorable, she acknowledged. But she wanted to keep up contrary impressions for Mum's sake. Why, she was not quite sure. So Sylvia had agreed, and she now had the slightly unenviable task of preparing David for this precarious introduction.

She had made her excuses swiftly after the park, needing to cross town before rush hour impeded a booked lesson with Giselle. She had been looking forward to this for over a week now and had been practising quite hard, with notable reward, she felt sure. It was becoming a little addictive, this music thing, she realised; she still chuckled at the thought of work not knowing what she really got up to in her spare time. Nah. She wasn't gonna tell them, not yet. Hurrying across to the far side of the park, she began to feel a bit overheated in her copious scarf and child-sized gloves. Ripping off woollen fingers one by one, she startled when she saw 'POST' scribbled on her left hand. She winced, now ashamed that yet more days had passed since she had remembered the letter on the bus. She scolded herself to remember to buy a handbag which didn't dissipate its contents into oblivion. With rapid and urgent resolve, she extracted David's letter from her bag.

Without further ado and clasping it firmly, she strode over to pop
it once and for all in the tall red sentry box which stood stoutly
on the pavement beside her. Its wide mouth was open and also,
Tess felt sure, smiling.

Chapter 44

Half an hour earlier, Giselle had risen to pick up her 'cello, always an instinctive destination when troubled. Now lost in complete absorption, she was darting furiously through a Bach suite, her right elbow flapping rhythmically, her left fingers dancing jerkily to keep up. It was a perfectly industrious confluence of thought and sound.

She had been unable to believe her eyes. That they had thought she was the poor swollen and bloated corpse dragged from the Seine beggared belief. *Or did it?* she wondered. *Bon alors, je suis mort.*

She knew that she had acquired some notoriety from her performing days, albeit on a subsidiary circuit, so she was improperly amused at the elucidation 'renowned cellist.' *What a perverse means of discovering one's reputation,* she pondered wretchedly. Loose ends flapped all around her, as she sought to decipher the thread of the police investigation.

Of course, she had had to flee. There had been no question at all in her mind about that. Better by far that he remembered her as she had been, infused with vibrant and youthful vigour, and unflawed reminiscence. For she was likely going to die, that is what the Parisian doctors had told her. She had never disputed their judgement then, ignorant as she was of this insidious prognosis, with its terrifying symptoms and nerve-jangling manifestations. Life was being savagely snatched from her at the pinnacle of an accomplished prime. And she had told herself then that nothing, but absolutely *nothing*, would allow her to sanction him any further grief. She had absorbed the anguish of his past with a fierce and almost maternal loyalty, his pain had fused into her very soul, and she could not, would not, allow him to suffer the psychological torture of watching her die. And yet, with the deepest and most bitter irony, she conceded that he had probably done just that.

Mais jamais j'ai pense que cela se produirait, she lamented violently. I never realised this would happen.

Her thoughts turned to who the genuine drowned culprit might be. Surely, they could trace the inaccuracy from her dental records. So why did they seem so confident of her identification, or was this watery grave making even that impossible? She doubted it.

She had changed her name, of course. It had been surprisingly easy. Once she was in England, she had registered with a local doctor, no questions asked. Then, as symptoms progressed, she was referred to the specialist unit at the teaching hospital, where they had never seriously questioned her, especially when she had fabricated a tenuous tale about orchestral employment to a sympathetic neurological team. She had reluctantly disclosed a distant next of kin to keep them diverted. No, it had been undeniably straightforward. She reckoned that her demise in Paris would ultimately have concluded as a missing person, as had indeed been suggested at the time. She had no nearby relative to trace her, and their enquiries had been short-lived. But two years had passed, and now, suddenly, this.

Her thoughts were interrupted by a sharp buzz at the front door. She jolted. Tess. Of course. She had completely forgotten. Sweeping a slender hand through her soft mane, she stood up and tried to compose herself as she went to open the door.

'Hey,' Tess said brightly, stepping into the hall with undisguised enthusiasm.

'Entrez!' Giselle replied, pressing back against the wall to let her in.

Soon they were chatting cheerfully whilst Giselle made Tess a quick cup of tea before the lesson. She didn't normally do this for pupils, but Tess was different. Especially now, she was glad that she had come. They walked through to the lounge.

'So how are you feeling?' Tess asked. Her cheeks were flushing rosily, glowing from the exertion of having walked up the steep hill.

Giselle observed her rude health enviously.

'Ah, hmm, okay. Peut-être. Actually, I 'ave some good news,' she said and described the day's unlikely forecast from the hospital.

'Wow, that's amazing!' Tess responded gleefully. 'Brilliant. You see, doctors can just be plain wrong sometimes,' she proclaimed, glad that David wasn't listening. 'I'm *so* pleased.'

She genuinely was. Tess was compassionate to her core, such that work was just an extension of herself. 'A born nurse,' Sylvia had said once, ranking as one of the nicest things Tess ever could remember her saying.

'Oui. It is so good,' Giselle agreed, chewing her bottom lip with cautious optimism.

'I think you should celebrate,' Tess suggested. 'I mean, what would cheer you up most?' she added innocently.

Giselle swiftly deflected the truth but found herself answering spontaneously.

'Alors. I don't know. Maybe … I would like to perform again?' She paused. 'Yes. I would like to perhaps do a leetle concert?' she said hesitantly.

Tess pounced on this eagerly.

'Yes. You really should. That would be just fan*ta*stic,' she said warmly. 'Tell you what: I will come and … I could even bring David, perhaps?'

She smiled at Giselle, an eyebrow raised.

It was a bonkers suggestion. David, she knew, wasn't especially musical, but even so, she was sure she could rely on his support. Intrinsically, she knew he had developed an interest by proxy, plus she was equally keen to introduce him to her new hobby. It was the perfect opportunity.

Giselle beamed, her battalion of beautiful teeth smiling appreciatively. She liked the idea too. Optimism swept over them both.

'Okay,' she said. '*C'est genial.* I will see what I can do.'

Already, ideas were forming like rivulets, alive with hope and animation. Giselle visualised everything in notation; it was her primary language. Notes and words. Thoughts and notes. She never could quite decipher when either stopped or the other started.

'And Christmas isn't too far away, either,' she added dreamily as an afterthought.

She had noticed today for the first time the spangled lights in town and the brazen bold signs of impatient Christmas trees bedecked and twinkling, showing off brazenly in front terraced windows. It had somehow made her isolation acute and lack of purpose in contradiction. Now perhaps she could rectify this.

After Tess had packed up her 'cello and left, Giselle returned for the second time to the sofa, where the paper lay folded up on the coffee table, shielded from prying eyes and pregnant with possibility. She gazed at it for the longest time.

Then, reaching for her mobile, she scrolled down her contacts with a delicate index finger and, with minimal hesitation, tapped Dial.

'*Louis? C'est moi. Oui. Es tu occupé? J'ai besoin d'un accompagnateur.*'

Chapter 45

Brian had nodded off in his armchair. His slippered feet were up on a leathered poof, and a crocheted blanket was hanging ineffectively over them. Sleep was preoccupying him more than he could ever remember. They all said he should rest more, but it was alarming how often he found himself waking up from a nap he couldn't remember taking. In the kitchen, cups and saucers clinked as Maureen busied herself making tea. He heard the kettle whistle to a crescendo.

'Sugar, love?' she called, peering through the hatch.

He stirred at her voice and opened one eye slowly, thinking about sugar. The other half of him was still in a sleep where he felt sure he had been thinking of something rather important, although he couldn't quite recall what it was. He had congratulated himself for eighty-odd years that he had never taken sugar, but now they were all telling him he needed it. That he was too thin was an understatement. He sighed with a humph.

'Okay, then,' he replied unenthusiastically, forcing himself to add, 'Thanks.'

Maureen appeared in the doorway, carrying a tray of very wobbly teacups and saucers, and a plate of Battenburg slices, cut too thickly. He smiled weakly. He had always hated Battenburg: a parcel of neon sponge wrapped into a dense marzipan brick. How much more bilious could it be? He heaved slightly, feeling trapped, and a twinge of nostalgia hit him. Chrissy would have understood. Well, she wouldn't have bought it in the first place. But dear Maureen. Here she was, eager to advance his recovery with calorific infusions and his absolute worst cake. He hadn't the courage to resist. Putting the tray down on the coffee table, she returned to the kitchen to find the teapot. Brian lowered his legs slowly to the floor and sat up stiffly.

'I was thinking, Brian,' began when Maureen she reappeared with the warm teapot, hugged by a striped woolly cosy, 'why don't we ask David to take us put for a drive a bit later? Might be nice to get out for a bit, don't you think?'

'Hmm. Maybe,' he grunted, but he looked across kindly at her as she began to pour the tea. She plopped two sugar cubes defiantly into his cup and started stirring vigorously.

'I mean, we could just go out for short while, change of scene and all that?' she fussed, her spectacled eyes full of concern. 'I'm sure David wouldn't mind.'

'No, I don't suppose he would,' Brian agreed. He had actually been thinking of the same thing himself.

'Fine, pet. I'll go and ring him in a bit.'

She picked up her cup and saucer carefully and sat back to assess Brian with the sort of faithful attention that an adoring sheepdog might give a farmer.

Brian had told Maureen about the letter. In fact, he had told Maureen about everything. It had been good to have a confidante to share it with. Maureen had never been able to have children of her own, so she was all the more intrigued by his. Somehow, she was a third party to all this and slightly detached, or so he assumed, but sometimes, it was hard to tell. Since his heart attack, she had hardly left his side.

Maureen finished her tea and got up to make the call, her skirt swishing as she went.

'Have some more cake,' she cajoled, oblivious to the three squares that still lay uneaten on his plate. He had forced down a yellow square first because it wasn't quite so, well, pink.

He watched her disappear into the hall and heard her pick up the phone. His mind began to wander. It had been several weeks since David had posted his second letter. Both of them hardly dared to admit to each other what each of them was thinking. He had never been awfully good at being honest with David, or Richard, for that matter, when it came to emotional conundrums. Best to shut up and put up, which had been his Mam's mantra throughout the long war years and forever after.

'David says he can pick us up in an hour,' Maureen announced, returning to the room. 'That's kind, isn't it? I think I will just pop out to the chemist now and pick up your prescription. If that's okay?' she added, a little uncertainly.

'Fine. I'm not planning on going anywhere,' he said, covetously eyeing the unread paper on the coffee table. 'And thank you, Maureen. Not sure how I would manage without you these days.' He looked up at her appreciatively.

'Okay, love; well, I won't be long.' She smiled, gratefully.

She wasn't sure how she would manage without Brian, if truth were told. Losing Ken had been far worse than she could have imagined. Nearly losing Brian as well had been too much, too soon, so she had a vested interest in helping him convalesce. Plus, it gave her something to do: a focus, a plan, and a welcome occupation. She started to pull a chiffon triangle round her head and tied it deftly into a knot under her chin. Then grabbing her shopping trolley and handbag with determination, she walked out to the hall in search of her coat. A few minutes later, Brian heard the front door click behind her, and then, all he could hear was the quiet tick of the clock on the mantelpiece. He reached for the paper with one hand and his bifocals with the other.

***

He glanced at the headlines, but nothing really grabbed his attention. He was never quite sure why he looked forward to reading the paper when all it usually did was dispirit him. He began to flick through the pages. A squalid daily diet of violence and crime, a tedium of paedophilic exposure, and the predictable politico-economic doom. As if to confirm his thoughts, he started to read about a woman washed up in a river. *Awful way to go,* he thought, refusing to read anymore. *Where's some good news?*

Before his collapse, he had genuinely thought he was onto a good thing when he had shared the contents of Christine's letter. David had seemed to take it so well, and they had taken up the quest of discovery together. He did feel wretched for not having shared it with the boys before. But that's just what had happened, for better or worse. He had put off any thoughts of a search for so many years, even after Chrissy had died and the law had changed. He was never quite sure why. Was he just afraid or a coward? It was all too complicated, and Brian always resisted complicated things.

He thought back to those terrifying days, when he had first met Christine. He had been so scared of girls until then. Oversized, sassy schoolgirls who made him cringe and stutter, exposing his inexperience and shyness. He had left school and become a junior bank clerk, and she had been a nanny for a posh family in the suburbs. They had met at a dance, and he had thought she was the cutest creature he had ever set eyes on, as she stole his first kiss. He sighed. Those heady post-Elvis sixties, when Beatlemania roared through every street and province like a tornado, and traditional morality was hung out to dry. As if they had all been swept along on fast-flowing rapids that were impossible to resist, a kaftan of flower-powered hedonism which had crept up like an unexpected monster, a fairground of risk and thrills to which he was wholly unaccustomed.

Being the cloistered and unadventurous lad that he was, no one had been more aghast than he when Christine had told him, trembling with tears and fright, that she was pregnant. He couldn't speak for nearly a week. Neither could she. It just couldn't be possible. He felt sickened that they had all been intoxicated by some kind of madness. 'Free love' was now anything but free, it seemed. They had buried their secret in endless clandestine conversations after work in smoky cafés, both paralysed by fear and anxiety and totally unsure of either the outcome or even each other. They had only been together for six weeks. Finally, she had told him through red-rimmed eyes that she needed to go away. She was going all the way to her aunt's house near coastal Worthing to have the baby, who she would then give up for adoption. There was no other choice, and she was adamant. It wasn't yet 1967. Even if it had happened after that, Brian knew with certainty that for this nursery nurse, Chrissy would never have considered any other option. No. She was born to be a mother.

He had thought about getting married. But they were barely just twenty, and he hardly earned enough to help his parents out with board and lodging, let alone fund a wedding or a wife. Neither did his cautious nature allow him to commit to someone he hardly knew. Plus, he couldn't live with the guilt. Everyone would know or would find out. He imagined her walking down the aisle, a symbol of remorse like a sinful meringue.

So it had just happened. Her parents had been distraught, and he hadn't told his. They wrote to each other, of course, long and anguished letters, where decency propelled him to support her rather than churlishly run away. He had come to dread the sight of her letters arriving at work (he had suggested she didn't write to his home): a sombre reminder of what in reality was burgeoning down by the seaside, miles away. They had even met a couple of times. Train trips and secret Saturdays spent pacing the promenade, as Christine sought to hide her shame beneath an oversized duffel coat on windswept beaches that seemed determined to expose her belly to the world. *How different it all was then*, he thought wretchedly. *How inconceivable now.*

And then 'she' had been born, and he had only found out a week later, by which time she had been carefully taken, dispatched, and removed, like an unwanted boil that had been clinically excised. He never even got to see her. Christine had cried herself inside out, until there were no more tears left to shed. And yet they still came, in unexpected and odd moments over the years that followed. The years where he had tried to salvage her grief by persuading her to walk up that aisle, persuading her that they could wipe the slate clean, only knowing in their depths that they couldn't ever forget, even when the boys were born a few years later. It was a primal wound that no amount of words or loving could ever truly erase.

He put his paper back on the coffee table and looked up at them both, smiling back at him now from a faded black-and-white wedding photograph, where lilies hung down from her petite waist to adorn a simple taffeta dress. The mask of smiles, the pain and pretence of what few people knew. But he had loved her so much and possibly the more for what he had made her suffer. Then when she had gone, he knew he simply had to fulfil her dying wish and make this journey complete.

Now he was thwarted again. No response to the letter which he and David had carefully concocted, and a stubborn sorrow threatened to cast charcoal shadows over his past again. He had never considered that perhaps she wouldn't want to see him. He had buried that scenario with fierce denial. David had concealed his own disappointment, determined to keep persevering, and they had agreed to send another letter. Just one more. Brian wasn't sure he could endure any more sadness. And so they were just waiting, like Godot, for something that might never actually happen.

'Coo-ee!' called Maureen, as he heard the door unlatch.

'Hi love,' he called back, interrupted.

He looked guiltily away from the photograph and towards the door, which would frame her arrival within seconds.

'David will be here soon,' she reminded him, entering the room looking rather pleased with herself. The trolley trundled in behind her. It seemed to be bulging with a little bit more than just pills.

'I saw some lovely pork chops at the butchers,' she explained. 'Well, just in case we can persuade David to stay for some supper afterwards?'

'Great idea,' Brian responded cheerily.

He was impressed by Maureen's efforts at hospitality. He knew David was still struggling to come to terms with her.

She turned, smiling and satisfied, to deposit her shopping safely in the kitchen.

'Now then,' she called back as she disappeared again. 'Do you want to find your coat and hat, while I will get this meat in the fridge?'

Chapter 46

Kitty was on spin cycle. It had been another fruitless day in which the entire world was getting on her nerves. Swamped by the incessant demands of five children, two incontinent dogs, a houseful of clutter, piles of laundry, a grumpy husband, and her adoring oldies at the day centre, she was ready to resign. On all of them. Not to mention an irate editor who had been particularly stroppy on the phone today because she was two weeks behind with an assignment. *God help me,* she prayed. Her head had been pounding all day, which had been the reason she had bought two Krispy Kremes at the garage store, all willpower having evaporated before midday.

The morning had begun with worse havoc than usual. Sam and Lucy had fought violently at breakfast over driving lessons and Lucy's boyfriend (whom Kitty had never heard of), Toby had been in tears, and Tilly had announced that she had overshot the deadline for her art coursework because someone had nicked her original portfolio folder. *What?* Angus had been streaming with a heavy cold and was probably brewing a temperature, though he had insisted that he wasn't missing rugby club after school (his legs were already a patchwork quilt of multicoloured bruises). No one had had their lunch boxes ready because, guess what, they had run out of the bread, which Nick had promised to pick up on his way home from work the night before. Into all that melee, Helen had rung for an inappropriately long chat about her latest urinary

195

infection. This took twenty minutes which she didn't have, and the children were late for school.

When she finally got back home, the phone was ringing even as she came through the front door. Kitty stared at it in disbelief and then simply picked it up and slammed it straight down again. Whoever it was could wait. For the sake of sanity, if it was Helen again, then surely her symptoms couldn't have got worse in just half an hour? Kitty had simply run dry on sympathy. She wondered, and not for the first time, if she perhaps was menopausal after all and then shuddered at the thought. It seemed like only yesterday that she was breastfeeding Toby.

In the kitchen, her mobile started its *Star Wars* ringtone in protest. Kitty glared at it and briefly considered throwing it out of the window, before she caught sight of the word Yani flashing back at her from the screen. She grabbed it quickly.

'Yani?' she said, a little breathlessly.

'Hello. I'm sorry, I couldn't seem to get through on za landline,' he said, his voice sounded soothing and familiar.

'Are you okay? I mean, are you back now?' Kitty deflected, shelving her rudeness but blushing nonetheless.

She didn't want to sound too interested, even though she had been thinking of little else recently. She just couldn't decide if Yani was a closet criminal or haunted victim, and she needed some resolution to fend off her mounting insomnia.

'Yez. I came back last weekend, actually. I'm sorry, I've only just heard your voicemails. I couldn't access them from France, for some reason.'

'Don't worry. I just was wondering whether you might be free for another lesson? Sam is driving me insane,' she said, trying not to sound needy.

'I'm sorry. Actually, it's short notice, but are you free this evening? My rehearsal got cancelled, so I suddenly 'av a free zlot.'

'Sure. Best news of the day so far,' she added truthfully. 'Sam is free too, I think. Shall we say seven?'

'Done,' Yani said, helpfully.

The day certainly ended better than it had begun. Nick had come home on time with two loaves of bread and a small bunch of apricot carnations by way of apology. The children had eaten supper voraciously and without one single altercation, and Angus was proudly showing off two more whopping bruises on his shins, undeterred by two streaming green nostrils. Toby had got a sticker for his poem from Miss Hicks, and the girls were talking about their favourite *Apprentice* contestants. Even Basil and Roger had twisted themselves into a tangle of legs and tails in their basket, sound asleep. *What a day*, Kitty mused in bewilderment.

Yani had then arrived and cast an inexorable spell over Sam, who had come out of his lesson afterwards and impulsively given his mum a hug. Kitty wasn't sure when that had last happened. Was it last Christmas?

'Bye then, Sam,' Yani said, slipping his music into a bag.

'Fanks,' Sam had muttered, the right side of his mouth smiling.

'My pleasure,' said Yani. 'Keep it up. You are doing zo well.'

The other side of Sam's mouth now drew a mesmerising arc. This was such a rare occurrence that Kitty wanted to photograph it. But before he could get trapped in further small talk, Sam turned gruffly and went back to the piano. Kitty knew this was his guise to impress. She ushered Yani through to the kitchen.

'You really are *amazing*. What's your secret with him?' she hissed.

'He's doing really well. I think I understand him quite a lot.' Yani nodded slowly as he spoke.

'You *do*?' Kitty sounded a little incredulous. She had to rely on telepathy.

'But yes. Don't forget, I was his age once too.' He smiled.

There was no need for either of them to make a comparison; it was simply not possible. Kitty couldn't countenance that Yani had ever resembled Sam in any shape or form. But she was intrigued nonetheless. She sidestepped slightly.

'Did your mum ever struggle with you at this age?' she asked.

Yani looked at her and considered the best answer. Then he simply confessed.

'I never knew my mother,' he said abruptly.

Kitty stared at him. She screwed up her eyes a little, so that her irises almost disappeared.

'*Really?*'

'Really.'

She sighed. Somehow it felt safe to confide.

'Me too,' she blurted back. 'I never knew my mother, either.'

***

Two sets of eyes looked at each other for several lingering moments before they both burst out laughing. Kitty dived in first.

'So what happened? Did she die?' It sounded blunt and invasive, and she regretted her candour immediately.

'I don't know. Perhaps.' He was spinning it out. 'How about you?' he said quickly.

'I was adopted,' Kitty said matter-of-factly. She wasn't sure why it was still so hard to actually say the words out loud, even now she was forty-five.

'Oh,' Yani said. 'I see.'

They both paused again.

'Did you ever meet her, your mother?' he offered.

'No, sadly not. Well, not yet,' she replied.

'I see,' said Yani again, although he didn't really see at all.

'Um, so what happened with you, then?' Kitty began hesitantly.

'Well, I guess I was kind of adopted too,' Yani explained, 'but then, zat mother definitely *did* die.'

'Oh dear. I'm sorry.' Kitty didn't know what to say. Silence descended between them.

'Yes, it was very sad.' He broke his gaze to look out of the window.

Kitty hovered, waiting.

'But still. Here I am now,' he said, looking back at her. 'Life is full of mystery sometimes, don't you zink?'

Kitty didn't want to get distracted into the present.

'Yes, it certainly is. I still find it all quite unsettling really. Even now.' She shrugged.

'I understand zat,' Yani said quietly. If only she knew. But perhaps she did.

Kitty went on.

'My parents both died a while ago,' she explained, 'and so the unsolved riddle remains. But I really would like to find her one day,' she admitted, slowly. The depth of that wish hung weightily between them.

'Have you tried searching yet?' Yani asked, cautiously.

Kitty looked at him some more, unsure of what to say next. For someone so spontaneous, this was a private compartment which she very rarely opened. But she trusted the synergy between them, on this subject, at least.

'It's complicated,' she began. 'There never seems to be the right time to be honest. I keep putting it off, but then again, it's funny you ask because it's all come up again recently. And now I don't really know what to do.'

Yani was listening intently. Kitty sighed.

'It's just that I got a letter a few weeks ago. From someone who said he was my brother. So weird. But if you can believe it,' she said, looking glumly over at the dog basket, 'the letter got destroyed.'

Chapter 47

Tess had rung Lizzie and left a message. Sisterly irritation simmered a little as she pursued a well-rehearsed attempt to communicate, which was almost always thwarted. She was always either too busy, too abroad, or too distracted by some errant boyfriend. Tess wondered sometimes what mileage was left in their relationship. Perhaps if they had both settled down and had kids by now, things would be different, she pondered. But she didn't hold out much hope. She reckoned that even mothering itself would widen rather than close the gap. Her thoughts were interrupted by the phone. It was David.

'Free for a movie on Friday, by any chance?' David sounded happy. It was already Wednesday.

'I might be,' she said cautiously, disguising some delight.

'Fine. You have a choice,' he began and started to rattle off a list of hopefuls.

Tess suddenly remembered Sylvia and sighed.

'I'm afraid there might be a bit of a hiccup with Friday,' she said, hesitatingly.

David listened to her sheepish and half-hearted enthusiasm for a meal with her mother and chuckled. He had, in fact, secretly been looking forward to meeting Sylvia. He was intrigued after all Tess had told him.

'Listen, I promise to behave,' he tried to sound reassuring.

'It's not you I'm worried about!' Tess said, laughing.

Lizzie had finally responded in a voicemail, from Gran Canaria. Futile apologies and breathless explanations that she wouldn't possibly be able to get back to UK for another three months. That Tess had landed the lion's share of looking after Sylvia was never aired. It was just a given, and Tess had long learned to ignore it, but it festered nonetheless.

They had driven over together to fetch Sylvia, who on arrival, Tess noticed, had made a brave effort with both some lipstick and scented candles. Buster was out on the town, and the house looked, if she wasn't imagining it, as though it had survived a little spring clean. Tess wondered if they should have perhaps braved Sylvia's kitchen after all. No matter, she had a stew bubbling back home, and it would be good to get Sylvia out.

'Mum, meet David,' she enthused, as David entered the house, his right arm extended.

Sylvia eyed up his suave good looks. *He'll do*, she thought, without a moment's hesitation. She beamed up at him, glasses perched squiffily on her nose.

David smiled warmly back. He always quite enjoyed meeting the families of girlfriends, although he had to shudder when he remembered his former mother-in-law. She had been a tricky one, a tyrant even. Still. It had given David much fuel when the sad end eventually came.

They had driven back to Tess's little flat where, true to form, she had contrived to create a tidy and welcoming ambience, in stark antithesis to Sylvia's dust and grease, which Tess felt sure could be easily remedied by just a little Jif and polish. Tess loved to clean; it was just what she did, from work to home. She prided herself that she could wage a triumphant war on all germs. She was never quite sure if it was just an overwhelming desire to disinfect herself from the hospital or to protest against childhood memories. Either way, David seemed pleased. Sylvia, if she but knew, just felt edgy and uncomfortable in pristine surroundings.

Feelings of inadequacy lurked close to the surface, but she made a brave attempt to quell them.

'So David, go on, tell me all about yourself, then,' Sylvia began, as they sat down at the table, festooned with chintzy serviettes and flickering candles. She was longing for a fag. Her glasses were still roosting crookedly, and Tess resisted the urge to straighten them.

'How long have you got?' David replied jovially.

He could be quite beguiling when it suited him. Sylvia seemed as antithetical to her daughter as it was possible to be.

An hour later, they were sitting back relaxed and contentedly, whilst Tess cleared both empty dishes and an empty wine bottle from the table.

'That was delicious, pet,' Sylvia said warmly, making no attempt to help carry things through. She hiccupped. She was a little nervous that she might drop something.

'Thanks, Ma,' Tess said as David rose to help her.

'Truly exceptional,' he echoed.

That Tess could cook well slid her right up to the top of the list as far as he was concerned, like a plastic button on a snakes and ladders board. Evie had nearly poisoned him on more than one occasion, and Laura had showed no interest in food whatsoever.

They had driven Sylvia back across town afterwards, David driving slowly to impress, and Tess breathed a sigh of relief. Tick. She could relax. Meeting Lizzie wasn't likely to happen for months, and there was no one else she needed to worry about, being so sparse on relatives. Sometimes, it was a blessing.

'That seemed to go okay,' David suggested hopefully, as they drove back.

'Aha. Yep, I think we can safely say you got the job,' she said, grinning. 'Not that there's been a lot of competition,' she reminded him firmly.

David had often wondered about that. How this beautiful and vibrant creature had escaped the long-term clutches of another man was a mystery to him. Meeting Sylvia, he began to see perhaps why. Was Tess trying to protect them both? Or perhaps not meeting a father was the reason? David was struggling to imagine him. It was true she had pitiful faith in the male species as a result. Either way, he felt sure he'd won the lotto. He gazed at her with increasing affection. She was a survivor; he knew that. He pulled her over to him for a long embrace, whilst outside the car, dark rain drizzled silently over the bonnet. Reluctantly, they pulled apart. Tess had an early shift the next day, and he had to take Brian for a check-up first thing too. It was late, and they were both copying yawns. With a wink and a flick of her trim bob, she had hopped out of the car and was gone, slinking swiftly inside.

Lying in bed half an hour later, she reached for her phone to send him a final text, but it wasn't there. She hummed. Getting up again to look in her bag, it wasn't there, either. Or in the kitchen. *I must have left it in his car*, she wailed, cursing her forgetfulness. She needed to ring Giselle in the morning to change her lesson time. And she didn't have time to get to David's before work, either, and he wouldn't be there, anyway. She sighed and lay down, reaching out to snap off the light. *Tomorrow's another day*, she thought. Pulling the soft duvet over her shoulders, she wondered how to contact Giselle and then drowsily recalled that she still had her business card downstairs in the hall from that first lesson. *I'll ring her from the landline,* she decided, before sleep quickly stole consciousness and anaethetised her rapidly.

Chapter 48

It was raining at the station by the time Giselle got out of the taxi. She glanced at her watch. With luck, she would have time to grab a quick snack before boarding the East Midlands train south. If she didn't pick up something now, she knew she would forget to eat later. Her 'cello was slung over her back, entombed in a shiny purple case. She stuck out a mile, she realised miserably, pulling her woolly hat further down till it was firmly halted by her nose.

She had heard back from Louis, who was now based in London. It was easier to arrange the concert down there, not least because he had contacts and had been able to book a large church venue near Waterloo Station for the event. She wasn't sure she could command such an audience in Sheffield, where she was virtually unknown, whilst he seemed to know everyone. Everyone who mattered, anyhow. It was tempting to use her real name, but she daren't. Not with the recent news, which had paralysed her predicament. It was easier to deny any of this was happening, but she couldn't erase what Yani must be thinking or going through. It was too unbearable to contemplate and was certainly now keeping her awake in the small hours. But her response had frozen. Everything in her wanted to call him, to reassure him, but how could she when she didn't know whether he would ever forgive her for all she had put him through? *Hope is so fragile*, she realised. But there wasn't enough hope in her to return. Not yet. Maybe not ever.

And Louis hadn't a clue who she really was, either. She smirked at that. They had met quite by chance through a Hungarian violinist called Bianca, who had needed a cellist for a chamber music charity event. She had met Bianca when depping for the symphony orchestra, and the two had forged an unlikely friendship. Bianca was breezily unrestrained and eccentrically bohemian, but she had salvaged Giselle nevertheless and had shown raw and touching kindness concerning her health. She hadn't told her too much. But she had been terrified and enthralled in equal measure when Bianca had suggested the piano trio. There was really no good reason to turn it down, and she needed something to while away the long hours in the caged walls of her lonely home.

She pulled out her phone and glanced at two messages from Louis. He would be there as arranged. She was indeed grateful to him. The trio had been so much fun in the end, and also being French, they had shared many jokes, often at Bianca's ignorant expense, whose command of English was even worse than hers. It had been so good to speak French again. She recognised that her English still had a long way to go, although she now managed to grasp most things, at least the gist. One bleak advantage of exile, she comforted herself drily. She had told him the truth about her professional background, merely changing names and dates and vaguely changing the subject of her past whenever it came up. It was a massive disguise of her real achievements, but better that way, and he hadn't guessed anything. Having Bianca there detracted her from making comparisons with Yani, but now she realised that this concert would be a true test of that, just the two of them. Playing her favourite pieces without him with her would have been unthinkable a year ago, but maybe now it was possible. Could she pull it off? Her mind slithered off again.

The last fortnight had been a whirl of practising and lessons. Giselle had suggested the programme, and Louis had dutifully obliged. He had an accomplished breadth of repertoire, even if he was a little full of himself as a consequence. But he had done the circuits and knew his stuff. More combative and forceful than Yani, she had struggled to stay with his tempo at times, and she didn't always challenge his interpretation, as he did hers. But she buried the irritation. Truthfully, she felt less entwined and certain, recognising a depletion of synergy, which she knew she could only explain to herself, least of all Louis. She simply couldn't mimic imitation. For absolutely no one could replicate what they had both had had together. Louis had been enthralled by her playing, eager and animated to supplement her innate gift, the one Yani had worshipped in her too. But he was no threat. His boyfriend had accompanied him to every concert and pub afterwards. She remembered nostalgically the many times she and Yani had tumbled into a bar for a drink after each concert and felt her heart pumping again. His brown eyes twinkling at her in relief, exuberance, triumph. And for her, he was the nearest she had ever experienced to perfection. In both craft and in love. Just practising their signature tunes again in these last few weeks had brought him closer, and she had treasured it, though at an agonising and tearful price. It was enough for now, and it was all she could bring herself to do.

Que Dieu m'aide, she pleaded, sincerely hoping that she had the necessary strength to do this.

Je dois le garder en vie. I must keep him alive. Keep us alive, please God.

She reached Louis eventually, after a frenetic cab ride which had made her head spin. She had tried to stop lurching in the back seat by grabbing the door rail firmly, willing herself to calm down and stay focused. She had to get this right. For herself, for Louis, for him. She was glad to finally arrive. She was deposited on a pavement outside a large austere building, and she climbed the steps carefully, her alter ego straddled obesely across her back.

Inside, she could hear sounds of Louis practising. She paused outside the double doors to listen and steeled herself. Those phrases, so dear and so familiar, threatened to disentangle her before she'd even begun. Notes. Those beautiful, exquisite, and unmistakeable notes. She shut her eyes and thought of him, breathing him in through her ears. *Just remember him*, she willed herself. She held his smile on her face. *Think only of him.* She took a deep breath and swung open the doors.

Louis looked up from the piano, a little startled.

'Giselle, you've made it!' he exclaimed warmly in French, hopping up and leaping down off the platform to rush over and kiss both of her cheeks, noisily.

'Hello comrade,' she replied, pleased to see him again.

It had been at least six months. He looked thinner and even more mannequin'd, but just as warm and effervescent. She felt a rush of reassurance as his confidence spilled over, obliterating her apprehension. He was animated and a little feverish with excitement.

'I can't *wait* to do this,' he said, grinning enthusiastically.

'Me too,' she said, honestly, invigorated by his energy.

'How are the headaches? Any better?' he asked politely.

She had fobbed him and Bianca off with a migraine history on more than one occasion.

'Mostly okay,' she replied. 'Nothing a little music can't help with.' She smiled and tried to sound more confident than she felt.

Two hours later, she certainly did have a headache, but this time, she knew it was just from tense concentration. Louis had worked her hard, too fast as always, but she had gone with him in a full quasi-gymnastic workout. She was exhausted. He was pushing her, but she needed it. Too much time had passed since such an intense rehearsal, and she was obviously out of practice. She was almost relieved when her phone went off. Louis glared at it.

'Sorry, Lou; forgot to turn it off,' she said, laying down her bow and slipping it under an ear. She didn't recognise the number. 'Better just take this,' she insisted, trying to make it sound important. They needed a break, anyway.

It was Tess.

'Hey, is this a good time? Sorry to disturb. I just wanted to check about next Tuesday's lesson; you said you'd confirm?'

Giselle had completely forgotten.

'Ah oui, of course. I'm sorry. That should be fine. Urm, where are you?' she asked, confused by the number.

'Sorry. I left my phone at David's by mistake. You can use this number for now, until I get my mobile back.'

In her distraction, she failed to remember that the number would be stored anyway, but instead grabbed the pencil she had been using to scribble all over her scores and looked for the nearest blank piece of paper. She saw the pile of flyers that Louis had prepared for the concert and snatched the top one.

'Give me the number again,' she said, wedging the phone into her shoulder and scribbling the number down carefully on the back.

'Thanks. I'll look forward to next week, then,' she said, glancing over at Louis, who was already jerking his head back to the piano. 'Better, go Tess. See you soon, oui. Adieu.'

Forty-five minutes later, she interrupted Louis again. She suddenly noticed the time.

'Non! *Excuse-moi*, Lou, I must go!' she exclaimed. 'I need to catch this train or I won't make it back tonight.' She looked at him apologetically.

Louis understood, although he would have liked just one more run-through of the fourth movement. Her playing was exceptional. She was completely in a class of her own. Intuitively, he knew the concert was going to be phenomenal.

They rounded up quickly, Giselle packing away her 'cello and music stand, talking hurriedly about a final rehearsal on the concert day itself. She really couldn't afford to come down from Sheffield again before then. He grabbed the pile of flyers and promised to circulate them widely. Giselle thanked him profusely. Louis gathered his belongings and slung on his leather jacket. She picked up her music and followed him out, turning off the lights behind them and shutting the door, before stumbling out into the dusk, where the street lights were just beginning to flicker hesitantly into life.

Chapter 49

Sam heard the postman at the door and the sound of letters being stuffed through the letterbox. He had the day off from college and was in the kitchen, scavenging for food an hour after breakfast. Lucy had sneaked off to see Jack, and he suspected the two of them were probably on their way into town right now or having a fag in the park on the way. He didn't like Jack at all. Although only a year older, he treated Sam like he was a prize prat. Resentment gnawed away at him even thinking about him and Lucy together. Jack with his poncey clothes and pretentious swagger, Lucy indifferent to his flirtatious intentions. Such a plank. Sam had kept a wide berth from girls, who secretly terrified him, but Jack was the ultimate playboy: nineteen years old and all revved up. He'd tried to warn Luce, but she was having none of it. He wanted to warn Mum too. But the invisible twin cloak of confidentiality had restrained him, so he'd kept quiet in the end.

Which reminded him, where was Mum? The house was quiet; even the dogs were snoozing. He hadn't seen her all morning. She normally left a note or text or something, but the house was strangely silent. It wasn't Monday, so she wasn't with her fossils. He wandered aimlessly into the hall in the direction of the post, picked it up without looking past the first two leaflets of junk mail and a handwritten letter to Mum, before returning magnetically to the piano and plonking the letters on top of a rather overladen lid.

In truth, his music was strewn all over the piano, on top, on the rack, and all around the stool too. The post simply fused into the tablecloth of manuscript which was covering it, whilst the piano itself looked as if it might disappear altogether, obliterated by layers of paper feathers. Kitty's irritation over the mess had been slightly tempered by the overall objective, and she had admonished herself that the end really did justify the means, even if it meant some temporary disruption. Plus it surely gave Yani the impression that Sam had become fanatical about the piano. Which was true. This was one of the rare things that both mother and son now agreed upon.

An hour later, Kitty came in the back door to hear *Dr Gradus* being played at breakneck speed; Sam's fingers tumbled over each other in their haste to fall down the octaves, before landing in a walloping crash at the bottom. Although wildly unsteady, it was still enormously satisfying to hear that he wasn't upstairs and plugged into Google. She debated interrupting him, but he had heard her come in too.

'Mum?' he yelled from the lounge. 'When's lunch?'

Kitty took a deep breath and rolled her eyes.

'I'm not eating lunch,' she called back unhelpfully.

Speciously, she eyed up the opened pack of Jaffa cakes which were peeping put of her handbag. There was a minute's pause before Sam appeared in the kitchen, hair ruffled and looking cross. Before he could kick off, Kitty interjected. She hadn't the energy to fight him and hated herself for her compliance.

'Look, Sam, just because I'm here now doesn't mean you can't fix your own lunch,' she wailed, realising that she was giving conflicting signals. Only yesterday, she had chastised him for helping himself to nearly a whole packet of cold ham and the last loaf of bread.

'Where *were* you?' he asked, annoyance fuelled by rising hunger.

'Pilates,' she said. 'With Jen.'

'Whassat?' he demanded, still scowling.

Kitty glared at him and swallowed an explanation.

'Exercise?' she said, completely unwilling to try and describe the convoluted movements she had been twisting her reluctant body into for the past hour. She doubted that Sam had ever heard of core strength. She sighed.

'Look. There's a spare pizza on the bottom shelf,' she proposed, wondering what she would now give Angus and Toby for tea later on.

Sam looked as if he needed to decipher code.

'Pizza?'

'Yes. Think you can get that into the oven?' she said rather unkindly, regretting the words as soon as she'd said them.

She was weary of these responsibility battles but was even more weary keeping abreast of Sam's appetite. Inside, maternal guilt scuppered her resolve. Sam looked sullenly on.

'Okay, okay. I will pop it in now while I go and shower. Can you keep an eye on it, though? They don't taste quite so good burned.'

Sam glowered at her sarcasm.

He looked at her implacably. Corkscrew curls shot out at all angles from her head, incognisant of the pink headband which tried to contain them. It looked suspiciously as if she might have borrowed one of Lucy's lycra tops, which was several sizes too small, rendering an unflattering display of abdominal squidge. He started to laugh.

'Mum. You look *ridiculous!*' he said, chortling insensitively.

Kitty rose up to his shoulder and aimed fire with her nose.

'Sam. When I need you to give me compliments, I will politely ask. Now I am going upstairs to make myself even *more* presentable, and when I come down, I would be so grateful if you can manage not to set the smoke alarm off.'

Sam shrugged and turned towards the fridge, whilst Kitty kicked off her trainers and headed for the shower.

***

In a warm and stuffy office on the seventeenth floor, Richard was sitting in the middle of a very dull board meeting. He had said his bit and now had to sit out at least another half an hour before they could adjourn for lunch. His eyes strayed over the monotonous balding colleague opposite him to the window and London skyline beyond.

A sister, David had said. Nothing could have come as more of a bombshell. Well, he for one wasn't going to overreact. David's curiosity had bordered on childish glee, and it had irritated him enormously. Not only that, but he felt miffed that Brian had chosen to tell David first, and it rankled that his father had also shown surprising exuberance about it all. No, he was not going to be so easily fooled. He had chatted it over with Olivia, who had been adamant that it would open a can of worms, about which he was inclined to agree. Grief. Whatever Dad and Mum had done, it was too late now to start delving into the past. He wondered what she may be like now and, for some reason, shuddered. The only women he had any real respect for were like the ones sitting round his table now: fierce and perfumed, driven and well-manicured.

Resisting an urge to slip a hand into his breast pocket for his phone, he knew he would have to wait until the meeting finished. Instead, making a mental note not to forget, he decided he would text David and say he was too busy next weekend to come up and see them, after all. Too busy and too unwilling to chase a sister he wished he never had.

Chapter 50

The train was uncomfortably full. Yani had been lucky to get a seat, and he was deliberating whether to get the Schubert score out of his briefcase for a mental drill before meeting his operatic diva in town. She had booked a practise room at the Barbican, yet during the past week, he had barely had time to study the accompaniment. It wasn't one he knew especially well, either, and he sighed. He was dreading her theatrics already. She was just one of those. He was beginning to wish he hadn't agreed, but impeccable manners nearly always contrived against him at times like this. Saying no had been a lifelong struggle, possibly ever since leaving the orphanage, he reckoned. He couldn't really fathom why. Perhaps he felt he owed it to the world, this necessary repayment against a deeply treasured and lavish redemption. Whatever the reason, he was stuck with this current obligation now, and he stared out of the moving window, frowning. Deciding to ignore stares from fellow passengers, he fished out his music and began to concentrate, flicking over the pages methodically, before sepia'd thoughts interrupted the page of dots in front of him.

She wakes him softly, teasingly, with a whisper of a kiss on his nose. He is sunk into her sofa, where daylight hours have stolen a night of sleep. He stirs, remembering. A midnight train which has rattled through long inky hours to reach her after weeks of separation from a tour. Arriving first, he has waited for her return, resting on her couch

before sleep finally drowns him. Then, as he opens his eyes, she is there,
gazing down at him. His arms reach up to pull her close.

The train tooted a whistle, and Yani was jolted back to the
station. Two notes blasted a jarring interval, snatching both his
reflection and memory. He stared at the manuscript before him,
batting off perceived curiosity. *Heaven's script*, he mused, *and my*
language too. Her language, ours.

And yet he still couldn't (or wouldn't) believe that she was
gone. *No.* She was still alive to him, and he would fight until
his final breath to keep her existence real. Taunted as he was by
her memory, he felt his soul being lanced again. Thinking of
her now was indeed a living death, a haunted ruin of such vast
proportions that there was no quantifiable measure for its grief.
From somewhere far on the horizon outside of himself, he knew
that denial held him firmly in its grip, but he was powerless
to resist. Glancing at the city buildings sprinting past him, he
checked his watch. They would soon be at the terminal, and he
would have to rush to catch the Tube in time. He pushed his score
back into his case and stood up, edging his way slowly down the
crowded aisle towards the closed door.

Battling through pedestrian traffic to the Underground
entrance, he ruefully acknowledged, as he had done endlessly
before, that the police hadn't made any obvious progress with
the investigation. He had spent nearly a fortnight in Paris, long
exhausting days spent in endless interrogation, where he had
answered their repetitive questions with the same answers. He
knew nothing. Only that she had suddenly disappeared. No, he
had no explanation; there had been no note, no discernible motive.
He had wanted, needed, to know the truth. As did they. So he had
tasered them with his question: Was this her body? They couldn't
say conclusively.

This final suspense had almost suffocated him, as he absorbed
their suspicion with the instinct of a leopard. For she had certainly
led a solitary life. He knew that, and the reasons for it, but they

had seemed unimpressed, rounding on him like a wretched toro. It was unbearable, but they had finally let him go, unable to detain him further. However, he was certain they were watching him, even now. Hunted and furtive, he felt increasingly paranoid. Even as he was walked through crowded streets now, he tossed frequent glances behind him.

Two hours later, he walked wearily across Blackfriars Bridge and hesitated at the mouth of the Tube. He couldn't face the crush of any more suffocating carriages and paused. Tired from the predictably irritating rehearsal, he reckoned that if he walked across, it may just help clear his head. It was already dark, but the river was well lit up, and he could hear boat horns in the distance, calling across the water. Crossing onto the bridge, he breathed in the fumed night air as cars sped past him, tail lights braking impatiently. He stopped and leant over the thick iron railing, looking down to the long fall beneath, seeing only a fluid blackness which entirely mirrored his heart. He imagined her as Millais's *Ophelia*, drifting silently past reeds and debris, floating beautifically on the surface. But that was not how the body had been found. A naked and strangled corpse had been dredged from the river, marred from any recognition or identity. There had been no dental records for Sabine, either, not that could be traced. He doubted whether Sabine's translucently perfect teeth would have ever needed a dentist, anyway. An incandescent and white anger burned inside of him as he considered who might have done her harm, but he endeavoured to banish his imagination before it harrowed him further. Ahead lay Waterloo Station, and he could already hear evening trains thundering over ground, clattering into the night.

He crossed at the lights and made his way, lost in thought, along the well-worn pavement. It was so dark that he almost didn't notice the huddled shape of a homeless man beside him, submerged under a dark sleeping bag. A sad dog with empty black eyes sat beside him, keeping watch. Yani shuddered. It was a picture of hopelessness, and that emotion ran very deep. It had been there all his childhood years in Albania, until the day he had met Viktor Papadasi and stumbled across God. Yet perhaps it was God who had had found him? From that point on, nothing else had mattered. It had been like falling into a dream that was even more real than being awake. And he had given her to him. The most wonderful and breathtaking gift, beyond any of his wildest dreams. Only now, his faith hung on a precipice.

He walked on another fifty yards before looking up to his left. As if synchronising with his thoughts, he noticed that he was, bizarrely, standing outside a large church. Its drabness was punctured only by the yellow lights that were on inside, seeping out through the high stained glass windows above. He gazed up. He must have walked past this place hundreds of times and never noticed it. *How peculiar*, he thought. Standing on the step outside the solid front door, he stopped to listen. It didn't sound as if there was activity inside, but you never could tell. He leaned nearer and waited. Looking up beyond its silhouette to the sky above him, he found himself whispering, inaudibly, '*God, help me. Please help me.*'

Intuition told him this was a déjà vu. Slowly and cautiously, he turned the door handle and stepped inside.

***

It was larger than he had expected and surprisingly welcoming, despite its emptiness. Perhaps it was the contrast with the fallen dusk outside. Ahead of him lay a decorous altar with wooden choir stalls flanking the walls in front of it. Under an imposing golden lectern, his eyes were drawn to a covered grand piano on a raised platform, which was both silent and inviting. He hovered at the back quietly. Lights were on throughout the church, so he guessed someone must be about. He walked slowly up the main aisle towards the front, warily looking around for signs of life, and resisted any thoughts of being an imposter in God's house, however unfamiliar the building might be.

He heard a door close quietly from the vestry on the left and froze. Then a dark-robed verger appeared out of it and looked up at him, slightly startled. Yani smiled at him cautiously. The verger smiled warily back but said nothing, carrying a heavy pile of hymn books towards the empty choir stalls. He was clearly busy, and Yani detected that he was an unwelcome interruption.

Yani had almost reached the front pews, but in order to avoid further interruption, he slipped into the third row on the left and sat down. With elbows on knees, he cupped his head in his hands, fingers burrowed into unruly locks, and looked down at his shoes. It was hard to pray whilst being watched. He shut his eyes.

In the blackness, he saw the face of Viktor Papadasi, looking lovingly at him. Suddenly, he missed him with overwhelming nostalgia. He really should go back and visit. He had tried after Adile died to visit him and Pjeter regularly, but the visits had stretched into ever longer gaps such that now, he realised regretfully, it had been nearly two years since he had seen them both. Two eventful years, but still, it had been too long. Age must surely be overtaking him now, Yani thought anxiously. Odd as that thought was, for he had always seemed entirely ageless. But Pjeter had never truly recovered. The last time he had visited, evenings were spent in unwelcome quietness, conversation awkward and laboured. Yani had tried everything to ease his bereavement, but the truth was he couldn't. Nothing could erase either Adile's absence or her memory.

He heard a door shut again and looked up. The verger had disappeared back into the vestry. Head still in hands, he gazed up at the beautiful stained glass scene ahead of him, a mosaic of blues, greens, and whites. A shepherd Jesus, staff in hand, who straddled a lamb across his elbow. It comforted him. As if God was surely holding him too. Even now.

Instinctively, he stood up to remind God that he was still

there and return the Shepherd's gaze, who he sensed was surely looking down at him. An indefinable reassurance washed over him. Then passing out of the pew, he started walking towards the back of the church, eyes swinging like a lighthouse beam over the empty rows, until almost at the back, he saw something on the floor out of the corner of his eye, peeking out from the penultimate pew and trespassing into the aisle. Just a piece of paper. Yani reached down to pick it up and found himself looking at it, bemused. It was a flyer about a concert, of all things. No photos. Smiling with association, he glanced at the names. No one he knew. But the pieces? His eyebrows knotted, staring at the programme, transfixed. How could anyone else know their programme? It was as rare as it was unique.

He turned the flyer over for any clues and then drew the most sudden gasp. For the longest time, he stared at what he was seeing. It was inconceivable, but if he wasn't mistaken—yet these things were so intimate—he was looking at Sabine's handwriting. *But it couldn't be.* Yet unmistakably, it *had* to be. It *was* her writing; he recognised it instantly. Yet all he could see was that she had simply scribbled down a girl's name. A girl's name he didn't recognise, and a phone number.

Chapter 51

The answer phone was flashing as Tess came through her front door. She glanced at it wearily. For some, energised as they were by attention, the intermittent red light would be welcomed, but today, on a day off, it was simply undue pressure. She knew it wouldn't be David, as she had retrieved her phone from his car, and it couldn't be Sylvia, as she had spent a tedious day shopping with her at Meadowhall in a vain search for a new winter coat, one of those shiny padded ones, that Sylvia had had her eye on for some while. So it was probably work, asking for a last-minute spare shift, and she sighed. Not today.

Feeling unusually rebellious, she decided to ignore it and went in search of her running stuff instead. If she didn't sit down, she could pound a couple of blocks before meeting David at the cinema later. Sheer willpower succeeded in goading her out of the house ten minutes later, and she set off purposefully in order to get back before it got dark. Short winter evenings had always conspired against exercise, which she knew was psychological; but ever since the accident, she doubted whether she would ever run again after dark. That night's memory, although fractionally dulled, still haunted her, especially as she approached any traffic lights. Looking firmly ahead of her, she tried to concentrate on the music, which she now never ran without. Her headphones fitted snugly. She remembered that it was Giselle who had said that, only last week, reminding her to 'focus on the music.'

Tess had been growing tetchy and frustrated miscounting rhythms and forgetting time values, as technicalities seemed to mitigate against all progress. There was just so much to think about when learning music, she realised. A whole new language to be grasped, and she sometimes wondered if she was just too old to learn such a complex skill. Yet Giselle had encouraged her with simple logic. Shutting her eyes, she had played a short phrase and told Tess to shut her eyes too. Ironic how the process of shutting her eyes had made her see it. Suddenly, she could comprehend the music through raw sound, unhindered by manuscript. She marvelled at this auditory memory, remembering the power of those long, beguiling notes she had heard so many months ago in the taxi, the day that this extraordinary musical journey had begun.

She now wondered what would have happened if she hadn't been in that taxi on that day and heard those heart-stopping notes. Would the music have eventually found her? She wasn't sure she could answer that. Perhaps. But too many what-ifs confounded her. What if she hadn't been on duty the day Brian had been admitted? Or had taken her lunch break when she did? There seemed too many coincidental threads. She had always believed in fate, but now she was beginning to wonder if there was something more. Was it just destiny or merely luck? Or were the events of her life prescriptively unfolding by some other force which she was striving, yet failing, to understand?

Her steps lengthened as she tried to pace them rhythmically with the piece she was hearing. Slender lithe legs thud-thudded along the pavement, and her sleek hair swished to the beat as she made her way round the second block and headed back home. Half an hour later, she was showered and perfumed, and a glance in the hall mirror rewarded her with satisfaction. She could sense that she was glowing. Love's debut was certainly potent, but she had never known it this way before, not even close. Whether it was David, the 'cello, or both, she knew sunshine was creeping into her soul, with every day a little bit more. Subliminally and at a cellular level, it was just good to be alive. She felt more revitalised than ever before and watched, bemused, at the eyes which sparkled back at her. Never had that truth reinforced itself so strongly since she had watched it so brutally snatched away before her own eyes. Since then, she had endeavoured to live each day more purposefully and gratefully. Time now seemed precariously short and indisputably precious. Thoughts of the afterlife still bothered her, though: unending questions and unsolved answers which, until faced with direct mortality, had never remotely bothered her before. Delving into the fridge, she poured herself a slimline tonic to await David's arrival. As she wandered through the hall to the lounge, she noticed the phone light blinking and swore at its persistence.

Taking a slow sip from her glass, she ventured towards it, as intrigue replaced reticence. After the briefest hesitation, she picked it up and pressed the button. There was a long pause before she heard the stilted accent of a man's voice.

'Excuse me, my name is Yani Belushi, and I am trying to contact Tess Gibson? I believe you may 'ave the details of a friend called Sabine Dubois, who I am trying to contact. Forgive me if ziss number is wrong, but if you could help me, I would be grateful if you could call me back? Zank you very much.'

After he had left a number, the machine clicked off.

Tess frowned. Sabine Dubois? *Who was that?* Taking a long sip of her drink, she wandered through to her sofa and sat down, kicking off her shoes and pulling her legs up underneath her. She had recently put up a little Christmas tree on a coffee table, and she flicked on the lights. They twinkled reassuringly. Still puzzled, she wondered how on earth he had got her number or her name, for that matter. She had never heard of Yani Belushi, either. *How weird.* She shuddered apprehensively.

Glancing at her watch, she jumped up again. David would be here any minute. If she didn't deal with this now, she would simply forget. Worse still, he would keep ringing and pestering her. Without further ado, she went back to the answer machine and replied, leaving her own brief, bland message:

'Hi. Thanks for your message, and sorry I can't be any more help. I'm afraid I don't know the person you mentioned or how you got this number, so please don't call again.' Click.

It was a bit rude and perhaps invidious, but she didn't want to take any chances. There were some total weirdos out there, and she really didn't like the fact that he knew both her name and number. Odd how he sounded foreign. The only other person she knew with a foreign accent was Giselle. *Yes*, Tess thought, *maybe I should ask her. She might shed some light.*

Her thoughts were interrupted by a rappity-rap at the door. She smiled in anticipation. Pulling on her heels again and grabbing her coat and bag, she hurried outside the door and into the eager arms of David.

Chapter 52

A week had passed since Yani had been in London, and since then, his feet had hardly touched the ground. Being the festive season, he seemed in constant demand and had rather overbooked himself. He berated himself for this overcommitment, but work was a double-edged sword. He could throw all his energies into it and buy welcome distraction, which numbed thoughts of Sabine a little, but since he had stumbled across that note, he had completely imploded. Over and over, he had rehearsed in his mind the possible scenarios as to what it all meant. That it was her handwriting was undeniable. He had rummaged around to find old letters she had written and compared them, side by side. The handwriting seemed identical. But then the sheer impossibility of it being so came crashing down on him like a hammer, as he searched unsuccessfully for answers.

He was also exhausted. Nights spent tossing and a couple of days away for a school concert series in Eastbourne had left him spent. He had wandered along the blustery promenade, where pebble skies and pleated waves had created an amalgam of grey density, and he wondered how Debussy had ever composed *La Mer* from this insipid shoreline. He struggled to imagine sunshine droplets on water, the sky as vibrant as it was now dull, and the happy sound of children as they tore over the sandy expanse, playing chase with the teasing waves. It was a world away. All he could hear now was the dull engine of the sea and the shriek of gulls overhead as they swooped and dived, oblivious to the weight of his despair.

For there had been the phone message. He had raced back from London like a jail-free lunatic, restlessly willing the night hours to pass swiftly by so he could make the call, finally sleeping fitfully with the piece of paper sandwiched under his pillow.

He had stood quietly in his flat as he tapped the number. Time lingered for him to press the call. What he was expecting he really wasn't sure, or even what to say. How could he ask a complete stranger the most important question of his life?

Then, disappointingly and unremarkably, an impersonal voicemail instruction had spoken back to him. He had hesitated a little but left as much information as he dared. He had hardly known how to occupy himself whilst waiting for a response. All his thoughts seemed now incapable of control, resembling a large bunch of balloons which tugged determinedly until they broke free, drifting off in all directions into the ether above.

He had been on his way to Kitty's the next evening, and wondering how he was ever going to be able to concentrate on Sam, when he picked up a missed call. Darting into a deserted bus stop, he sat down to compose himself, willing solitude as never before. Then, he had heard the most demoralising message he could possibly imagine, which had meteorically scuppered his trail. Like a giant metal door to a huge castle slamming finally shut, leaving him in utter defeat and desolation on the outside. Was it possible that this pain and grief would never end but become ever deeper and stay unresolved? His eyelids filled with an unfamiliar sensation of damp tears, surprising him starkly. For he truly believed he had long ago lost the ability to cry. He stopped abruptly and pulled out his handkerchief, normally used for wiping the sweat off his brow and neck during performances. He snorted into it loudly, willing the stubborn moistness away, whilst instinctively knowing he needed its healing tincture too.

But now was not the time. Coughing, he took a deep breath and walked on.

He had trudged on to Kitty's house with lead in his shoes, and almost rang to bail out. He had no energy for her benign yet warm prattling and knew he would be no match for Sam's heady exuberance, either. But where was there to go? He couldn't face the emptiness of his own company, certainly not this evening. Diversion had always somehow protected him from a nadir of despair, but right now, it would require all his strength and more to mask his cataclysmic dejection. As he thought of the challenge ahead, he remembered Kitty's unexpected empathy the night she had told him about her adoption. Underneath that frazzled facade lay more depth than he had at first detected, he perceived with some comfort. Plus, she was about the only woman he knew to confide in just now. The only other options were hapless admirers or truculent divas, and he had had more than his fair share of those. He rang the doorbell with a heavy heart.

'Yani! So nice to see you. Come on in,' Kitty enthused merrily from the other side. She was holding the tea towel that seemed to follow her wherever she went.

'Hi,' he said, stooping his head to avoid her gaze as he entered.

The hall still resembled a landfill site. Sidestepping several school bags and coats that had never encountered pegs, he headed straight for the piano to avoid unnecessary interrogation. Only there was no Sam sitting at the stool.

'I'm so sorry, Yani,' Kitty, began. 'I just picked up a message that Sam's bike got a puncture, but he's wheeling it back as fast as he can. He'll be here in a tick. Can I fix you a drink?'

She looked at him apologetically, noting for the first time a slight pallor in his face. He looked shattered.

'You okay?' she added, looking worried.

'Fine, yez. Coffee maybe? That would be great.' He smiled absently.

'Sure. I'll be right back.'

Kitty hovered, but Yani turned towards the piano and began ruffling papers in his bag.

'I'll just warm up before he comes, if you don't mind,' Yani called over his shoulder. 'Never enough time to practise at the moment, I'm afraid.'

Kitty retreated to the kitchen. She admired his dedication and refusal to waste time, yet she sometimes felt snubbed by his aloofness. This was one such example. He seemed wary to let down his guard, and since their unexpected conversation, he had clammed up again when it came to more than small talk. Kitty sometimes couldn't work him out at all. It was probably just the artistic temperament, she reasoned reluctantly.

She filled two cups hurriedly from a recently boiled kettle and returned to find him, but paused on her way as she heard the most beautiful music streaming towards her. Chopin perhaps, or maybe Liszt? She wasn't sure, but at least it answered her own question. This was surely Yani exposed. How was it possible to make those notes sound so sweet, rich, and full of articulation and meaning? It was a gift quite beyond her understanding, and it moved her deeply. She paused at the doorway, feeling like an intruder in her own home.

'Here we are,' she whispered eventually. She didn't really want him to stop.

'Zank you,' he said, without stopping or turning to look at her.

'That really is ... beautiful,' she said softly. 'So lovely.'

The unexpected tenderness in her voice made Yani pause. He swung round slowly to look up at her. His eyes were underscored by dark rings, and his hair looked as though it needed a shampoo.

'It's the music which is beautiful,' he explained. 'I am just a technician, really.'

'Nonsense,' Kitty countered. 'Technicians don't make sounds like that. Chopin?'

'Liszt,' Yani corrected politely.

'I just don't know how anyone can dream up music like that,' Kitty said sincerely.

'Yez, I agree. In a class of their own. But luckily for us, they left the notes behind.' He looked admiringly at the score.

'Funny that, isn't it? Leaving notes behind,' Kitty said.

Yani looked at her, thunderstruck.

'What do you mean?' he said hastily.

Kitty thought the statement was obvious.

'Well, they could have just kept it in their heads, couldn't they? Or just played it by ear until it got lost in the mists of time. But at some point in time, they chose to write it down and pass it on. Bravo for them! And besides, you've always said that music must be shared,' she added coyly.

'Hmm, I 'ave. It's very true,' he said honestly. Then without a flicker of hesitation, he suddenly blurted out, 'Kitty, thinking of zat, do you mind if I share something with you?'

Kitty was surprised by this unusual request. She stared at him in surprise, flattered even.

'Of course not.'

Yani hesitated, pausing to construct his words with sufficient emphasis.

'I need to tell you about a note I found left behind,' he said gently.

Kitty looked at him. There was simply no knowing with Yani what would come out with next. He was as unpredictable as the weather.

'Well, go on,' she said cautiously.

At that moment, the front door crashed open loudly, and Sam burst into the room. Yani and Kitty looked at each other in wide-eyed exasperation.

'So sorry, Yan, I mean Yani,' Sam said breathlessly, before Kitty had time to deliver a withering look. His spiky dark hair shot out at all angles, producing a remarkable resemblance to Dennis the Menace.

'Until later, then,' Yani said with a wink to Kitty.

'Of course,' she replied quietly.

Sam looked nonplussed.

'Okay, Yani, just wait until you hear what *I've* been practicing!'

He sat down clumsily at the long piano stool next to Yani. Kitty wondered if it might break under the weight of them both, it was so old. Yani rose respectfully.

'All yours, Maestro,' he said, ushering an arm to Sam, whilst simultaneously taking the cup Kitty was holding out to him.

Kitty smiled at him. The intrigue was captivating.

'Let's chat after the lesson,' she suggested, adding by way of diffusion, 'and I'm afraid you really do need to give me an invoice.'

Chapter 53

Nick shifted in his seat. This car was giving him increasing backache. He even wondered whether he should join Kitty for a Pilates class but hadn't dared voice it for fear of her triumphal reaction. She had tried to persuade him for ages. He wasn't sure he was succumbing to midlife wear and tear very well. A keen athlete in his youth, he had strongly resisted as his body had imperceptibly slowed down over the last decade, but it was just too easy to blame it on the kids and the maelstrom of their activities or their ridiculously congested lives. With dogged persistence, he had kept his fitness as best he could by running and cycling when time afforded, and he played squash with Jen's husband Mike, but those weekly sessions were becoming harder and harder to fit in.

In truth, it was Helen who was becoming the main focus on his crowded horizon. The last two months, he had been increasingly hounded for visits, as well as the endless moral support required on the telephone. High maintenance was what Kit had always said, but that seemed a churlish reaction now that her mother-in-law was fighting a battle which the cancer cells were clearly winning. Her cluster of robust friends helped, but living so far away still gnawed at his guilt. Overnight visits were compulsory, as it was just too far to make it in a day. So that meant weekends, and each time he went, he felt he was losing her in little pieces. It was a slow, premeditated grief, vignettes of abstract goodbyes which were unspoken but real, nonetheless. He wondered if she sensed it too. For all her demands, when all was said and done, she was still his Mum. And he didn't want her to go.

Ahead, the traffic was sluggish. He wanted to be home in less than the sluggish eighteen minutes the satnav claimed it would take. *Time rules everything*, he thought glumly: *never enough of it*. His phone jingled. Probably Kit wondering when he would be home. Why she insisted on sending the same message every night when she knew he would be sitting at the supper table within a half an hour, irritated him daily. *She probably doesn't even realise she does it*, he thought accurately, reminding himself to tell her yet again not to bother. But he could never stay angry with Kit for long. She was his life. She salvaged everything by just making him laugh, and few people could do that.

He wondered repeatedly how he had ended up with such an amusing and gung-ho woman, for which he was indeed grateful. Marriage was such a risk, he had often concluded. It seemed, to his casual observation, that there was a suspicious element of dice-rolling involved. Or perhaps it was just good old-fashioned tenacity. After all, who in their right minds knew what they were taking on when they walked up the aisle? Couples they both knew well had fallen by the wayside recently, and unexpected ones; crashed irretrievably on the rocks of infidelity or ennui. Somehow, the thought of straying had never been an issue for him and Kit. Perhaps they were naive, and maybe he should be worried that he thought like this. But he knew that for him and Kit, they just belonged together, like a cup and saucer. It's just how it was, even though he knew he must never take it for granted. His own parents' parched marriage had been empty, strained, and poisoned by boredom, so he had dared to dream of an entirely different model for himself one day, which he felt lucky enough to have achieved, through no real choosing of his own. It had just happened. And one thing was for certain: no one else would be so much fun for the ride, even if he never knew which mood he would find her in at the end of each day. He looked ahead appreciatively as the familiar neighbourhood came into view. Also, he was ravenous.

When he arrived, he found the kitchen strangely quiet; Kitty was sitting poised and purposeful over a mug of tea with Yani. They seemed to be in deep conversation. Why this sight unsettled him, he wasn't sure, although he instinctively sought reassurance from his most recent thoughts. He needn't have worried, though. Kitty got up to give him a lavish hug, pulling him, as she always did, into every conversation, especially when his opinion was required, which to his pride and delight was fairly often.

'Hon, you *need* to help us,' she began, gauging Yani's face for approval.

His smile hinted with assent. Kitty explained carried on an explanation, with arms waving in her usual animated and theatrical fashion. Her zest for adventure always made life exciting, even at the dullest of moments. It is what he absolutely loved about her.

'Yani is sooo very near to finding his lost love!' she exclaimed triumphantly.

That Yani had a love at all wasn't something Nick had remotely considered. He looked across at Yani awkwardly, if a little relieved.

'Yes, it's all so extraordinary,' she continued. 'You just *won't* believe it!' She thumped her fist down on the table so that the mugs shook nervously.

Over the next few minutes, Kitty regaled Nick with the story and Yani's predicament, which the musician had to privately concede perhaps embroidered events in a charmingly flamboyant sort of way. The despair he was feeling had been tempered by Kitty's implacable belief that he would find Sabine again. She made Yani sound like he was part of a crime thriller which had a resolutely happy ending. This he was desperate to condone. However, he let Nick absorb the situation, eager to glean his response.

'So,' Kitty went on, 'I told him he just *has* to go to the concert.

Don't you think? It *may* just be a clue.' Her face was flushed with melodrama.

Yani and Kitty stared at Nick, waiting eagerly for his reaction.

Nick sat down and poured himself some water. He would have preferred to eat first, but manners prevailed. He coughed courteously.

'Yes, well, that does sound like the best bet,' he agreed guardedly. 'When is it?'

Kitty explained it was the weekend after next, flush up to the week before Christmas.

'Well, then,' Nick said, secretly eager to discover the contents of the oven before too long, 'I suggest, Yani, that you take the evening off and get yourself to that show.'

Chapter 54

Tess giggled to herself in the bath. Alone in her flat, she was wallowing in some foamy luxury on a much-needed day off. David was making such monstrous compliments about every part of her body these days that it had swelled her head quite successfully. He was the most polished and professional flirt, but she relished it. No one else had ever made her feel quite like a supermodel. It was just ridiculous, and she chided herself for believing his extravagant flattery so patently. Sinking further under the bubbles, she sighed. It would be another few days before she saw him again, with three long shifts ahead of her before the weekend. She had booked a last-minute lesson with Giselle that afternoon, knowing that once Christmas descended, the diary would be suffering from indigestion.

She wrapped a towel around her as she sauntered into the bedroom. The week's laundry pile in the corner lay untouched and neglected. *What is happening to me?* she wondered cheekily. That she didn't even care, was unheard of. She tossed the towel defiantly on top of it and pulled on her jeans. She was eager to see Giselle again; it had been over a couple of weeks. She had planned to get an hour's practice in before heading across town on the bus, stopping for a quick bite with Sylvia on the way back. Then she was determined to catch an early night, in order to combat the following morning's alarm.

She found Giselle in good spirits too. This was pleasing,

as Tess found it increasingly hard not to worry about her, the closer they had become. For Giselle had become both friend and teacher, quite imperceptibly. The two women provided each other with invaluable support, both thinking the other to be the more indispensable. Tess was constantly amazed by Giselle's incessant patience with her feeble mistakes, and Giselle was secretly delighted with Tess's progress, enjoying her companionship gratefully. They greeted each other warmly, Tess growing accustomed to the smack of kisses Giselle always planted successively on both cheeks.

The lesson progressed happily, Tess pleased to be feeling her earlier practise had paid off. Giselle confirmed it. She was delighted.

'Alors, this is so good, Tess,' she said encouragingly. 'Well done. *Cinq etoiles.*'

Tess flushed a little. She was so unused to all this praise coming from all quarters. Even her boss had congratulated her last week. It was all a bit heady, and she knew she must bottle it for a rainy day. Still, she must surf the wave while it lasted.

'Hey, guess what?' Tess said, after another half an hour of hard work had passed, and they had both paused for a break. Giselle looked interested, glad for the distraction. Her fingers were hurting, and she needed to rest them for a few minutes. Tess had forgotten to tell her about the phone call.

'A really funny thing happened to me the other day,' Tess continued, resting her 'cello carefully against the sofa and looking absently out of the window.

'*Quoi?*' Giselle asked, looking intrigued. She often forgot to speak in English, even with Tess.

'Yeah. This man phoned me. Looking for a woman I'd never heard of. So weird.'

Giselle looked at her carefully.

'What kind of man?' she asked innocently.

'Well, hard to tell, but he was definitely foreign. Not French, I don't think.' Her voice trailed off a bit as she considered.

'Definitely European. Yes, I'm sure he was, maybe from Eastern Europe?' she concluded, trying not to sound vague.

'Who was he looking for, then?' Giselle stared at her enquiringly, her eyebrows almost touching.

'That's just it, I didn't recognise the name at all. I think her name did sound a bit French, but I can't be sure. It was something like Sabrina? Or was it Sabine, maybe? I can't exactly remember, let alone pronounce it,' she confessed.

Giselle stared, her eyes frozen wide.

'Excusez-moi? *Sabine*?' Her face didn't flinch.

'Yes, something like that. Why?' Tess looked at her, puzzled.

Giselle was looking at her, transfixed.

'Did he leave a name or anything?' she asked, her hazel eyes intense with curiosity.

'Yes. That name I do remember, I think. He said his name was Yani.'

'Yani?' Giselle's head dropped into her hands, and she let out a soft groan which sounded like a spaniel whining in pain.

Tess looked on, frowning.

'What? What is it?' she asked. 'Do you know him?'

'Did he leave a number?' Giselle queried quickly, her face full of questions.

'Well, I didn't give him a chance really,' Tess explained. 'I was worried how he had got my number, so no. I just deleted his and told him not to call back.'

It had seemed sensible at the time, but now she was not so sure.

This time, Giselle seemed as though she really was going to faint.

'I need to lie down, please,' she said weakly, moving slowly towards the sofa.

Tess steered her into a horizontal position and placed a cushion under her head. She certainly had gone very ashen, blending like a chameleon with the cream cushion underneath.

Oh no! Tess wailed internally. *What did I do?*

'I'm sorry if I said the wrong thing. Do you know Sabine, then?' she added as an afterthought.

'Oui. I know her very well.'

Tess looked down at her, somewhat astonished.

Giselle continued to look up at her. 'Tess, please don't be scared or surprised,' she said, '*but I am Sabine.*'

Chapter 55

'*What?*' Tess found herself saying. 'You are, wait, *who?* I don't understand.'

Her face was riven with confusion, and Giselle felt wretched in every conceivable way. She hadn't wanted this to happen. It seemed like such a betrayal.

'I can explain,' she began slowly, 'but I do need you to forgive me. I had no choice but to use another name. Like I told you before, I couldn't take a chance that he would find me.' She tried to remember what she had already told Tess about Yani and realised she had never told her his name.

'Why not?' Tess asked.

'Because he thinks I'm dead. And that's the awful truth.' She closed her eyes.

'*Dead?*' Tess's eyes widened in disbelief.

'Oui. He probably thinks I drowned. It was all over the news a few months ago.'

Tess vaguely remembered something about a drowned musician, but now she was completely bewildered.

'The police seem pretty clear that Sabine Dubois drowned,' Giselle continued, 'although the case closed without absolute certainty.'

'So you see, I couldn't advertise as Sabine Dubois, because technically, she doesn't exist.'

'But then who *did* drown?' Tess needed to ask.

'That's just it," she replied. 'I don't know. Seems she was an unexpected alibi, for me, at least. But Yani is bound to think that it was me.'

Both Giselle's eyes now emitted deep perplexity. Her forehead had criss-crossed into a tangled frown.

'What I can't understand, though, is how he got your number? If it was really him who called,' she added, still unsure.

'Me neither,' said Tess.

It was definitely a mystery. But what was slowly dawning on her was the spectacular way she had now destroyed all means of discovering the truth. Yani must have been trying to contact Giselle, but Tess was at a loss to understand how she was the missing link. It was all a crazy mess.

'Giselle, oh goodness. I'm *so* sorry,' she began wretchedly. 'I didn't know. I just didn't realise.'

'It's okay,' Giselle responded magnanimously. 'How were you to know? I doubt 'e will call back again, and if 'e does, will you please tell me?' Her eyes brimmed with concern.

'Of *course* I will. Although you must surely still be able to contact him?'

Her question hung in the air. Giselle paused.

'Yes, it's true, I could. But I made a vow that I never would. Just in case I don't make it, you see.' Her voice trailed with poignant sadness.

'Yes, but Giselle, I really think he deserves to know. *Seriously.*' Tess looked earnestly at her. 'Love can find a way. It's not just a cliché, you know.'

'Do you really think so, even now? And after all I've put 'im through?'

'Even now.' Tess looked strangely confident. 'And anyway, who says you're not gonna make it?'

She grinned buoyantly at her. Giselle smiled wanly back.

'Who knows, Tess? The prognosis was really not good. I know I 'ad a pardon recently, but I cannot be sure it will definitely last.'

She sighed, before more forcefully adding her final verdict:

'No. I don't think I can go back. Unless, of course, 'e finds me first.'

Chapter 56

Suddenly, all Yani wanted was to see Viktor Papadasi again. Instinctively, he just knew that seeing him would give all the resolution and clarity he needed. But there was no possible way he could get out to Albania before Christmas, even if he could get a flight for the coming weekend. He was more than tied up with rehearsals over the next few days. It wasn't even possible to call him; he had suggested once that he buy a mobile phone. Viktor had just laughed.

'A cell phone? Me?' he had tittered, as if the very thought would tip him out of a previous century.

'Yes, even you,' Yani had retorted. 'That way I can keep an eye on you, *Monsieur*. Come on, you know it would really help.' *Me, at least*, he thought.

But Viktor had been adamant.

'My dear Yani, whatever has happened to your faith? Cannot God take care of me?'

It wasn't really a question. He had looked up to the ceiling above, as if a reminder were necessary.

'You are far too busy to worry about me,' he had said; screwing up his eyes a little, he had added, 'neither do I want you to.' His gentle face was full of kindly compassion.

Yani had looked at him with both love and exasperation. How was it possible not to love this dearest of old men, the one person who had given him so much, everything even? Yet how could he ever forget his welfare, especially from a long distance? It was impossible.

So they had agreed to keep writing good old-fashioned letters, because even Yani knew that never in a million years would Viktor enter the digital age. He belonged to something altogether more timeless, more yesterday. More sacred, even.

But he couldn't stop worrying, whenever he thought about him. Pjeter sent him the occasional email, as did Adile's sisters, so he knew they would let him know if there was any concern. Yet that was just it. Viktor's simple faith in divine providence and protection was so concrete, so absolute, that he transmitted more peace than anyone Yani had ever met. Death didn't faze him, not in the least. He had told Yani too many times that he wouldn't die anyway, not in the spiritual sense. Yani found that deeply comforting as he thought about his own pilgrimage. He had wondered as a teenager how you could be so sure, so definite about immortality. Viktor had patiently listened to his questions time and again, not imposing bland or religious answers. Yani needed to know for himself.

'You see, my son,' he had explained one evening, when the darkness was punctured only by a flickering candle and dying fire, 'truth can only be revealed.'

Yani had listened, as ideas hung suspended. He had waited a long time for such disclosure, for his own answers to the mysteries of life, which there were too many to count.

'Where do I find it, then, this revelation?' he had asked innocently.

'That's the thing. Perhaps it's not entirely up to you,' Viktor had replied intriguingly, out of his storehouse of wisdom. His brown eyes sparkled as they teased the thoughts out of Yani's head.

'So I just sit around waiting for it to happen, then?' Yani had asked, stumped.

'Yes … and no,' Viktor had simply said.

He had pulled his own worn Bible down off a shelf and flicked over the tissue-thin pages, which crinkled as he turned them, the dim light casting shadows around him.

'There are plenty of clues,' he had said quietly. And holding up the old book, he had said softly, 'This is one of them.'

Then placing a stout index finger in one of the rustling pages, he had read him a verse. Yani had never forgotten it.

'Draw near to me, and I will draw near to you.'

It sounded warm and inviting. Yani had listened, mesmerised. Viktor had looked up, his kind eyes smiling warmly.

'If you can believe that, then you have just stumbled before the gate of heaven, my son.'

'It's that simple?' Yani had asked.

'It's that simple,' Viktor had said.

'If God is real, Yani, your search will be rewarded. And.. here is a map,' he said softly, tapping his old Bible lovingly, as if it contained secret treasure.

There were no more words to be said. It was a promise. A promise which was outside of time, and one which he had never since erased.

Since then, over the years, Yani had taken many detours on his journey but never forgot what he had learned that night. He had seen too many miracles, if that's what you called answered prayers, to count. Too many coincidences, too many moments when he had sensed a watching presence. Now he needed every ounce of divine help to heal a broken, bleeding heart, which had been smashed into so many shards. If God hadn't given him the gift of music as a salve, he was not sure how he would ever recover. Not even music, though, could always console him. It always left him wanting more. Touching another world with his fingertips. A key perhaps to heaven, the language of the angels. He thought about heaven often and wondered whether Sabine was there now.

'It will be more beautiful than any place you can ever imagine,' Yani had insisted, one blisteringly hot summer's day when they had sat on a bench in the Jardin des Tuileries, listening to the fountain spray before them and watching children run barefoot and carefree across the lawns.

Sabine had smiled her radiant smile, loving this spirituality about him, understanding it so completely now, and deeply infected by his faith. There was a unity in their belief, even though paradise had appeared prematurely to them both, it seemed. The sun had washed her face with joyful illumination, and he had always held fiercely to the memory of it. She believed it too.

Now he needed a final answer. If she was still alive, which that note tantalisingly suggested, only God could find her. If not, he needed to know she was safely home, happy, and waiting for him. He did not know if could ever endure the long years of his life ahead without her, but he would try. Just as Viktor had modelled, perhaps it was possible to live with God being enough. Maybe that was the lesson of her vacuum. He would treasure her memory until such time he could see her again, forever reunited in a place they could only dream about now.

He had thought about what Nick had said. The only link with Sabine and the note was the building in which he'd found it. He would have to retrace his steps; it was the only hope left. And the programme completely mystified him; surely no one would ever play their repertoire so specifically, but maybe it was just a fluke. Irrationally, he doubted it. The G minor Andante was well known, but the Piazzolla, Dohnányi *and* the Ginasterra? It just couldn't be.

The day of the concert, Yani found himself torn between agitation and excitement. And abject terror. He knew the music would undoubtedly pierce his already fragmented heart, but his greatest fear was the possibility that he would discover nothing. Instead, he would listen to two young artists play music so sacred to him, that it was virtually a prized possession, although music could never be owned, he knew, even by the composer. It was a gift, given only to be shared. Viktor had told him that when he was just a boy. He knew it was so true, even though some artists tried, with arrogance, he had always felt, to turn the spotlight on themselves.

He found himself once again in dark London streets, but now ablaze with Christmas lights from every lamp post. Light into darkness, he mused. He really hoped so. Taking a longer route this time, he had stopped in a bar for a drink; he was not sure why, for he never drank much. He had seen too many colleagues propped up by it, and it scared him. He needed the adrenaline to perform, but right now, he needed it tamed. A buffer? Against what? He wanted the concert to have both begun and ended all at once, and he chastised himself momentarily. This was probably a complete blind alley. *If only he hadn't told Kitty and Nick*, for they had now forced him into a corner. Kitty would no doubt be ringing him tomorrow, desperate for a report, and he would have to tell her it had been a dead end. He brushed the grim thought aside.

Crossing over the road, he waited at the bollard in the middle until it was safe to cross. Ahead the church was lit up, doors open, and groups of anonymous strangers huddled in winter coats were making their way in. He had dared to presume he could get a ticket on the door, and he was correct. Classical concerts were rarely sold out unless in a theatre or concert hall. He queued for a few minutes, envious of those who were greeting each other in recognition, absorbing their seasonal glee, aware they had probably tumbled out of wine bars on their way in, as he himself had done too. Friday nights were surely the same in every city throughout the known world. *Strange to be in the audience for once*, he thought. Yet he felt alone, so very alone.

***

David had arranged to meet Tess at Monument Tube Station, and they would walk to the concert together. She had raced down to London from work, and it was going to be tight for time. They weren't able to travel together, as he had gone on ahead to see Richard and Olivia the night before, paving the way for their first meeting of Tess that night. He had been glowingly effusive in his description of her but sensed an unspoken censure from them both, nonetheless. That he was divorced and had left Evie for a younger woman (although that wasn't the case, he knew) was just what they had automatically conjectured. *Richard was probably just jealous*, David thought. Boyish envy had never really dissipated between them. Being stuck with the haughty Olivia couldn't be much fun, either, he reckoned. Oh well, he didn't care what they thought. Tonight was going to be sublime, not least because he hadn't told her he had finally handed in his resignation. He had been toying with the idea for a while, but in recent days, the decision had almost ceased to be a choice. There was only one continent he wished to be living in now. And this evening, he was going to tell her, exuberant at the thought of her reaction. That Tess seemed so enthusiastic for him to hear her teacher was both irresistible and charming to him, knowing his own paucity for musical appreciation. Whatever she loved, he would too.

Tess arrived breathless and windswept but on time, just. They kissed like unabashed teenagers at the top of the Underground, before huddling together and hurrying briskly to the church. It was only a few minutes away, and David steered her confidently, his time spent living in London second nature even now, years later. Tess was impressed. She had rarely travelled south, and it thrilled and terrified her in equal measure. But she clung to David's muscular bicep gratefully. Her heels clicked rapidly as she tried to keep up with his stride.

They reached the church just as a few stragglers were contemplating a last-minute entry. There was only a small queue, and they waited in line, conscious of the unfamiliar context in which they found themselves, which merely added to their feverish exhilaration. Tess felt as if she was literally floating on a current of happiness, although she wondered empathetically how Giselle must be feeling right now. She felt sick with nerves on her behalf. It was one thing to be a teacher, but quite another to be the soloist, and she truly hoped that Giselle would have enough stamina for the performance. It was sheer agony knowing the back story.

Looking around, she was intrigued by the audience. A whole spectrum of ages seemed represented. There were even a few children too, she noticed. Ahead of them were a group of white-haired dames, clearing enjoying a night on the razzle, lipstick and bling out defiantly. She glanced behind her. A solitary man was following them, looking a bit withdrawn and reclusive even, dark floppy hair tossed backwards. She wondered who would come to a concert alone.

Maybe he is a pupil like me, she thought, although he seemed too old to be a student.

He looked sad, distant. She turned away from him abruptly, not wanting to absorb his mood. Hugging her secret proudly inside—that she knew Giselle—made her feel a little superior, ludicrous and irrelevant though it was.

***

In a room in the hall behind the church, Giselle was warming up. She was nervous, but not musically. She knew the repertoire blindfolded. What unnerved her was playing these pieces without *him.* Louis would never, could never, be Yani. He was strutting around, pacing across the back of the room, clutching his music as if it were a buoyancy aid. Yani had never played this music with a score. She had it all in her head too. She wriggled her fingers and wiped sweaty palms away, giving her bow one final resin. In loyalty to him, she was wearing his favourite dress, the pistachio satin ballgown she had worn for their first concert together, as she remembered his whistle of admiration. Her pale shoulders were sculptured perfectly under its simple straps, and her brown hair was loose, falling with a silky sheen down her back. No make-up or jewellery; it wasn't needed. She stood up as the stage hand entered, her heart beating faster, and she pictured Yani's face before her. That last intimate smile before they went on stage. He was there in her mind; he would always be here in her heart, and she was ready.

***

After an usher handed Yani a programme, he made his way through the crowded church to a seat at the end of a pew on the right. The piano was on stage left, but he had no desire to see the keyboard. He was surprised how full it was, guessing that proximity to both London Bridge and Christmas must make a difference. Sitting down carefully, he assessed his neighbour with a sideways glance, searching for some leg room to accommodate his long limbs. In the row in front, the young couple who were before him in the queue had taken their seats, his arm protectively draped around her shoulder. She was young and pretty, flaxen hair shaped perfectly around a heart-shaped face, full lips adorned with pink gloss. She looked up at him, and he kissed her nose. A few grey streaks glistened from his dark sideburns, but he had handsome and arresting features, honed by middle age. Yani watched them, catching the faintest whiff of her perfume from his seat. New love, he presumed perceptively. Yet strangely, instead of feeling regret, he celebrated this with them, sensing instantly the power of association. There was an energy radiating from them which they were oblivious to. He knew this, for he and she had had that vivacity too, that infectious fragrance and intoxication. He shut his eyes.

He is backstage and watching her glisten, utterly captivating in rustling sea green swathes of a full satin skirt. She has never looked so beautiful. Her hazel eyes are dancing, and he holds them in his. There is no fear, only jubilation at what is to come. Holding the 'cello firmly in her left hand, she suspends her bow in the right, tantalising him. Come on, she is teasing, let's dance!

A hush fell over the audience, and now Yani knew it was time. He couldn't bear to look as the musicians came onto the stage. Instead, he stared down at his programme, the typed repertoire which was so familiar and tender to him, although he didn't recognise the names of the artists at all. *Why am I here?* he wondered. A ripple of applause spread with a swell across the room, as he absentmindedly turned the programme over, seeking photos of the performers. But looking up, what he saw instead stopped his heart beating.

Giselle walked slowly onto the stage, as the crowd showed their welcome. Louis followed behind her confidently, and they both paused for a short bow before he purposely took his seat at the piano. Giselle raised her head and turned to sit on her chair. The stage light was bright and hot on her face, and she could only see blackness in front of her. They tuned swiftly. There was a long pause as Louis prepared for his sonata entry. Giselle looked down as the notes began and then up again at the darkness.

For you my darling, she said to herself. *This is all for you.*

In the fourth row back, on the aisle, a man was silently weeping. *Sabine.*

Chapter 57

A week and a world later, Tess was sitting in Giselle's front room, her 'cello lesson long forgotten as she listened incredulously to what she said. It must be the most sublime love story she had ever heard. Giselle—no, Sabine—was transformed. Tess stared at her, unable to mask her delight at what she heard. It was too impossible, more than she could have ever dreamed for her friend. *True love really does conquer all*, she thought, and yet. Such a price paid for this depth of joy. And so much that has been beyond their control. Was it just destiny?

Sabine's eyes swelled with tears as she remembered leaving the stage, after the final encore, the rapturous applause and the sweat pouring down Louis's face. His back was soaked too. She had taken her last bow, alive in the music still, and nearer to him than she had ever felt. Desperate to hold the moment, she went backstage to the rehearsal room and laid down her faithful steed, who had transported her to this incredible place. She was now hugging Louis with gratitude, when beyond his squeeze, her eyes clasped hold of the one face dearer to her than any other in the world. Over his shoulder, she saw a vision at the back of the room, which could surely only be a mirage. *It was not possible …* but somehow, it was. She beheld Yani looking at her, standing at the back of the room with tears streaming down his face.

Eternity stood still. She dropped her arms from Louis's shoulders, absorbing in a fraction of a second that she was not actually dreaming. His arms opened wide, as she cried out, her shriek matching his, and ran into his embrace. They clung, entwined, for the longest time, before any words were feasible, as her tears mingled with his. Forever after, and for as long as her life lasted, she would hold this memory as her most precious. It became his too.

***

For it had indeed been an absolute triumph. Even Tess could tell that. She had watched her friend, transported, enthralled by the sheer force and beauty that she had coaxed from her instrument. It was totally inspiring, knowing as she did now, the gargantuan effort and years it must have taken her to play to that level of expertise. Let alone the physical endurance. No one would have ever guessed her vulnerability that night. There had been a strength and power that defied her tiny frame, superhuman even. She had wanted to find Giselle afterwards to congratulate her and introduce David, but she had mysteriously vanished. Now it made sense. She listened, unable to really believe that Yani has finally found Sabine again. Or that she had in some inextricable way been part of it. For Yani had told Sabine about the note. It seemed almost miraculous. Perhaps it was.

'I just can't get over it,' she had said, like a stuck record.

'I am just so happy for you both, *so* very happy.'

The two women had beamed at each other, smiles pinned secure, incapable of slipping from their faces.

'Thank you, *chère* Tess,' Sabine had said.

She wanted to tell the story over and over, not sure she would ever tire of it.

She had told Tess some, but not all, of what had followed since the day of the concert. It was too sacrosanct even to share with a friend. She only knew that life had returned to her, undeserved by his forgiveness, and that her deepest prayer had been answered in the most extraordinary way.

'I wish I could write a film script for this!' Tess had said, laughing.

She had thought long and hard about reunions, especially since David had been agonising recently about finding his sister. It all seemed so hopeless. There had been no response to either of his letters. David had tried to put a brave face on it, but deep down, Tess knew he was hurt. Can't be easy for either of them, she had suspected. She had told Sabine about it.

'I wish there was something I could do for him,' she had said, letting her smile slip temporarily. 'Guess we will just have to wait and see. But the longer he doesn't hear anything, makes me wonder if he ever will?'

'Don't give up hope,' Sabine had quietly replied.

David had also been riveted not only by the concert, but also by the events succeeding it. Tess had phoned him as soon as Sabine had told her the story. It seemed incredulous, even to him. He was always a fan of happy endings; who wasn't? But deep inside, he was also beginning to doubt whether he would find his own resolution, as far as his sister was concerned. He was growing suspicious of her rejection now and pondered whether it was perhaps for the best not to be confronted with it.

Possibly too much time had passed, and too many years of the unknown. He had also been dismayed by Richard's pessimism over it all. Yes, for everyone's sake, maybe it was better to let sleeping dogs lie.

Chapter 58

The last few days had passed in a complete blur for Yani. He was still wondering a week later whether, in fact, it was all a reverie.

He hadn't let Sabine out of his sight. Time had fused into oblivion as they had reunited and reminisced over every possible detail since the fateful night of her disappearance. He understood it now, her deepest fears for him, and her reason for leaving. Not even imminent death could make him less willing to face the future for as long as she may have left. He just wanted to be by her side, to share it with her, wherever it may lead. *A day can last a lifetime*, he had told her, and now, finally, Sabine understood this too.

They had eventually phoned the police. Sabine would be needed for further questioning in Paris, but it could wait until after Christmas. Relief descended on them both. Her case would be transferred, accelerated by Yani's witness and medical evidence to support her disappearance, although Sabine knew she was still likely to face a barrage of psychological interrogation. Somehow, it didn't worry her anymore.

A couple of days later, Yani had suddenly had the idea of taking her back to Albania. He wanted to share this immeasurably dense happiness with Viktor Papadasi. More than that he wanted, no needed, his priestly blessing. He wanted a *proper* wedding, in a church full of friends and witnesses, a celebration of their love and story, and confirmation of what had happened by the lake in Ohrid.

He had even slipped out the day Tess had come for a lesson on a secret trip to buy a ring, disappearing before she arrived. He had always known what he would buy her: a diamond trilogy symbolising him, her, and the Other, the one who had returned her to him. Christmas would frame his surprise perfectly. The old jeweller had smiled knowingly; absorbing Yani's excitement yet undimmed by familiarity, he had wished them both well. Then he had wrapped it carefully in a small leather box. *She is a jewel beyond any price*, Yani had said to himself on the way back. He had sprinted through the busy streets full of harried shoppers with it hidden in his breast pocket, trapped beside his full and bursting heart.

When he got back, Tess had gone. Sabine was singing softly in the kitchen. He tiptoed up behind her and pulled her into his arms. She swirled round to embrace him, their kiss lingering for the longest time, his eyes so full of tenderness that it broke her heart, even now.

'Is it really you, my Yani?' she said, breaking free to look into those copper eyes which melted her now more than ever before.

'It really is,' he had said, sweeping her into both arms and carrying her weightlessly through to the sofa.

'But my girl needs to rest,' he had said gently, laying her carefully on the sofa and detecting with shame and guilt that she had hardly slept for days. He knew he was treating her like a porcelain vase, but as far as it was down to him, he would fight with every cell in his body to protect her and make her strong again.

Sabine looked up adoringly. It was simply too good to be true, to see him really there again, holding her, loving her. She hadn't wanted to let him out of her sight, either, but she knew she had wanted to see Tess. Yani had worried it was too much, but she had promised it would only be an hour, and in a flash, his inspiration and her lesson had provided the perfect excuse to slip out.

'She's been such a good friend to me,' Sabine said to Yani, telling him about Tess's kindness when she had been ill, and her solid companionship when her spirits had been low.

As for the note, she realised that it must have slipped out of her arms when she went for the rehearsal that day. Why Yani had chosen that particular church on that one day to slip into would be an unsolved mystery. *Only God knew.*

'She didn't sound all that pleased when I rang,' Yani had countered, awkwardly.

'Why would she, *mon cher*? You were a strange foreign man, who had somehow got her phone number. I don't blame her for being abrupt,' Sabine had laughed. 'But she's also found love recently you know,' she added with a sly smile.

'*Really*? Then I am very happy for her,' Yani said with genuine warmth.

'Yes. He's a doctor. They even came to the concert.'

'Really? Did you tell her what happened?'

'Of course. She was overjoyed to hear about our reunion.'

Sabine looked out of the window, thinking of what Tess had told her about David's sadness over his sister.

'Though it seems that the boyfriend is looking for his own reunion too,' she said, explaining.

They both said nothing, remembering instantly those feelings of tortured and buried longing which only a few days ago had threaten to destroy them both.

'I'm so glad she was here for you, Sabine,' he had said, suddenly serious. 'You don't know how many hours I spent wondering if you were alone.'

'I was never alone, Yani. Although I might have felt it, God never left me. Or us.'

'I felt that too,' Yani said with a whisper, stooping down to kiss her tenderly again.

Chapter 59

Kitty sat at the kitchen table, busy making lists. Christmas was fast approaching, and as usual, she was well behind schedule. It was tipping down with rain outside, and she had forty minutes before the school run to scramble some ideas together. Roger was cosily asleep on top of her feet, and the dishwasher was needing to be emptied, but it would have to wait. Her biro hung suspended over a notepad whilst she racked her brains, berating herself at how little time she had left.

She had started collecting bits and bobs over the last few weeks, stuffing them in her cupboards and wondering, as she did every year, what all the faff was about. She sometimes wondered if all the effort was worth it, feeling sacrilegiously that she, rather than Baby Jesus or Santa, carried ninety-nine percent of the Christmas responsibility. Five stockings that nearly finished her off. Every year, she determined to have them wrapped ahead of time, but invariably, each year found Nick and her awake at three o'clock on Christmas morning, with an abandoned bottle of prosecco, still wrapping them. Last year, they had only just made it in time before Toby woke up at 4 a.m. One year, she had tripped spectacularly into Sam's bedroom with a rustling sack, only to hear him grunt from under the covers, 'It's okay, Mum. Just leave it outside.'

Such gratitude. For the sake of the younger ones, she had tried to retain the magic of it all, but as time went on and the children grew, she had lost her former enthusiasm. This year would be more stressful than ever, as Helen was coming to stay, probably for a final Yuletide, so the pressure was on. It would have to be picture-perfect, and she groaned inwardly, knowing with absolute certainty that such a likelihood was impossible. She had a reasonably healthy relationship with her mother-in-law, but there were was vast differences when it came to organisation. Kitty performed best under pressure, whereas Helen just fell apart. Which meant that Helen had all her presents chosen, bought, and wrapped in August; she couldn't for the life of her understand why Kitty left it until mid-December. And now cancer had also made a guest appearance, rewriting all the rules. Kitty would no longer be able to insist on the final say, needing to pay deference to what she knew Helen would prefer, which was order, quiet, and tidiness. Especially in her current condition. She doodled an angry face on her pad, with a tongue sticking out.

Thankfully, Amazon had rescued her magnificently in recent years, but she still had plenty to do. Normally, she didn't bother with homemade preparations, but this year, she wanted to make some walnut chutney for Helen, so she scribbled down jam jars on her list, remembering crossly that she had just recycled the last lot away. She wondered about some new lights for the driveway but decided she couldn't face Nick's wrath. There was a whole box in the attic—none of which worked, for mysterious reasons—and he had banned her from buying anymore until she had checked the bulbs. Which she absolutely did not have time to do. It really wasn't worth ruffling Nick's patience at this time of year; he was swimming upstream just to pay for it all. She glanced wearily at her watch, as she hurriedly jotted down more thoughts, suddenly remembering that it was Thursday and Sam's music night. She scraped back her curls, twirling them forcefully back into a band, and realised that she was eager at the thought of seeing Yani again. It was not a little disconcerting that he hadn't bothered to reply to her texts following the concert, other than one the next day, which simply said 'Speak soon.' He was being evasive as ever, and quite honestly, it infuriated her.

A few hours later, she had reason to forgive him. He had arrived at the house, grinning from top to toe, and had swept into the kitchen before the lesson. She didn't have time to ask.

'Kitty, you are *not* going to believe what I have to tell you!' he had exclaimed so loudly, that she wondered if he was drunk.

Then the whole extraordinary story had spilled out. He had come all the way down from Sheffield this afternoon to see them, teach Sam, and tie up a few last commitments before heading straight back for Christmas. No *wonder* he had been out of touch.

It was true. She really hadn't believed him, other than his countenance was so transformed and euphoric, that she was in shock. For once, it was Kitty who was silenced.

'Yani, this is just ... *incredible*!' was all she could say, words untypically failing her.

'I know. Tell me about it!' Yani had agreed, laughing loudly.

He now wondered whether he should have invited Kitty and Nick to the concert too, sensing her delight and animation. Not that he would have had the power of speech to communicate the wonders of that night, but he was certainly touched by her heartfelt reaction.

'This is simply the *best* news ever,' Kitty had proclaimed emphatically, reaching for one of the Chateauneuf bottles she had bought on special offer for the season. Glasses quickly followed. Kitty always viewed any good news, however minimal, as a perfectly good reason to celebrate, and this was a magnificent excuse.

'Steady on, Kitty,' Yani had protested. 'I still need to teach Sam!'

'You may need it' she said, pouring a large glass and handing it to him.

'And I have made a big vat of chilli for dinner, so I absolutely *insist* that you join us after the lesson. Why don't you stay over too, until you need to get back? There's loads of room.'

She held up her glass and added, 'Cheers,' looking every bit as pleased as she felt.

'Santé!' Yani said, as they clinked glasses.

He looked at her, realising acutely the debt he owed her. She had provided him with a home away from home when he had been a stranger, an exile even. She had welcomed him so warmly into their family and demonstrated a mothering heart, which he had sorely missed. He thought fondly of Adile and knew she would have loved to meet Kitty too.

'I really am so grateful to you, Kitty,' he blurted out.

'Grateful for what?' she had answered, unsure what he meant.

'Just, well ... your friendship,' he admitted.

Kitty smiled back appreciatively, wondering afresh at the way things had turned out. Even she had to admit that events had been remarkable. Meeting Yani so unexpectedly in the cafe all those months ago, when she had no reason to, had often made her ponder. Life was now so much the richer for that chance encounter. Who knows where Sam would be now without his music? She shuddered to think. It was just brilliant to hear this news; and gave her renewed hope that the other unresolved issues in her life might follow suit. Her face betrayed her thoughts.

'What is it?' Yani asked, as if reading her mind.

'Oh.. nothing really,' she fibbed, then added more honestly, 'I just wish I could also find the person I am looking for.'

She bit her lip and looked across at the dogs, who were vying for the nearest place to the range.

Yani paused. He knew immediately that she was thinking of her brother. Something flitted across his mind.

'Never lose hope,' he said, with more meaning than he felt able to convey.

'No,' said Kitty thoughtfully.

'Sabine never lost hope, and neither did I—although it's easy to say that now, I suppose.'

He remembered what it was that had chimed with Kitty's predicament.

'Funny you should be looking for a brother, though,' he said, frowning. 'Sabine was telling me about someone she knows who is looking for his sister.'

Kitty looked up, nonplussed.

'How so?'

'Oh, just her pupil's boyfriend. He is trying to trace a sister, but that's reached an impasse too.'

'Oh.'

Kitty struggled to imagine the uniqueness of someone else in her situation, but it was comforting nonetheless.

'Maybe he should try Facebook,' she suggested. 'It wasn't any good for me, sadly, as I got no response.'

She had certainly tried that avenue in desperation but had drawn a blank.

'I will indeed pray that you find him,' Yani said, unexpectedly.

'Know that prayer is the greatest power in the universe,' he added sincerely. He could almost feel Viktor smiling at him.

'Thanks, Yani.'

Kitty looked at him thoughtfully. Faith really was found in the most unexpected of places.

She had actually exhausted herself praying. God seemed very elusive on this one. Not that she doubted, exactly; it was more like she wasn't sure whether she should still be searching. Things were meant to be or not. She'd always believed that.

A few hours later, when they had all eaten and Kitty had made up a bed for Yani in the den, she climbed wearily up to their bedroom, which was a large attic conversion that Nick said was the best financial investment he'd ever made. She was inclined to agree. He was sitting in bed, reading the paper with glasses perched on his nose, waiting for her. The sight of him made her dissolve a little, feeling as tired as she was. Dear, wonderful Nick. Such an anchor, and now more than ever, she needed his stability. She determined that this Christmas, she would really try, for his sake and more than ever before, to be the wife that he deserved.

Chapter 60

A few days later, after Yani had gone back to Sabine and just before Helen was due to arrive, Kitty was pottering around the house, making last-minute touches to the decorations and adorning the house with tea lights and scented candles in every nook and cranny. The tree looked magnificent, a bigger one than normal, showing off ostentatiously in the large hallway. The girls had been requisitioned to decorate it, but not to be outdone, Angus had stealthily added a few of his own daredevil creations, only Kitty pretended not to notice. She wasn't sure that a papier mâché Darth Vader was really appropriate, but she didn't have the heart to take it down.

Later on that afternoon, she would join Nick for the boys' carol service, as he had taken the day off to go and collect Helen and bring her there to join them. She had insisted on coming, even though Nick and Kitty weren't sure if it would tire her out before she'd even begun. But loyalty to her grandchildren was absolute. *How the kids will miss her*, Kitty thought sadly. *And we will too. Poor Nick.*

But ignoring all thoughts of loss, she determined to banish the inevitable for the next few days, commandeering her innate cheerfulness to carry them all through on a wave of final festive optimism.

Outside, the weather had turned nippy and raw. There had even been a light frost on the car that morning, as Kitty willed a snowy surprise for Helen's sake. She wandered into the lounge and sat carefully down on the piano stool. Her last job was to clear away Sam's music and allow the poor piano, for a few short days, to come up for air. Her fingers touched the ivories, and a swell of familiarity came over her. The only time she ever got to sit and play now was when Sam was out. She didn't dare play when he was around. All of a sudden, she ached to see her own parents again, now long gone. How they had loved to hear her play, especially at Christmas. The memory of this gift of the old piano made her miss them with an unanticipated jolt.

Notes wrapped themselves easily round the chords as she played, and before she knew it, carols were forming their timeless sounds. She thought about the angel harps of gold, picturing them hovering as 'still their heavenly music floats, o'er all the weary world.' Heavenly music. Yes, it was. *But certainly a weary world.*

She thought about her life, its peculiar tapestry, her losses and gains. There was so much to be grateful for; she couldn't deny that for a moment. But deep and hidden things still haunted her, things she couldn't really explain to anyone, mysteries that she would never understand; perhaps it was best not to try. Unbidden, salty tears began to roll down her cheeks, as they rallied to her aid. She was profoundly moved as she listened to the melody; hearing the age-old lyrics remind her that 'man hears not the love song' which the angels sing. How sad. But probably true, she thought, wondering how anyone could truly refuse a love song.

Then in that moment, she had clarification, an epiphany which came in sacred form. *Love.* The gift of it, and a baby's fragile life. She looked up at the wooden nativity set above her on the mantelpiece. Little carved figures which told a story that she had heard a thousand times, but right now, in this moment, as if for the first time. The incarnation. It suddenly became real and made urgent sense to her now.

Her fingers stopped on the keys and rested as her thoughts paused. Moments dissipated as she privately stooped before that first manger and encountered her own personal nativity. *All would be well*, if she only trusted; even over the unresolved issue of an untraceable brother.

She stared down at the gold necklace around her neck, on which was hung her mother's wedding ring and cross. Love, a baby, and a sacrifice. The symbolism wasn't lost on her in that moment, as she held them tenderly.

The silence was popped by Basil, who suddenly started barking aggressively from the kitchen. *Who needs a burglar alarm?* Kitty thought, pondering for the endless time about this little scruffy dog who had literally turned her life upside down.

She looked up at all Sam's music littered atop the piano, groaning as she noticed there was even some junk mail poking out from underneath the manuscripts. Standing up, she scooped up all the sheets and tried to shape them into an orderly bundle. There was no time to sort them now; she just wanted them out of sight.

The piano stool compartment was absolutely crammed to bursting. Sweeping up the entire pile from on top of the piano, she took the whole lot through to the kitchen. Then she shook it down on the table and tried to condense it into a methodical mass, which was difficult, as there was so much of it. She noticed some odd strays peeping out of the pile, glimpsing with despair Sam's college report and, with relief, his provisional driving license. There it was. Honestly, *what else was buried in this pile?*

Still, there was no time to sort it now. It would all have to wait until after Christmas. Grabbing a spare cardboard box from the larder, she popped the whole lot inside and hid it back on the bottom shelf, next to her rows of neatly packaged and proudly labelled chutney. Then, knowing full well she might then forget it was there, she paused.

Going back to the kitchen, she hastily scribbled a Post-it note to herself and stuck it on the fridge:

'Music – sort. TBC.'

To be continued. It was the only thing she could do.

Outside, something fluttered across the window, catching her eye. She stared, as a slow smile began to sweep across her face. Snowflakes. As if on cue, she absorbed their soft, transcendent magic. Thousands of them, falling silently, their individual designs representing to Kitty the endless possibilities which now lay before her. Endings and beginnings, death and life, the old year—and the new one which lay ahead. A field of white on which no footsteps had yet trodden. Somehow, that pristine image brought deep comfort, as she finally absorbed the opportunity of the unknown ahead. She walked over to the piano and quietly closed the lid. The future was enough, and it was those tomorrows, in which she would place her hope.

"Life is a song. Sing it"
—Mother Teresa